"A cracking debut thriller with pace and heart ~ an author who really knows her stuff. Hi~¹ ~
Zoë Sharp, author of the *Char¹*

RED HAV
Crime Writers' As

The CWA Dagger logo is a registered trademark owned by and reproduced with the permission of the CWA.

RED HAVEN

METTE MCLEOD

METTE MCLEOD

for Tormod and Freya

PROLOGUE

NINETEEN-YEAR-OLD DMITRI PAVLOVICH VOZNESENSKY KNELT, back straight, feet slightly apart. His arms flexed as he adjusted his hands around the waist in front of him. He closed his eyes.

The music was all too familiar. First the bassoon, then the oboe and the flute joined in. The four cygnets would be dancing across the stage in near perfect symmetry, four pairs of pointe shoes tapping the wooden stage in unison.

Dmitri took a deep breath and lifted the body in front of him as high as he could. But it wasn't high enough. Down again. Sweat was running down his neck now, soaking through his threadbare shirt. He couldn't see them any more, the ballerinas, but he knew they'd be zigzagging across the stage. The wind from the open window cooled his face and brought with it the scent of the tulips and violas at Revolution Square and the park in front of the Bolshoi theatre just north of them. But the bird song that used to flow through the window with the smell was drowned out by another, wholly man-made music; the rumbling of tanks from Red Square a few blocks away.

Dmitri adjusted his grip. Inhaled and exhaled.

Swan Lake would never be the same.

Not after this.

It would be the soundtrack of the day of the coup for generations to come. The only thing people all across the Soviet Union would see and hear when they turned to their televisions to find out what was going on.

Dmitri knelt down again, fingers pushing through the flab to get a better grip. Up, up, up, as high as he could reach. His shoulders were seizing up, he was standing on tiptoes now.

There. He'd got the man onto the window ledge.

Dmitri held onto the body with one arm before he climbed up himself. Then he hauled the heavy suit-clad man up, inch by inch, into a standing position. It seemed to take forever, but Dmitri knew from the sound from the television that the cygnets were still dancing, the oboe and flute still playing.

The backyard was empty, only a few crows picking at some rubbish. Dmitri didn't take any chances. He nudged the body forward, kicking its feet gently to make it seem like the man had jumped, not been pushed. It was a common mistake to think you could stage a suicide by simply throwing someone out a window or off a roof. They would land all wrong. A last push at the lower back, and the body was flying in the air. Dmitri jumped back inside. There was a thud from the backyard as the body hit the ground. No screams. No shouting. Everyone was busy looking at what was going on at Red Square.

Dmitri wiped the sweat off his forehead with his sleeve. He picked up the syringe, took it apart and put it back in the little case with the spare one. He had to give it to Sorokin. The drug he had provided Dmitri with was frighteningly good. Ten seconds was all it had taken from injection till the target had stopped resisting. In those ten seconds, a corrupt Communist Party official by the name Viktor Petrovich Lebedev, had stared at Dmitri via the reflection of the window he'd just been looking out of. Lebedev had been whole head shorter than Dmitri.

Dmitri would never forget that look. The grey eyes that seemed to say both; 'do you know who you're dealing with' and 'my God, they have come for me' at the same time.

Maybe it was because it was broad daylight, and Lebedev's pupils had been tiny specks of black in the big grey eyes. Maybe it was because Dmitri had seen the exact same eyes on the photo on the desk, the photo of the target's two little boys. Dmitri had his rules. He would never kill women and children. But he had just deprived these boys of their father. Just like someone had taken his own father, years earlier. But those eyes, those grey eyes, would stay with him. He knew they would.

Dmitri ran back to the filing cabinet in Lebedev's office. Sorokin had told him to take everything, but it was far too big. He started opening drawers. The files were in alphabetical order, the Latin one.

Damn.

Dmitri had never been abroad. Never been to any of the other Soviet republics even. The only English he knew was the words to Metallica's *Enter Sandman*, which his older brother had bought on the black market. But if he got this job right, there were more exciting missions to come. He spelled his way through the names in the top drawer. Antigua and Barbuda, Belize, Bermuda, BVI, CI. He didn't understand the names, maybe they were codewords? Sorokin hadn't said what Lebedev was in charge of, but it was obvious that money was involved. Foreign money. American dollars.

There wasn't much time. Lebedev's driver cum bodyguard could be back any minute, he'd only popped out to pick up a briefcase Lebedev had left behind in the swanky Party-issued Chaika.

Dmitri made a snap decision and cleared out the top

drawer. He took his own well-thumbed version of Bulgakov's *Master and Margarita* out of his backpack before he filled it with the folders. As he shoved in the last one, the seam of his bag looked like it was about to tear. Sweat was running down Dmitri's back again. The cygnets were long gone from the TV screen, and the stage was set for the ball. The third act. He had to get out.

He zipped up his bag, put his book in his jeans pocket and glanced around the room. He'd used a sleeve whenever he had touched anything, so there shouldn't be any finger-prints anywhere. His gaze lingered at the desk. The photo of the two boys; a similar age gap to that between Dmitri and his older brother.

As he lifted up his bags to leave, he noticed a thick, brown envelope that must have fallen out of the filing cabinet. He was about to put it back when the elastic band snapped, revealing photographs from a holiday. A young woman in a bikini, lounging on a beach somewhere. White sand, palm trees and blue water. Colours so vibrant they looked unreal. She didn't look half bad, and was topless in several of the pictures, so Dmitri shoved the lot into his pocket.

Tchaikovsky's music followed him out of the office, down the stairs. The music echoed around him, from the office he had left behind, then it crescendoed again as he got to the caretaker's booth at the bottom of the stairs. She was safely closed up inside the booth, watching the TV screen and waiting to hear something, anything, about what was going on in the streets of the city outside.

It was a big day. A monumental day. The day the hardlin-ers, Sorokin and other patriotic KGBshnikis, were taking back control of the country from the weak Gorbachev. Dmitri leapt out the main door and slowed to a stroll when he'd put a few metres between himself and the building. He puffed his chest and lifted his chin. He'd done it. His first high-profile kill.

And no one, apart from Sorokin, would ever know it was him.

Dmitri didn't know it then, but it would be three years before he would see Sorokin again.

1

THE BLACK FABRIC stuck to the sweat on her upper lip and chin as Rory inhaled the soft, spice-scented air of the souk. Cinnamon, turmeric, paprika tickled her nose even through the thin fabric. A group of men sat at a plastic table with their water pipes, watching a game of football on a small television in the corner of a stall. Rory looked at the cups on the table. Even the sweet local tea would taste divine right now. She tried to stop herself from fiddling with the earpiece, but it kept coming loose. Or it felt like it did. She had complained about it, asked for a new one, but as she was only here as backup, she'd had to settle for the faulty one. As usual. Sweat was running down from the nape of her neck, and soaking the top of the burkini she was wearing underneath the tent-like djellaba. And every time she turned her head, it took a millisecond for the niqab to follow. She blinked a few times to make sure the brown contact lenses covering her grey-blue eyes moved freely. Aurora "Rory" Conroy had her Norwegian mother's eyes and dark blonde hair, but her British father's smile. All hidden under the niqab.

Rory gestured towards a man selling water, and exchanged a few dirhams for a dust-covered bottle. She paused. Wondered if she might be able to get away with lifting the face veil so she could take a sip, but dismissed the thought. The vendor looked at her, and reached for a plastic cup filled with straws. They looked as dusty as the bottle, but she took one anyway, and manoeuvred the bottle and straw up underneath the veil. Tepid and flat, but still the best water she had ever tasted. She closed her eyes for a second, and a breath of wind that had snuck through the gaps between stalls blew away the heavy scent of spices. Then a piercing sound burst into her ear.

'Target is on the move. Three in the group.'

The voice ended with a crackle.

Rory stood up, and had a quick look at her phone. They were a few rows over, and further north, maybe five minutes' walk away. Rory muttered to herself as she walked towards them. Street names, the layout of the souk, the way to the beach. She had gone through it a million times, both on the map and in real life, even if she was just the backup. This was the section with tea sets, up ahead was an array of colourful hanging lamps. When an older man in a group of grey haired tourists bumped into a water pipe, it almost knocked over a row of tea sets standing on the table next to it. The vendor was yelling at the tourists in Arabic and Rory had to slalom her way through the red faced westerners. The voice came back.

'Abort, abort. They're all wearing niqabs. We can't make a positive ID.'

'We're moving to plan B. That's your cue, Rory,' Dick's familiar voice made her shudder.

'I know. I'm on my way,' she muttered into her veil.

'Just remember to …' Richard's voice faded into the argument behind her.

Rory adjusted her djellaba so she wouldn't stumble in it, and disappeared into the souk. She kept visualising Leyla's face, focusing on her eyes and the curve of her nose. Richard didn't believe there was such a thing as super recognisers: this was Rory's shot at proving him wrong. But even for her, a woman wearing a face veil was a challenge.

Rory checked the tracker on her phone. The target was a few rows over. Breathing through the niqab was getting harder, the sweat a result not just of the heat, but of her nerves. She took a deep breath before she wound her way through the crowd. There. She could see Dario. Rory scanned the people around him, and spotted the group of three dark shapes standing in front of a spice stall. Two younger women, girls, judging by their gait, and one a lot older. The grandmother. Both the girls looked about the right size and age, and one of them was tugging at the grandmother's hand.

Rory moved over to browse the stall next to Dario, who gave her a slight nod before she headed towards the women. It was all up to her now. She only needed five seconds to get lost in the crowd once she'd found the target, according to Richard's plan. But first Rory had to find out which was 14-year-old Leyla from Bromley.

The three women had picked up some ginger and turmeric and the bouncy girl was leading the way towards the jewellery. Excellent. Mirrors. Rory joined them, looking at a necklace with turquoise beads. She stole glances at the young girl in the mirrors, searching for the little peculiarities that she had seen in the photos. The left eyelid hanging slightly lower, the flecks of green in her hazel eyes. But the girl flitted around, so getting a good look was nigh on impossible. There wasn't enough light either, to see the eye colour. But something felt wrong about her. The girl might be related to Leyla, but Rory didn't think it was Leyla.

'Rory, have you got an ID? Time's running out here,' the voice in her ear said.

As if she was looking at jewellery just for fun. Rory took another deep breath, and let her shoulders drop again. She pretended to spot something on the other side of the stall, sidling up to the other two. Held up some earrings in front of a mirror to see how they matched her eyes, and almost forgot that her blue eyes were hidden brown lenses. She zoned in on the passive girl, who didn't seem to want to look at anything at all, and who kept her eyes to the ground.

Look up, please. Just for a second.

A gust of wind got the roof cover flapping, and let the sun through just as the girl looked up in reaction to the noise.

It's her.

Rory's heart rate shot up, and she signalled to Dario. He came over, and started chatting to the tradesman, asking for something special for his daughter.

'No, that's too childish, I don't think my daughter would like that. She is fifteen, after all. Beautiful green eyes, just like her mother,' Dario continued, moving closer to the other girl who was now pointing at a few necklaces in suggestion. That was as much as Rory caught of the conversation in Arabic. Dario kept chatting, and the older woman moved over to get in-between the bearded stranger and her mindees, leaving Leyla's side. Rory bumped into Leyla so the girl turned slightly and spotted the picture on Rory's phone. It was of herself, fifteen months ago, sitting with her mother and Luna the cat in their South London flat. The last picture taken before her father had kidnapped her and taken her here. Leyla started to turn, but Rory put her hand on her back, whispering in her ear.

'No sudden movements, we're just going to walk sideways, slowly, and get out of sight, ok?'

Leyla nodded, but her knees almost gave way as Rory led her between the stalls. As they rounded the corner Rory grabbed Leyla's hand, and walked so fast Leyla started running next to her. Then the screaming and shouting began. People started scurrying through passageways and between stalls to see what was going on, and Leyla stopped still. Rory had to get her moving, and out of the way, before reality hit.

Before Leyla's family started mobilising their connections in the police. They were just a minute or so away from the car.

'I can't leave her here, I can't leave her!' Leyla started wailing in English. They were already getting curious stares, two young women in niqabs rushing around on their own.

'We have to go, Leyla,' Rory said, and dragged the girl through a narrow alley. The car was waiting at the far end with Ahmed behind the wheel. The back door was opened from inside, and Rory pushed the girl inside in front of her.

'I can't do this, I can't leave her,' Leyla said again.

Rory leaned over and tugged Leyla's hands off the door handle. The car shot through the streets as Rory wrestled with the girl.

'We have to go. I'm really sorry about the other girl, your cousin?'

'It's not her I'm worried about, my uncle is the head of police, dad wouldn't dare touch her. I worry about grandma. My dad will kill her for not looking after me.'

Rory put her hand on Leyla's shoulder, but the girl shrank away, as if she had hit her.

'Has he hurt you?' Rory asked. 'Leyla, does your father hurt you?'

The hazel eyes welled up with tears, and the girl fell in on herself.

'Oh, sweetheart, he is not going to get to do that again. We're taking you home, home to your mum. Home to Luna. Okay?' Leyla was leaning into her now, sobbing, and they were rocking back and forth in the backseat as the car wound through traffic towards the beach.

Rory stroked her head. 'I need you to do something for me, ok? We're going in the water, so I need you to wear a burkini. Just picture your mum and Luna. You will be back with them in no time.'

Rory grabbed the bag in the front passenger seat, and got Leyla to sit up again. She pulled out the all covering swimsuit and the matching hood, arranging it so it would be easy for Leyla to figure out how to put it on. The loose-fitting tunic was attached to the trousers in a way that meant it stayed down in the water, but made it difficult to put on. Even if her djellaba was loose fitting enough for her to change in the seat.

'I, sorry, I can't. This thing.'

Leyla's hands were fumbling around, leaving a pile of swimsuit fabric in her lap. Rory rearranged the burkini again, and guided Leyla's legs and arms into the right openings, before Leyla managed to get the hood on herself. Then Rory stripped off her own djellaba and niqab.

'Remember to smile. This is a happy day, the first in the rest of a happy life,' Rory said.

Then they heard the sirens. Blue lights were reflected in the shop windows around them, but they couldn't see where the cars were. Ahmed turned around.

'Has she got a phone on her? Did you check for a phone, Rory? Tell me you got rid of her phone?'

Rory had forgotten about the phone. Had assumed Leyla wouldn't be allowed one.

'Leyla, where's your phone?' she asked.

'I don't know, it's here somewhere, in one of my pockets. Or at least it was.'

The traffic around them almost came to a standstill, which kept the blue lights at bay. Rory searched through the clothes at Leyla's feet, and found an Iphone under the driver's seat. A small green light was blinking in the top corner of the screen. Find my phone had been enabled. Traffic was moving again, and a few rusty motorbikes were finding their way in between the cars. The blue lights came closer.

'Turn that damn thing off, Rory. Now!' Ahmed had turned around, the blue lights reflecting in his eyes.

Leyla was crying hysterically, trying to open the door again. The sweat on Rory's face had turned to ice, and she leaned over Leyla, pushing her back towards her seat. Then she rolled down the window and tossed the phone into a basket tied onto the back of a passing motorbike. It disappeared into a pile of fresh bread, and only seconds later it was headed back into the souk.

'Nice job, Rory. Smooth. Keep your heads down though, till the police have passed.'

Rory pulled Leyla close, and shushed her, humming a lullaby that her Russian grandmother had sung for her. The police sirens came closer, and it seemed like the sound and the lights were all around them, echoing between the buildings lining the road. Then they passed them, and faded. The heap in Rory's arms turned limp, and as the car approached the beach, Leyla had calmed down again.

'You ready?' Rory wiped away Leyla's tears before she gave her some sunglasses.

'Yes, I'm ready. I'm ready,' the girl nodded.

With large sunglasses covering their faces, Rory and Leyla walked arm in arm across the beach. There was nothing to indicate that this was anything but two girlfriends or sisters having a fun day together. Jack stood at the water's edge with the jetski, and a few hundred metres off the shore, the yacht was floating on the waves. A crew member was hoisting the jib, in no great rush.

'Hold on to me,' Rory said as they both got on. Leyla grabbed her waist so tight Rory almost had to tell her to loosen her grip. They got some curious stares from people on the beach, so Rory started out doing slow turns and figures of eights. She did a few hazardous turns, making it look like they almost fell off, and then headed for the far side of the yacht. More blue lights were speeding past in the direction of the souk.

'Be ready to jump into the water,' Rory shouted as she flung the jet ski around behind the yacht. 'Now, Leyla. Jump!'

But Leyla froze, and refused to let go of Rory's waist.

'You have to let go of me, and get into the water. My friend Sam is right there, he will help you.'

Rory tried to get out of Leyla's grip, but wouldn't be able to get her off without hurting her.

'Leyla, sweetheart, you have to let go of me, so we can swim over to the yacht. Once they find the phone they'll start looking everywhere for us. If you don't let go, we'll be jumping into the water like this, ok?' Rory started standing up, lifting herself and the girl on her back.

Leyla's arms went limp. Rory dove into the water, then Leyla climbed off the jetski with Sam's help.

Sam set off, driving the jetski along the shore, and would continue doing so until the people on the beach had forgotten about the two girls and the yacht was long gone. At least that had been the plan, but this was taking too much time. The girl clung onto Rory, and pulled her under the water.

Bloody girl can't even swim properly.

Then Rory stopped herself. Leyla hadn't asked to be taken in the water. Not asked if she could swim. And she was only 14. And the incident with the phone was her, Rory's, fault. She probably deserved that dunking.

Rory spluttered, and gasped for air before she grabbed Leyla's arm, and spun her around so she could swim her towards the yacht. Mike was leaning against the railing at the back of the yacht, his back to her, eyes closed towards the sun.

'Mike, what are you waiting for? Where's the line?'

'Calm down, dear,' he said as he tossed a buoy over the side.

Mike dragged them the last few metres and lifted Leyla up on the deck.

'Not very professional,' Rory said through gritted teeth as she climbed up herself.

'Oh, come on. You gotta enjoy the little pleasures you can

have in this job. Eases up the tension. By the way, want help with that, uh, wetsuit?'

'Nice try.' Rory said, and ushered Leyla down the stairs, where Richard was waiting.

'We're all set to go. Customs and passports were done in the harbour, as you predicted, so we shouldn't face any difficulties,' Richard said.

Rory took Leyla to the front berth, closed the door and helped the girl get the wet burkini off. The towels were warm, and Rory took out the new clothes she had bought Leyla before they left London. The sails flapped for a minute, then the yacht turned, and all they could hear was the sound of the keel cutting through the sea.

'Can I talk to my mum?'

'Not yet, sweetheart. We need to get away from here first. Out of Moroccan waters. Then we'll get the satellite phone out, and call her together, ok? Now. Are you hungry? No? You must be exhausted though, why don't you try to have a little rest?'

'Okay,' Leyla said with a sob.

'Your mum gave me this, though I'm not sure if …' Rory said and reached into the bottom of the bag, where an old rabbit with one eye missing was hiding. 'You might be too old for teddies, but I thought it might be nice to …'

Leyla grabbed the rabbit out of her hands, buried her face in it and crawled under the covers. Rory smiled through the tears in her eyes. She stayed for a while, going through everything that had happened that day in her head, letting Leyla's small hand grip tightly onto hers. Her burkini was getting cold, but she waited until Leyla's hand was relaxed and the girl fast asleep, before she left the berth.

Still wearing her own burkini, Rory went into the tiny shower. Her job was not over: the best bit was yet to come. As she shimmied out of the burkini, she heard the bell from above. The one that said: We're all clear, out of Moroccan waters and the reach of Leyla's father.

Rory let the warm water rinse over her head one last time, tears of joy and relief mixing with the water. She turned off the water and wrapped herself in the small towel, thinking about the cup of tea she had been looking forward to. She might be only half English, but not when it came to tea. Builder's, extra strong, a splash of milk. And one sugar, when she was working. Then she remembered that she'd left her bag outside the tiny shower room. She could hear Richard moving around in the galley, and was hoping she could just reach out and grab it, but as soon as she opened the door, he was right there. Between Rory, wrapped in a small microfibre towel, and the bag with her dry clothes.

'Rory,' he started.

'I'm sorry, can we do this upstairs? Leyla's sleeping,' she tried.

'I just wanted to say that you did an amazing job today, with the planning, organising. Everything really. The thing with the phone, it happens. But good thinking to get rid of it. You've really proved yourself on this one,' he continued. He was no longer talking to her face.

'Thanks, I appreciate that. But if you could just …' she said, trying to nudge him aside enough to get her bag.

But his arm blocked the way, so they stood there, swaying with the movement of the boat. And on the next wave he just happened to bump into her. Full body contact, his heavy, plump belly pushing her against the door frame. She had to grab onto the towel so it didn't come undone. She could smell the stale coffee on his breath, the mix of sweat and Old Spice.

Then it happened.

It was a reflex more than anything. A result of the training she'd got in the army years before, the close combat training with Dario, Tom and the other ex-SAS colleagues.

As the yacht righted itself and there was a little bit of

space between them, her right knee shot upward, and hit him where it hurt.

Where it really hurt.

It felt softer than she had imagined, squishy, in a way. Until her knee met resistance. But Richard was already on the way down, and collapsed on the floor in a whimper.

2

DMITRI THREW his bag on the chair. The hotel room was like most others he had been in. Big, comfortable bed with linen in neutral, earthy tones, a shiny bathroom with the standard little soap bottles and the request to save the environment and reuse the towels. Dmitri thought back to the first times Sorokin had sent him abroad in the late 90s. How he had wanted to stay in bed, on the deep mattresses, forever. Watch TV, order room service. Get a little taste of a world he hadn't known existed before the Soviet Union fell apart. Now all he wanted was to get on with the job, and get out.

He pulled the antique cigarette case he had got from his handler at the airport out of his inner pocket and opened it on the desk. It contained, as Sorokin had said it would, three vials and a small syringe. He put the vials in the minibar fridge.

Dmitri had escaped detection for a long time. Too long, really. His handsome, bland looks had made it easy to disappear in the crowds over the years, but with CCTV and facial recognition everywhere, it was becoming a lot harder to stay invisible. Often he didn't even stay the night, just flew in one day, and did the job in as short a time as possible, before he grabbed the last flight out. He might catch five minutes' sleep in the back of a cab or on a bus, assuming there were no cameras. But this assignment required him to be at the same hotel as his intended victim, so if he was going to be on CCTV anyway, he might as well hide in plain sight and get a few hours' sleep. There wouldn't be many more after this one, anyway. Sorokin had promised him that once they found the documents, they would both be set for life. The job they had set out to do in 1991, when Dmitri staged his first of many 'suicides', would finally be finished. No need to work ever again. Not that Dmitri didn't enjoy his work. The creativity involved in staging situations and scenarios that would all seem natural; accidents, suicides, a bar fight gone wrong, was something he loved. He had only survived as long as he had because he was so good at it. Exceptional, even. Of all the other men and women who had worked for Sorokin over the years, none had lasted. Apart from Dmitri.

It was just getting a bit tiring with all the precautions, the counter-surveillance, the many different identities and passports, the travelling. He wouldn't mind never seeing another airport again. Quite a change from the little boy who had looked up at the sky, holding his mother's hand, wondering where all the aeroplanes taking off from Sheremetyevo were going. And if he would ever get to go on one. Dmitri was proud. Proud to be so good at his job. And proud to play such an important role in protecting his country, Mother Russia, from its many enemies. Some foreign. Most domestic.

He flicked on the TV. CNN were showing various state leaders arriving in New York for the big meeting at the UN. Dmitri had to admit, it was a pretty good cover. His target, Arkady Povarsky, had almost got away with the US trip. If only he hadn't been too indiscreet and bragged to his girl-friend about the yacht he was going to get her, once he got off the sanctions list. It didn't take long before Sorokin had figured out that Povarsky had agreed to reveal all about his

Kremlin dealings to the Americans in exchange for his financial freedom, the opportunity to spend his share of the plundered Russian wealth as he pleased. Traitor. The lowest of the low. Dmitri opened the minibar and double-checked the vials once again. There was enough in there to kill a horse.

Dmitri didn't like using the fast-acting poisons, like the one he'd been given this time. Radiation poisoning had been his favourite, but after those fools using polonium in London had left a radioactive trail all over Europe, they were off his list. The slower acting ones made the killing almost undetectable, but he didn't have that option in this case. Povarsky had already had his first meeting with the Americans, and the Kremlin didn't want him revealing too much.

Anyway, like many of the oligarchs, Povarsky wasn't a particularly healthy man. He both drank and ate too much, so helping bring on the heart attack that would probably kill him anyway at some point might fly under the radar. At least there would be enough doubt about the death for the Americans to not raise the alarm. That little grain of doubt was such an effective foreign policy tool. It threw the Western liberal democracies into a headspin, and made them waste their time 'looking at all options', just because something might not be what they all knew it to be.

Dmitri got into bed, and set his alarm to 2.30. He didn't want to risk Povarsky still being up watching a late night movie when he made his entrance. Sorokin's boys had hacked the hotel systems, so he knew Povarsky's room was just above his own, one further left. The Moscow team would also let him know if there was any activity on Povarsky's phone or other mobile devices, indicating he might still be awake. That fool. So vain that he refused to give up his gold iPhone even when preparing to betray his country. Whatever made Dmitri's job easier.

When the alarm rang, Dmitri went through the plan again before he opened his eyes. Then he checked his phone. The message from Moscow gave the all clear; no activity on the target's phone since he stopped browsing Washington escort agencies two hours earlier, and nothing heard or seen from the phone's microphone and camera to indicate that he was still awake.

Dmitri put on his clothes and the black climbing shoes. He put the vials and the syringe in the little pocket on his belt, and opened the balcony door. The city air felt cool and the sounds from the street below created a welcome background noise, and he quickly climbed from his own balcony to the one next to it, and up to the floor above. Two windows further along, and he found the balcony to Povarsky's room. He had drawn only the sheer curtains, and the faint light from the TV showed the silhouette of a man lying in the bed. The door was left ajar, so Dmitri pocketed his tools. This was almost too easy.

Povarsky stirred a little at the fresh air entering with Dmitri, but he quickly settled back into deep sleep. Dmitri walked over to the bed, and listened to Povarsky's heavy breathing. Too many cigars. And fatty foods. Dmitri would never have treated his own body like that. Dmitri grabbed the pillow on the opposite side of the bed with one hand, and the syringe with the other. He could see a vein pumping in Povarsky's neck, and just before he inserted the needle into the little point below the ear, right where a little mole was, he pressed the pillow hard onto his face. There was a quick gasp for air, sounding more like a snore than anything else, and then the drug had done its job. The man didn't even have time to lift his arms. The head and body went limp.

Not bad, Sorokin, not bad at all. The drug was even more effective than the boss had said. Dmitri felt a burst of national pride. Pride in his country, and their scientists, who were the smartest in the world.

Dmitri put a tissue onto the injection spot to soak up the little drop of blood that had followed the needle out, and checked that the pillow hadn't got any stains on it before he put it back on the other side of the bed. Then he packed up the syringe and left. The sound of the city below wasn't as beautiful a soundtrack as the Swan Lake had been back in 1991, but it wasn't bad either. When he got back into his own room, the clock said 2.45am. There was plenty of time for the drug to dissolve and disappear before the body would be discovered by housekeeping sometime around noon. And Dmitri would be out of the country and halfway way back to his mother's cottage by then. He'd promised to fix the roof of the banya; a corner of it had given way to the massive snowfall that had come in February.

As he got in the taxi, Dmitri logged onto his encrypted phone and checked the messages. A couple from his mum, as usual. She thought he was at a conference in St. Petersburg. He scrolled past them, to the top, then back again. There was one from Sorokin, with a single word in it; *Нашли*. He'd found it. Dmitri leant back into the leather seat and closed his eyes. Finally.

3

LONDON

'And that's when I kneed him in the balls.'

The laughs were even louder this time, stilettos and shiny trainers stamping on the dark wooden floor boards. Every new arrival at the table had demanded to hear the story, and every narration of it had generated a decibel-level the small pub in the City of London wasn't quite used to, even on a Friday after work. Rory looked around at the familiar faces of her allies, all women who'd experienced similar sexual advances at work. Women who all wished they could have done the same. Nikki, the Met detective. Sam, the European business correspondent at the *Financial Times*. Priya, her best friend and cancer researcher. Sally, the investment banker. Two corporate lawyers.

Their faces were flushed from the gin and tonics and the now empty bottle of rose. And from the story of the day. Her story.

'Best. Resignation. Ever,' Nikki had called it.

They had all got the giggles by now.

'A toast. To no more 'accidental' touching of boobs and bum.' Rory laughed, and the others with her.

She put down her glass, but couldn't quite let go of it.

Toasting victory, drowning failure. There would never be another job like that. It had been her dream job, where she got to use her military experience for something good. She'd got to travel and use her language skills and work alongside a cracking bunch of ex-SAS guys, reuniting kidnapped children with their parents in the UK.

The conversation around the table fluttered on, and Rory felt the need to be alone. She fumbled to find her bag on the sticky floor, and had to pause for a second to stop her head from spinning when she stood up. The cold air would do her good. Priya had put her coat on as well.

'You've got the experience you wanted from that job, there was no need to put up with that old perv any more. And it's not like you hadn't thought about leaving,' her best friend said as they stepped through the heavy, stained-glass doors.

'I know, it's just that I was hoping to have something new lined up before I jumped ship, you know. Not to have burnt all bridges and be left without a reference. Thanks for being here though.' Rory tried to smile.

What if Richard is right, that I'm not good enough to do this on my own?

Priya looked at her friend with concern. She knew her well enough to know there was more to the story. 'Do you want to come over to ours tonight? Hot toddy?'

'Thanks, but no. I need to get some air and clear my head. Go for a run, maybe.'

'It's not because my brother was mean to you about Tom is it? I can tell him to go out for the evening?'

'No, of course not. He's already apologised for that twice. Not that he needed to, he was just telling the truth. I just need to be alone for a bit. Think things through. And work out how to pay the rent.' Rory kissed her friend goodbye before she could say anything more.

———

As RORY CLOSED the door behind her in the Chelsea flat, just across the bridge from Battersea Park, she was tempted to just slump into the sofa with a bottle of wine. Then her eyes stopped at the photo of her grandparents hanging on the wall.

They'd not given up.

The beautiful Russian spy and the weathered Norwegian sailor. Rory could trace her own heritage in the photo. She had her grandmother's cheek bones, and her grandfather's eyes. They'd worked side by side in Finnmark in Northern Norway, to try to stop the Germans burning everything when they retreated south towards the end of the war. But a daring raid had made it too dangerous to stay, and they'd had to sail across the North Sea mid winter to stay alive.

Rory had inherited the flat after her mother passed away. She hadn't changed anything in it, wanted it to look much like it had when they lived there, and left it empty when she moved to Norway straight after graduation. Returned to her roots, just as her mother had before her. Though while her mother had gone looking for something, Rory had been running away.

Rory changed into her running kit and set off towards Battersea Park. The place of many happy holiday days with her grandparents. She ran on the circular road, forcing herself to run interval after interval, the alcohol in her blood disguising the pain in her muscles, the cold air rasping.

Rory's anger was not just with Dick and his chubby, ever-present fingers, but with herself. Angry for letting it get to the stage where she'd snapped and her left knee landed her without a job. She could have gone the sexual harassment lawsuit route, but what would that have got her? Compensation, maybe, after a long tribunal. Or she might have ended up with nothing. And no one would ever hire her again if she'd done that. Not in this business. The men doing this kind of work were all chums, drinking and swapping war stories. And the things he'd said afterwards, when he'd got back on his feet again, had really stuck. How he never should have trusted her with a man's job. That her failure to get rid of that phone had jeopardised the entire operation.

'You don't have what it takes. Never had. Never will have.'

It wasn't the first time she'd heard that.

And it was always the men who said it. Her own father. One of the admissions officers at the secretive military academy in Norway. Fellow soldiers when she got sent to Iraq before she'd even finished her course. Her colleagues, who thought she should stay in the intelligence vans, head-phones on, rather than working with the Norwegian Armed Forces' Special Command. They were a clear minority, these men. Most of the people she worked with respected her and judged her solely on what she achieved, but there were always a couple of guys who didn't. And it was usually the ones who saw themselves as the alpha-male, but didn't possess the natural authority that meant anyone else did. It had been easy enough to ignore them, but this time it was different. Richard was one of the best in the game, and he had headhunted her for the job.

Rory's thighs were aching; she hadn't run this fast in a long time, so she slowed down to a light jog just to keep the cold at bay. Her cheeks were stiff with the streaks of tears, and she had to pause for a minute to blow her nose. That's when she noticed her phone buzzing in her pocket. She looked at it. Three missed calls. Probably Priya. Though her number usually came up. Rory answered, almost on autopilot.

'Hello?'

'Hi, is this Aurora Conroy?'

'Who's asking?' Rory replied, half expecting there to be an automated message about her having won a lottery she'd never entered. No one used her full name these days. But the slight Russian accent threw her off. And there was something familiar about her voice.

'It's Masha. I was in the year below at the High? Sorry to call out of the blue.'

Rory had to think a second before she placed her. There had been a few Russian girls in her school, but Rory hadn't made many friends beyond Priya, and didn't expect anyone to remember her either. Then she remembered. Masha was the pretty girl who'd taken over as captain of the chess team. The one who'd made sure no one remembered about Rory's stint as the best chess player in school.

'Can I help you with anything?'

'I got your number from Natalya, a friend who said you'd helped her with a certain issue?'

'Is Natalya ok? And her family?'

Rory smiled at the memory of the happy little face of Natalya's daughter, the victim in a family kidnap case with a rather unusual resolution.

'Yes, yes, they're all well,' Masha continued. 'But you see, I'm in a similar situation…'

Rory cut her off. 'Not on the phone please. Face to face meetings only. Where are you?'

'I'm in Chelsea, off King's Road?'

'Can you come to Battersea Park? The tropical garden, in half an hour. And don't bring your phone, please.'

'Thank you. I'll be there in twenty.'

As the phone went silent Rory realised her fingers had gone numb from the cold. She took the phone apart out of habit more than anything. It was one of the simpler models, where the battery could be taken out. A just in case precaution due to her job. You never knew who could be listening, or what nationalities might be involved in the next case. The next case in job she no longer had.

It was a cold twenty minutes as Rory dawdled around a garden that seemed far removed from the Tropics. The palm trees were wrapped up in their winter coats and tarpaulin, and the occasional dog walkers that came through were in woollen hats and scarves. The Russia job. Again. The one where she'd met Tom for the first time. One of Dick's regular ex-SAS guys had cancelled on short notice, and Tom, who had just returned from a stint in Afghanistan, had filled the slot. It had been the start of the best two years of her adult life. And also what had given her the most pain.

A young woman dressed in a fur coat and matching hat entered the garden. 'Aurora?'

Nouveau Riche, Rory thought, but then stopped herself. She knew better than to pass judgement on first impressions. But Masha's perfectly shaped eyebrows and subtle makeup made Rory all too aware of her own appearance. The running tights wearing thin, her mousy hair all sweaty and slicked back in a ponytail and the smudged mascara. Not the prettiest sight, but then she hadn't planned on meeting anyone.

Rory stretched out a hand. 'Nice to see you again, Masha. Call me Rory, I haven't been Aurora in a long time. Before we start though, can I just ask where you called me from? It came up as a hidden number.'

'Oh, I called from a public phone, dialled 141. Natalya said you were a bit of a stickler for precautions.'

'Good. You did the right thing,' Rory walked them towards the darker paths in the park. 'How can I help?'

'My little brother, Sasha, has gone missing. He lives in Moscow with my father, and he was supposed to come over to visit, but never showed up. And I can't get hold of him on the phone either, I worry that something might have happened to him.'

'He probably just missed the flight, you must know how bad Moscow traffic is. Maybe his phone's out of battery?' Rory heard how patronising she sounded, and cringed at how she'd become like her former boss.

'You don't understand, he was supposed to be here two

days ago. No one has heard from either him or my father, it's as if they ceased to exist. Neighbours haven't seen them, the school hasn't seen him,' Masha wiped away a tear with a gloved hand. 'That bastard. My father promised he'd never drink again. I've always worried that he might drag my brother down with him, but didn't actually think it would happen. He's eleven years old.'

Masha looked at her through a wall of tears.

They stood there for a while, going back and forth, Rory suggesting things to try, Masha explaining she'd already done it, or why it was no use. This wasn't really the kind of case Rory used to work on. No known kidnapper, no custody battle. Just a boy and his alcoholic dad who'd gone off the radar.

'Ok, take me through this, every detail. When you last talked to either of them, when and where they were last seen by others you have talked to, known addresses. Everything,' Rory said with a sigh.

'Does that mean you'll help me?'

Rory hesitated. Bit the inside of her cheek. She knew this would lead to her taking an assignment without time to do proper background, but she could really do with the money. And Masha wasn't just a random stranger, and her little brother was missing. Moscow police wouldn't lift a finger with the father being gone as well.

'Yes. I'll go look for him.'

'Oh, thank you, thank you so much.' Masha grabbed her hands. 'Do you need money? Like straight away? I have cash in my safe at home. Dollars, euros. Euros are probably best these days.'

'Let's take it one step at a time, okay?'

————

ALEXANDR PAVLOVICH ABRAMOV, or Sasha, as his sister affectionately called him, was eleven years old and went to what sounded like one of the more prestigious state schools in central Moscow. The photo Masha had brought showed a grinning boy, in a bright white Tottenham Hotspur kit, in the stands of the old White Hart Lane. He was on the small side, slender, and had short medium blond hair and a gap between his front teeth. He had come to visit Masha several times before, so it was unlikely that he would have got lost trying to get to the airport. The ticket for the flight had never been used.

'I only have a few printed photos, but can send you more if you want. There's lots on my phone, but I left that behind as you asked.'

'That's fine. I'll give you the details to an encrypted site for you to upload them to, just to be on the safe side.'

The dad's name was Pavel Ivanovich Abramov. Masha had only one photo with him in it. It showed the three of them standing together; Masha, Sasha and their father in the middle. Pavel was wearing a *telnyashka*, the signature blue and white striped shirt that the Russian airborne troops wore. Veteran's Day then. The picture was taken in Park Pobedy, Victory Park, in west Moscow. The park named after the victory Rory's grandparents had contributed to. The Great Patriotic War. Pavel had a big smile on his face but looked more like mid sixties than fifties: the years of drinking had taken their toll. There were obvious similarities between father and son, and Masha had some of the same traits. The straight nose, the strong jawline. Then Rory noticed something on the father's right upper arm. A tattoo. It looked like a military one, with only a few rotor blades visible of what Rory guessed was a helicopter.

'Have you got any close ups of the tattoo?' Rory asked.

'Don't think so.' Masha looked through the photographs in her bag again. Most were of her and her little brother. 'No, not here. I can send you some older photos though, when I get home. I'll send some of Ivan, his best friend, as well. He should be in some old family ones I got digitised for my dad's 50th birthday.'

'And, your mother? Is she still, uh, around?'

'No. She died when Sasha was born. Sepsis.'

'I'm sorry.' Rory knew too well how it felt to lose a mother.

'Me too. This would never have happened if Mama was still around.'

The few relatives they had in Moscow hadn't heard from either son or father, and the next door neighbour hadn't seen them for at least a few days. There weren't many leads that Masha hadn't followed herself. Only one really. Her father's old drinking buddy, Ivan, or uncle Vanya as Masha called him, had no phone and no known address. He was still a heavy drinker, and Masha feared that her father's attempt at getting Ivan dry had backfired.

––––––

As RORY JOGGED BACK towards the flat, she tried to digest it all.

How was this happening? Taking on an assignment all on her own? But Masha and her brother needed help, and Rory needed the money. Really needed the money. Not to mention that it sounded like an easy job for a first solo assignment. A recovering alcoholic having fallen off the wagon, taking his son with him.

She did feel there was something Masha wasn't telling her, but brushed it off. All families have embarrassing secrets, her own in particular. It had taken years before her grandfather had returned to see his family in Norway, and to this day Rory still didn't know why. But the feeling of unease kept her on her toes. Even though the missing boy and dad might want to be found, she had given Masha strict rules about communication. No email, pay phones only. Standard operational security.

————

BACK AT THE FLAT, she started her planning as she did her stretches on the floor. Organised her travel, did her background checks. But first of all, she sent an email cancelling Sunday lunch with her father. At least she wouldn't have to tell him she'd quit her job yet. He would never understand. He had never approved of her choices, wanted her to be a doctor, or a lawyer, like Priya. Had threatened to disown her when she ran away to Norway, the country of her birth, instead of going to her Oxford University interview. She'd had to give up her UK citizenship to keep her Norwegian one, but Oxford had been her father's dream, not hers. Besides, Rory couldn't stand sick people, and would have died of boredom if she'd had to read thousands of pages on law. Her father had thought it was an excuse to avoid serious studies. And nostalgia for a mum who was no longer there.

But it wasn't a lack of ambition, or laziness that drove her. More an attempt at finding out more about her grandparents, her mother's parents. It had led to her signing up to the Norwegian army, and when her father reluctantly came to her graduation and heard the commanding officer describing her and her fellow officers as the elite, and Rory as top of the class, he had tears of pride running down his cheeks. And he had supported her decision to go to the Middle East and join the fight against IS.

They'd been on good terms the last few years, Tom had made that happen, but Rory knew it was an uneasy truce. Rory looked up at the photographs on the wall. At the family photos where most were dead. Only Rory and her dad remained. Maybe that was why Priya and her family had been so important to her. A backup family who'd taken her away from boarding school at half-terms when her own father was busy studying the biological diversity near volcanoes.

Priya. She had to send a message to Priya. Ever since Rory started working for Richard they had developed their own secret communication channel via one of the many Cats of Instagram accounts. Rory would post one type of picture to let Priya know all was fine, Priya would post a different one if she wanted Rory to get in touch. A few other friends were in on it too. Nikki Glass, who they called by her surname after she joined the police, was one of them. Cecile, who worked as a nurse, was another. Rory scheduled the post so it would go up after she'd left the next day.

Rory put her laptop away and went to her room to pack. She opened her closet, pulled out the suitcase and glanced at her clothes. This assignment was different. Not knowing where the boy or his father might be, she had to be prepared for all eventualities. Always blend in, don't attract attention. Dick's hated voice in her head again.

Finally ready for the morning's departure, she went to bed. Lying there, she vacillated between fear and anticipation, looking forward to running her own investigation, picturing success and failure with the same vividness. Then she sat up. *Shoes. I need the shoes.* She had never worn them, and had bought them on a whim after reading about the millionth celebrity wearing them on the red carpet. Christian Louboutin, the shoes with the red sole. She had always felt too self-conscious to use them in London. Worried it seemed like she was trying too hard. But in Russia they would be just the kind of item that could help her pass in places the rich frequented. She found the box, still at the top of the closet, and put the shoes in the suitcase. There, now she could sleep.

Rory got up early next morning. Even though she was all packed and ready, she wanted to have a calm and quiet start to the day. Another Richard thing. Save the adrenaline for the times when it really mattered. Not spend it on running to catch a flight. Then the doorbell rang.

Aurora pressed the speaker.

'Hello?'

'Morning hun, it's me. Got coffee. Can I come up before it goes cold?'

Priya.

Rory should have sent that message last night. She'd be annoyed when she found out Rory hadn't planned on telling her until after she'd gone. When it would be too late to talk her out of it.

Rory put the door on the latch and went into the kitchen to tidy away the washing up. The kitchen looked much like it had when her grandparents had lived there. 60s units with sliding doors and narrow shelves, a drying rack in the cabinet above the sink and a freestanding cooker. Her grandfather had kept it in mint condition, and she'd only given it a lick of paint to freshen it up. Her dad had offered to pay for a new kitchen, but she didn't want a new one.

'Hun?' Priya's voice as she closed the door.

'In the kitchen.' Rory walked towards her friend and gave her a big hug.

'How are you feeling today? Are you going to see your dad?' Priya nodded at the bags in the hallway.

'You won't believe this, but I've actually got my first solo gig. You know how you said I'd wanted to start up on my own? Well now I have. Flying to Moscow this afternoon.'

'Whoa. Today? Straight away? But ...'

Rory cut her off. 'Sorry, I can't say much yet, and I've got to leave in half an hour, but it should be an easy job to start with. No legal issues or anything like that.' She reached out her hand towards the coffee in Priya's left hand. 'Thanks?'

'Sorry, here.' Priya gave her the cup and took the lid off her own before she took a long sip. 'I know I said you should set up on your own, just didn't think you'd do it before I'd even got over my hangover. Are you sure about this? It's not something you agreed to when drunk, was it?'

'Pree!' Rory had to fight to keep from blushing. She had been under the influence. A bit sozzled. But not drunk drunk. She was a professional, after all.

'Sorry, it just seems a bit sudden. I don't mean to question you, of course you know your job better than anyone.'

'It's just a missing child case, in Moscow. Police won't lift a finger there unless the client pays them, so she'd rather pay me. And anyway, I need to be quick at starting on my own, before word gets out from Richard. He won't say what actually happened, it would be too humiliating to admit he got floored by a woman.'

They both rolled their eyes. It was all too familiar.

'But he's already started spreading gossip about why I'm unemployable, that I've been shagging half his employees.'

'Because of Tom?'

'Yep. Most won't believe it, of course. But I need to be proactive. Get out there. Write my own history.'

'Aw, hun, that is so unfair. But if the client didn't find you through Richard, how did she find you?'

'You remember the job where I met Tom? The client knows the mum. And she wanted me, not Richard, for obvious reasons.'

Rory finished her coffee, the caffeine giving her a sudden boost that drove away any sign of yesterday's G&Ts. Rory wondered if she should say who the client was, Priya might remember more about Masha, but she decided against it. Need to know only.

'Just goes to show, doesn't it. Richard might have treated you like an assistant, but that's not how the clients see you. Good on you. You will be careful, right?'

'Yes, mum. I will be careful.'

Priya pursed her lips at her.

'And I'll be in touch every week.'

Priya pulled her in for a hug. 'I can't help but being just a little bit proud of you, baby girl.'

Priya was two weeks older than her. A fact oft repeated. These days only in an affectionate way.

'And I'm proud of you. And grateful to have you, Pree.'

They left the flat together. Rory kissed her grandmother's old miniature icon that hung on a nail by the door. She wasn't religious, nor superstitious, it was more like a footballer wearing the lucky pants to a big match.

Better safe than sorry.

4

DMITRI PARKED his BMW and stood for a minute in the sunshine, closing his eyes to soak up a few rays of warmth after another Moscow winter. Across the street the tourists were milling about with their selfie sticks in the air, trying to get the best picture of themselves in front of the red walls of the Kremlin. It was a quarter of a century since he'd crossed the very same road, on his way to his first high profile assassination. Things hadn't quite gone to plan back then.

Dmitri took the last drag, threw his cigarette on the ground, and smothered it with his leather shoe. Twenty-five years. And it was finally coming to an end. What they had set out to do in 1991 had suddenly become relevant again. He liked the symmetry of it, the circle closing. His first high profile kill, the one that should have made them both a fortune, would now, twenty-five years later, be the job they could both retire on. Or at least that was what Dmitri hoped for. He buttoned up his suit jacket and walked around the corner, to the discreet entrance of Moscow's most exclusive gentlemen's club. He'd never been there before: he rarely met Sorokin in person. Maybe it was a sign of things to come?

'I'm here to see Deputat Sorokin,' Dmitri said to the young

man at the desk inside the stained doors. He didn't say his own name. There was no need to be careless now.

'He is waiting for you. Follow me, Gospodin,' said the young man and started walking into the building. The young man's oversized suit shuffled as he walked across the elaborately patterned parquet flooring. They went up the stairs and turned left at the top. The mirrors along the corridor had small brown speckles in the corners, and Dmitri caught the servant trying to get a look at his hand. The right hand that carried the evidence of Dmitri's having to get a new job whilst Sorokin had been locked up. He was no small man at six foot four, but up against the war veterans, former Olympic wrestlers and boxers who'd gone from being Soviet heroes to unemployed men with very specific skills, Dmitri's then 21-year old frame hadn't stood a chance. He'd lost half a finger pulling a crooked banker out of a hail of bullets, and gained a massive scar across his back dragging another client away from a nightclub brawl, before he'd realised that he needed to use his brain more than his body if he was to get ahead. To survive, even.

Three raps on the thick wooden door they had stopped in front of were followed by a stern, 'Come in'.

The room smelled of leather. Old books, old armchairs, cigars and scotch. Not one of the books had Cyrillic letters on them. It looked to Dmitri as if the whole room had been taken out of a Scottish country pile. The rumours must have been right then. The club's owner, Utkin, was said to have bought a stately home by Loch Earn in Scotland, and had shipped the entire library over to Moscow when he built a new gym for his mistress in its place. Dmitri had often observed this hankering for the British aristocratic lifestyle amongst the Russian elite. The ones who in public smirked at the waning influence of the British Empire, but sent their children to Eton and spent their evenings in this club. At least they had kept the mirrored hallway in the old, Russian imperial style, he thought. And the Scots knew how to distil.

'Ah, Dima, thank you for coming,' said Sorokin, a club regular if the servility of the servant was anything to go by. Dmitri had to stop himself from chastising the older man for using his name in front of an outsider. But the young man probably saw and heard a lot more interesting things than two middle-aged men meeting up for a drink. Rumours said the club had a deal with a prime escort agency, and sound-proofed bedrooms in the attic.

Sorokin stepped towards them, stretching out both his arms. A watch worth more than Sorokin's official lifetime earnings as a politician slipped on his wrist. Dmitri gripped Sorokin's right hand.

'Not at all, Andrei Mikhailovich,' Dimitri replied in return, still using the polite way of addressing the older man. Dimitri had promised to fix the roof of his mother's banya today, after having had to cancel because of the DC job. She had under-stood, of course. Work was more important. And she was still proud that he had such an important job at the Ministry. But he would have to make up for it later.

'I got your message, it seems we might have reason to celebrate?' Dmitri asked.

'Sit down, sit down.' The older man gestured at the two leather chairs, the only seats in the room. 'Celebrations are in order, yes, of course. But we're a little way off yet.'

'So you haven't found it?'

'No, not it. But I have found him. And there is only a question of time before we get to it, I am sure. But I might need your help.' Sorokin handed Dmitri a folded sheet of paper.

A handwritten note. So the room was bugged, might even have cameras. Dmitri wondered who might be watching, if they knew who he was. Not many did. It was the curse of being the best at being invisible. No recognition whatsoever.

There had been talk, once, of his being awarded a medal for his work. But Sorokin had advised against it, saying it was too risky. Dmitri would have liked to have had a medal. If nothing else, then to show his mother that whatever it was he was doing, it was something she could be proud of. Defending the Motherland, just like his brother had done in Afghanistan. Not that his brother had ever been considered worthy of a medal. He'd defected after being taken prisoner by the mujahideen, never to return back to Russia. He was dead to the family now. Dmitri felt his jaw tighten just thinking of it. Then he noticed Sorokin looking at him, head askance.

He smiled at Dmitri. 'I got you a drink, I know you're partial to a nice scotch. Utkin got hold of a few casks of the rare 1982 Talisker.'

The small table between them had two crystal glasses on it, with thick bases and thin rims. A solitary ice cube floated like an iceberg in the straw coloured liquid. A cigar, Cuban, of course, was smoking away by itself in the ashtray. And there was a stack of magazines. A Learjet catalogue, one for Dassault Falcon. And the most recent Tatler left open on a page from a recent art exhibition in Moscow. Sorokin must have been looking for himself. He'd been trying to establish himself as a patron of the avant-garde for a while, building up his credentials both in Russia and most importantly, in Europe. They couldn't all invest in premier league clubs.

'Any trouble in DC?'

'None. I assume he's been found by now?' Dmitri swilled the ice cube around in his glass and took a sip. *A shame it's so cold you can barely taste the peat.*

'Yes. Heart attack, the headlines say. He had a very heavy meal last evening. The usual suspicions are being raised, of course. But the drug did very well in testing. There should be no trace at all.'

The two men sat for a while, looking at the red Kremlin

walls on the other side of the road. They had known each other for almost thirty years now. Sorokin had become the father figure who saw in him a potential he never had seen himself. And as much as Dmitri wanted to be treated as an equal, as a partner rather than an underling, Dmitri was forever grateful to him.

'Everything else ok? You look tired,' Dmitri said.

'Just the usual. One of my protégés turned out to be an activist. A bit annoying. It made people question my judgment when he desecrated that church. Nothing a generous donation to the Orthodox church's efforts abroad couldn't remedy, but still. Annoying.'

Sorokin's battle with Volkov, his most recent rival from the FSB, was beginning to take its toll. It wasn't the first, but Dmitri knew that Sorokin was hoping it would be the last. The constant jockeying for position, for connections, for money making opportunities, was even more intense than before. It was the president's way of trying to make sure no one group got too powerful, making them all fight between themselves. Add in the international sanctions that had forced Dmitri's latest victim, Povarsky, to defect to the West, and you had a game so complicated no one really knew the rules any more. But Volkov was playing his cards well. He'd married the younger sister of the president's chief of staff. Went to church every Sunday and even knew how to do the sign of the cross correctly.

'He got into my computers last week. Must've bought someone in my team. Nothing to be found there. But just the fact that he thinks there might be something worth looking for. It's not good.'

'Does he know about me?'

'Yes, sort of. But they all know better than to try anything where you are involved. You're too useful. Your skills are appreciated all the way to the top. And anyway, anyone who's heard of you would do well to steer clear. No one wants to be the next one on your list.' Sorokin smiled at him and took a sip of his glass.

Was there a hint of deference in his voice? Or was it all just an act for potential microphones? 'All the way to the top, eh?'

'All the way to the top. DC was an important one. A reminder of how useful we are.'

———

DMITRI GOT UP TO LEAVE, the note burning in his pocket. On his way out he saw a beautiful oil painting of an old, wooden rowing boat on the banks of a river, mountains in the background. The ornate carved frame looked new. Sorokin had got up to follow him to the door, but froze when Dmitri paused by the painting.

'Beautiful. Just beautiful. I didn't realise Utkin had taste,' Dmitri said.

'Oh, he doesn't. This was a gift from Volkov to the club. He thought it might be 'fun' to remind me of my years in the wilderness after the coup. Painted to order, even. Don't think he realised how motivating it is to look at the place where I spent three long winters with forced labour. I am never going back there. Ever.' Sorokin spat the words out.

Dmitri had never asked Sorokin about his time in the labour camp. Nor had Dmitri said anything about his failed attempts at 'making it' in the early nineties, after the Soviet Union had fallen apart. When Sorokin was pardoned three years after the coup, and made his way back to Moscow, it seemed too soon. Later it had become awkward.

Dmitri stretched out a hand. He wanted to read the note, to see what had to be done so they could both get out of this game before it got to them. As Sorokin put his hand out again, Dmitri noticed a small nick on the webbing between

Sorokin's thumb and index finger. A slide bite from a semi-automatic gun.

'I had to hire a day labourer.' Sorokin said and looked at his hands, as if they were still soiled.

Dmitri had to smile. Sorokin hated doing his own dirty work. Never liked guns, found them too noisy.

'I'll be in touch.'

'Thanks again, Dima. I don't want to rush you, but time is of the essence. The wolves are gathering.'

5

MOSCOW

'MA'AM, you need to raise the back of your seat. We're landing.'

Rory felt the hand gently shaking her shoulder before she opened her eyes and saw the stewardess the voice and hand belonged to.

'Sorry, of course,' she said and fumbled to find the button on her armrest. As the stewardess walked away, Rory tried to collect herself. To remember what it was she had been dreaming about, what had made her so reluctant to wake up. Of course. She'd been dreaming about him again. Tom. About how they'd first got together, in the very city she was about to return to. From the beginning, she knew that the Moscow job would be unlike all the others. Tom didn't just follow instructions, he kept asking questions. Why were they doing this, why that. Did Rory think they always worked for the 'right' side?

They had found Leonora and her mother Natalya easily enough, in a run-down apartment building in a shitty town a few hours from Moscow. It was horrid, the playground as grey as could be, one single swing still in working order. And both mother and daughter had looked as miserable as the surroundings.

After a couple of days it became apparent that Natalya had no bodyguards, no family members who might pose a problem to Rory and her team. But during those days they also saw a mother completely devoted to her daughter, trying her best to make her days a little brighter. So, together, Rory and Tom had hatched a plan. Dick would have been furious if he'd known, but they weren't about to tell him. Rory approached Natalya when Leonora was playing with some other children, and it hadn't taken long before she had a sobbing Natalya in her arms.

It was what Rory was particularly good at; getting people to open up to her, even if she was a complete stranger. She'd got that from her late mother. It was the reason she'd been recruited to work as an interrogator. Soldiers and jihadis alike wanted to talk to her. She'd been sent to Iraq to work with SIGINT, signal intelligence, listening in to the enemy's communication channels, but then one of her instructors from the interrogation course had spotted her in the mess tent. It was just the one interrogation to begin with. Then came another. Soon enough she'd been transferred to assist the special forces with their newly captured prisoners. Rory had enjoyed it at first, felt like her efforts had real-time consequences and she could help save the lives of her fellow soldiers. The doubt came later. What happened to the prisoners afterwards? Were they treated as they should be, in accordance with the Geneva convention? After her second six month tour, she'd left the military. That was when Richard asked if she wanted to work for him. He'd heard about her from some of the SAS officers she'd worked with in Iraq.

It turned out that Natalya had never intended to leave Britain, never wanted to take her daughter away from her father, her own ex-husband. But neither was she willing to let her ex send their girl away to a boarding school. She'd taken

Leonora back to Russia with her to prevent it from happening. Rory suggested that maybe the father would reconsider, if they moved back to the UK. That some sort of amicable solution could be worked out.

'If I say no, you will just take her anyway, won't you? You and your bodyguards? I don't know how you found me here, I don't know anyone here. I haven't used my phone, bank account, nothing,' Natalya said and looked down at her hands: nails chipped, skin dry and cracked from having done any job that offered up a chance to earn enough to pay the rent.

'I've met your ex-husband. I'm not going to pretend that I know him as well as you do, but I don't doubt that he loves his daughter very much. And he's not so stupid as to not see that the girl adores you. I think it's worth a try.'

And try they did. Dick went ballistic, as expected, but had to contain himself as the client, a rich City lawyer, was part of the conference call. The client didn't take much convincing, even suggested getting two houses nearby a private day-school, so Leonora could spend as much time as possible with either parent.

How they had celebrated that night. Rory, Tom, and the two other guys toasted in vodka and washed it down with beer. And afterwards, when they got back to the hotel, Tom had escorted Rory to her room. Just to be a gentleman, of course. Not that she needed any protection: the guys had taught her enough self-defence and close combat to get out of most situations. But the gesture was still nice, so she decided not to dismiss him. Getting out of the lift he had put his hand gently at the small of her back, and she had felt the heat radiating, as if her skin was on fire. Neither of them knew what to say when they reached her room, and an awkward attempt at a goodnight kiss on the cheek had landed on her lips. Before she knew it she was halfway up the wall, slamming the door shut, her legs clasped around his waist, both tearing at each other's clothes.

When she woke up next morning, he had already gone. She'd felt like a mug at first, but then thought, what the heck. She might never see him again, and it had been a long time since anyone had made her feel like that. And Tom had an amazing body: well built, but not in the way you get when going to the gym. When she saw him at breakfast, with the other guys, she did her best not to blush. But as soon as he got a moment alone with her, he apologised for leaving so early and asked if he could take her out for dinner when they got back to London.

'Dinner? Why did you just leave then?' she asked.

'I didn't think it would be a good idea for the other guys to see me leaving your room in the morning. You'll probably get enough flak from Dick as it is.'

'You could have woken me up. But sure, I'll have dinner with you.'

That had been the beginning of two amazing years. The memories got Rory from the plane all the way through to passport control with a smile on her face. As always, there were no organised queues to get through the border, just a lump of people flowing from one line to another, everyone trying to outsmart the others in the great Russian game of queuing. Rory never even bothered trying to find the fastest line any more, and allowed herself the luxury of thinking about Tom for just a little bit longer. About the times before they'd split. Having lost her mother as a teenager she'd become an expert at compartmentalising. The sadness and grief was neatly boxed up and sealed away. The happy memories got to live freely. It would help keep her calm as well, in case the border guard should question the validity of the work visa she had bought online for a previous visit. It claimed she was here by invitation from the railroad workers' union. But the guard barely looked up at her before she stamped her passport, and her ease of passage continued through customs as well. No one knew, nor suspected that she had brought eight burner phones, her basic surveillance kit with microphones and trackers, and a large amount of cash, to the country. And a second passport, with her picture and the name of a Polish woman, hidden in her handbag.

———

RORY KNEW she should look for the father first. It was her best shot at finding an eleven year old boy in a city of twelve million people. A boy who might be lost, or might be hiding, from God knows what. But as much as her logic told her to look for Pavel, she also knew she wouldn't be able to sleep unless she tried finding the child first. Sasha. The smiling little boy in the white football shirt.

Masha had contacted Sasha's school and his friends and their parents. No one knew where he was, they all assumed he'd gone to see her in London as planned. And her father? He didn't really have many friends. Or colleagues. It was a bit odd, really. Rory thought he must be one of those Russians who lived in a privatised apartment in central Moscow, an apartment he could never have afforded to buy for himself but which had come to him as a result of the privatisation in the 1990s. One of her great aunts had lived in one of those. It was a shell of a home, her great aunt didn't have much money to buy furniture for it, but the high ceilings, ornate woodwork and parquet flooring gave it a feeling of grandeur that even the hard single bed in the corner couldn't detract from. Rory had stayed with her for a month. She'd come to visit with her mother and grandparents one summer, and had struggled with the language. Her great aunt, Lyudmila, had suggested she stay behind and learn Russian properly, and it seemed a good idea at the time. Two weeks in, Rory had cried on the phone to her mum about wanting to go home. Lyudmila was no gentle teacher; she expected a lot from her student. After four weeks though, Rory didn't want it to end.

She had been the same age as Sasha then. Eleven, twelve years old. Intimidated and fascinated by the great city in equal measure. She could spend hours walking through the metro stations, looking at the marble and chandeliers. Her favourite station had been Ploshchad Revolyutsii, where superstitious Russians would rub the nose of the dog statue for luck. The nose had changed colour from all the different people rubbing it every day, just like her own golden retriever's nose had changed colour from black to pink because he kept pushing open the heavy doors in the house to find Rory. Lyudmila had taken her to the ballet, which she liked, and to the opera, which she didn't like. To the theatre, which she struggled to understand with her limited Russian, and to see the Moscow Philharmonic Orchestra play. That had been the start of her love affair with classical music. It was the one interest she shared with her father. Classical music. One of the few subjects they could talk about where her mother's death didn't interfere.

But where would an eleven year old boy hide? A boy interested in football, chess and ice hockey, but who didn't have his phone and might not have any money either.

————

THE HOTEL RECEPTIONIST pursed her lips when Rory produced her fake Polish passport. A foreigner staying in a room intended for Russians. It was a trick Rory had learned years ago. Most hotels operated with one rate for Russians and one for foreigners, but if you could fool them into believing you were Russian when you booked the room, you'd get away with paying the local rate. As a quarter Russian, Rory felt like she was entitled to it anyway.

'Ms. Piwowarski? The room is on the 14th floor. Breakfast between 7 and 9.30,' the receptionist said with the pretence of a smile as she handed over the key. It was a key, not a key card, and the heavy brass ring attached to it left no doubt as to what hotel it belonged to.

Rory picked up a tourist map from the counter and walked through the foyer, past the plastic palm trees and white leather sofas that looked no different from two years ago, and pressed the button for the lift. It stopped on several floors before it reached the ground floor. Expecting it to be full of people when the doors opened, Rory stepped aside to let people out. But there was no one in it. She dragged her suitcase in, and the lift started its slow journey to the 14th floor. On the 8th floor, the doors opened for a man dressed in a suit that said money, but not enough for a tailor.

The man looked at her, and gestured towards the floor. 'Down?'

Rory shook her head, and pointed to the ceiling, but the man entered anyway. He looked at her via the mirror, examining her from top to toe. She couldn't help herself and stared right at him, so when his eyes reached back up to her face, he met her unflinching gaze. This one was not for sale.

'Sorry, sorry.' The man bowed his head several times and shuffled into the corner, keeping his eyes to the floor.

When they reached the 14th floor, Rory left the elevator and walked the opposite direction to her room before the lift doors closed behind her. Fucking idiot. What was it with men and Moscow, why did they think that every woman under forty was a prostitute?

Rory went back towards her own room, the ring clanking against the solid wood door as she unlocked it. The neon lights outside her window were flashing, illuminating her room in red, green and blue. She looked for somewhere to put her suitcase, but the bag stand was missing one of the straps, so she left the case on the floor. She could already hear the drip from a tap in the ensuite, and wasn't surprised to see the pink sink and bath had black grime around the wastes. Pretty much as expected in a local rate room.

Rory left her stuff in the room and ran back down the stairs rather than taking the lift. She preferred to have tried out any escape route, just in case. Blocked fire escapes were not uncommon in Moscow. As she walked towards the underpass she was amazed to see how much Moscow had changed in just a year. There were even more fancy cars, and a lot more middle class cars, around these days. And the old Ladas, or Zhiguli as the Russian market version was called, were few and far between. The driving was the same though. Crazy, chaotic, and obvious to even the daftest of police officers that quite a few of the drivers had never taken a lesson, but had bought their licence. So Rory took the metro whenever she could. It was faster, anyway.

———

THE APARTMENT BUILDING Sasha and his father lived in was as grey as the others around it, the courtyard both a parking lot and a place full of rubbish bins for the restaurants that were facing the main street, some overflowing. Someone had set up a little cardboard house between a bin and a corner, but there was no one in it. Up above she could see a sliver of grey sky, and a few sooty sparrows had settled in a lone tree. The only thing that said something about the state of the interiors of the flats, was the cars. Most were middle of the range, a Toyota Prius, a few Volkswagens and other family cars. And a Lexus and two shiny black BMWs.

The block doorbell had a handwritten note saying out of order. Rory got out the keys Masha had given her and found the fob. The door clicked open, and revealed a communal hallway as grey as the outside. There was a row of six dark green letterboxes on the left, and a pile of unwanted mail in the corner.

Rory walked up the stairs, listening out for any sounds, and could hear something from up above. A chair moving, perhaps. She looked up and caught a glimpse of a person looking down at her.

'Sasha? Is that you up there? I'm a friend of your sister.'

There was no reply. She scaled the stairs, there was one door to the left and one to the right on each floor. Six flats, three floors. Made sense.

Sasha and his father lived on the second floor. Rory looked up again, but there was no sign of the person above any more. He or she had been at the very top. As she turned the corner and could see the doors on the second floor, one of them shut without a sound. And whoever was behind it was now looking through the spyhole in the door. The door was opposite the entrance to Sasha's home. Rory rang the bell to Sasha and Pavel's flat twice, and could feel the eyes at her back. She made a point of showing that she had a set of keys before she let herself in.

The flat smelled of overripe fruit and rotten fish. The kitchen was on the right, and she found an oven dish half submerged in water, blackened pieces of food stuck to the half that was not under water. A few flies were circling the bin to try to continue their feast. Someone had left the flat thinking they'd be back to finish cleaning that. And quite a few days ago, judging by the smell and the brown bananas.

Rory went towards the living room. The wall was filled with photographs. Some old family photos, probably prewar. Others were more recent. And in the living room itself were what looked like a summary of the lives of the children. Two baby photos, one yellowed and old enough to be Masha, the other probably Sasha. First day of school. Masha with a red diploma. Her graduation picture. Both of them appeared in photos holding chess trophies.

The place looked tidy, but she got a feeling that someone had been in there. Someone who'd moved things around, who'd not put things back where they belonged. There were small signs such as the wooden shelf having been lightened by the sun, but the darker patch that used to be under a large picture frame was visible. She went through to the bedrooms. The father's room didn't have much in it. The son's gave a snapshot of a boy who loved football (Tottenham Hotspur shirt on the wall), chess (trophies on a shelf over the desk), ice hockey and movies. Nothing new to learn. There was a class picture taken not long ago, Sasha looked a lot like the most recent photo his sister had sent Rory. Rory looked at all the other children, examined their faces. Tried to guess which of them might be his friends.

As she left the apartment, she could hear movement from upstairs again, so she leapt up the two flights and found herself face to face with a man with a gun in his belt. The man reached for it, but Rory threw her arms up and stopped a few steps below him. There was a black folding chair behind him, a few dirty mugs and a full ashtray. A body-guard. Guarding whoever lived inside the top floor flat.

'I'm sorry, I didn't mean to startle you. I'm looking for the boy who lives below? Sasha? Do you know him?'

'Get off the steps,' the man said, signalling with the barrel of the gun.

'Of course, of course. I was just hoping that, maybe you, as a professional, might have heard or seen something in the flat below? Something others might not have noticed?'

'I'm not paid to spy on the neighbours,' he said and sent a blob of spit into the corner.

'Any chance your employer knows the family below? Could I perhaps ask him or her?'

'He's busy. Got company,' the bodyguard said and smiled as if it was him who'd lured a beautiful thing back home.

Rory heard the door open on the floor below, and decided

to give up on the bodyguard. 'Apologies, I didn't mean to disturb,' she said and walked back downstairs without turning her back on the pistol.

The door opposite Sasha's flat closed again just as she turned the corner. She knocked twice. Rang the bell. But nothing. The people in there didn't want to have anything to do with whatever was going on. She walked back down the stairs to the ground floor and looked at the letterboxes again. The top floor ones had the same name on them. Penthouse flat. Not that that got her anywhere. There was a letter in Sasha's mailbox, but Rory didn't have the key. She quickly got out her phone, turned the flash on and snapped a photo through the top flap. When she looked at the photo she could only make out a few words and letters. IM and Botkina. Some place named after Botkin, whoever that might be. She would have to look it up later.

———

RORY WALKED DOWN STARY ARBAT, the pedestrian street favoured by tourists and locals alike. Sasha's school was on one of the side streets, and its location alone was enough to prove that it was a prestigious one, at least among certain layers of Moscow society. Rory passed the Matryoshka doll sellers, the puppy vendors, the portrait painters. There. Spring holidays had just started, but Rory hoped she might still find a member of staff who could help her. Even if the headmaster had been dismissive when Masha had called.

Rory's shoes squeaked on the vinyl floors. A cleaner stood at the end of the corridor with a polishing machine, and chairs and desks had been stacked into the corner of the classroom she could see from the entrance.

'The sports hall is in the other direction,' the cleaner said over the hum of the machine.

'I was looking for the office?'

'Closed. There's no one there now. But I think there might be someone at the tournament.'

Rory walked in the direction the woman had been pointing. Then she followed the sound of voices down a flight of stairs and into a hall the size of a basketball pitch. There were wall bars on the far side, basketball hoops pulled up towards the ceiling. And rows of tables with chess-playing children at either side, eager parents waiting at the side.

Rory looked for the teacher from the photo in Sasha's room, but couldn't find her anywhere. But she did recognise a boy. Short, dark hair, little brown eyes behind glasses. The boy was looking at a couple of older girls who were battling it out in speed chess, and was smiling to himself as the game progressed. Rory walked over, pretending to follow the game, and manoeuvred herself next to him. The younger of the girls was on the attack and had her opponent fighting for survival. Then she brandished a knight, plonked it in the heart of her opponent's defence, and stood up to offer a handshake. The crowd around the table applauded, and Rory and the boy did too. As the girls shook hands across the table, Rory nudged his elbow.

'That was impressive, wasn't it?' she started.

The boy looked at her, and back at the winning girl.

'Yes, wasn't it. That's my sister,' he beamed. 'Our team captain.'

'Congratulations!' Rory leaned forward and shook the hand of the winner. The girl gave a brief smile before she turned to her peers.

'I thought maybe Sasha would be here,' Rory continued.

The boy turned and looked at her.

'Sasha? Which Sasha?'

'I think he's in your class? Blond hair, just a little taller than you. Plays chess?'

'No, he didn't sign up for this one. A shame. We could have beaten the other school if he'd played.'

'You know him well?'

'Sasha? Of course. We're best friends.'

'Ah, I'm good friends with his sister, Masha. Thought I'd pop in to see if he was playing today.'

'His sister? I thought he was with his sister, in London. At least that's what he told me.'

'He was meant to be. But something happened. He never made the flight.'

'Really?' The boy frowned, as if he was trying to add something up.

The girls had moved on, and another couple of school kids had taken over the table, setting up the pieces for their game. The boy looked like he wanted to run away, so Rory pretended to turn her attention to another game, and he followed her gaze.

'Sorry, I didn't catch your name. I'm Rory. The thing is, Masha has tried to get in touch with Sasha, to find out why he didn't come to see her. And she's very sad and worried. Thinks maybe he didn't want to go, after all. Any idea why he'd not call her to say he wasn't coming?'

'But I thought he'd left. That he was so keen he'd even left early.'

'Really? How come?'

'He hasn't been at school since Monday, so I thought he'd taken an earlier flight. And he's not answering his phone, which makes sense as it's so expensive to use it abroad. But maybe his dad took it away.'

'Why would his dad take Sasha's phone away?'

The boy looked around to see where his sister was. Spotting her on the other side of the room, he continued. 'We were playing *CS:GO*. When we were supposed to do our homework?'

Rory looked at him. 'A computer game?'

'Yes, Counter-Strike.'

'Were you together?'

'No, we play online. I was at home, in my room. Sasha doesn't have a computer in his room, so he logs on from an internet cafe.'

Rory kept chatting to the boy, Vladimir. They had played Monday afternoon, like they always did. And Vladimir thought Sasha had been caught not doing his homework, as he just disappeared without warning, and without logging off properly.

'I thought maybe his dad had surprised him, realised he wasn't doing his homework but playing with me. He's really strict, sometimes. Even when Sasha is top of the class.'

But Vladimir didn't know where Sasha had been. Just that he used to go to the same place each time. Whilst his father was doing something or other nearby.

Rory kept going through the conversation on her way back to the hotel. Internet cafes weren't exactly a scarcity in Moscow, and she assumed it would be some distance from their flat if the boy wasn't allowed to be home alone. If only she had the team with her, she could have gotten the tech guy to hack Sasha's CS:GO account and find the IP address of the cafe. Now she'd have to send a request to London. But she couldn't just sit down and wait for the results to come back, it could take a few days before she heard back with all the precautions. Rory dropped into an internet cafe on Old Arbat, pondering if it may be *the* one, but got down to contacting London. The out of office reply came before she'd had a chance to log off. It would be at least two days before tech would get back to her.

I'm going to have to start looking for the alcoholic.

Back at the hotel, Rory unfolded her map on the bed. She didn't want to depend on Google maps, couldn't risk leaving electronic traces all over the place in case her search rattled the wrong cages. Rory had already pinpointed the different locations Masha had said Pavel's friend Ivan used to drink, and had added a few from her own research. Then she compared it with a tourist map from the hotel lobby with internet cafes marked. No obvious matches. Though she hadn't expected there to be, the weekly activity a recovering alcoholic dad was occupying himself with whilst Sasha was playing Counter-Strike probably wasn't drinking.

She had to decide whether she should travel with or without a passport. Any foreigner should always carry his or her passport, or at least a copy, but she didn't want to be easily identified. She decided to bring a copy of the fake Polish passport she'd had made for the previous Russian trip. With a few rouble notes wrapped inside. Enough to bribe a cop or two to accept the copy. And she wasn't planning on looking like a tourist anyway. She had another look at the map, made sure she had memorised the watering holes and the nearest metro stations to where she was going. It had been a week now. One week with no sign of either father or son. Were they still together? Had Pavel pulled his son into the dark world of alcoholism? Rory thought about going to the zoo, or the state circus, but it really was like looking for a needle in a very large haystack. Rory realised she needed help. She sent a message to her journalist friend Sam, via the secure messaging service Signal. Sam's boyfriend should be able to find the IP address, and the physical location, of the internet cafe using Sasha's nickname in Counter-Strike. But he'd have to do so without being detected, and that took time. Rory couldn't just sit still while she waited to hear back.

———

THE NEXT MORNING, and six grubby, stinking bars later, and all Rory had gained was a thick layer of grime under the soles of her shoes, and the look of someone who might actually belong to the places she had visited. Her feet were aching, her neck stiff and she felt slightly woozy from all the beer she'd had to get through. She could still feel the hands of the two teenage boys who had taken her for easy prey when leaving the outdoor cafe under the ski jump just after midnight. Fucking idiots. She couldn't risk attracting too much attention to herself by beating them up, so had resorted to a bit of the on demand vomiting she'd learnt to master in her miserable days at boarding school. It was enough of a distraction for them to let her slink away into the darkness, where she quickly made herself disappear. She'd had to throw away the jacket she'd been wearing, and bought a jumper, a horrid, purple thing one of the old ladies at the nearest station must have been trying to flog for months. At least the road dust on it made the pattern on the front slightly less shimmering and looking like it belonged in an 80s pop video. The matted hair look she had tried to achieve before starting out, was now perfected. She reeked of beer and cheap cigarettes. Only one more place on her list, and she could go back to the hotel and have a well-deserved hot bath.

6

DMITRI LIFTED the axe above his head again. Drops of sweat were running down his temples, and his bare torso reflected the rays of sun that made their way through the birch trees above him. Thwack. The axe landed right in the middle of the wood, splitting it with one chop. He put another log on the wood block, his shoulder muscles flexing before he dropped the axe again. And again. The last traces of frost were thawing, but the ground still felt hard.

After hours on a plane and the tense meeting with Sorokin followed by a night of interrogating their prisoner, this was just what he needed. Dmitri rested the axe on the block and inhaled the scent of the trees and the flowers around him. Breathed out a cloud of condensation. It was good to clear his head, get the frustration out.

The prisoner wasn't talking. At all. Dmitri had tried the common methods, using carrot and stick in equal measure. Nothing worked so far. Dmitri knew himself well enough to take a break before he got frustrated. And he wasn't about to use extreme measures. Not yet. He wasn't a thug, and the results were not reliable either. So the wood had to pay instead.

Thwack. Half the log hit a nearby tree and Dmitri put the axe down to retrieve it. A single fat fly landed on his knee. His mother hated flies, had her fly swat always within reach, but Dmitri didn't mind. He grabbed for the water bottle by his feet, but it was empty. The piles of wood on either side of the wood block made him realise he'd been at it for quite a while. The fly flew away as Dmitri picked up a stack of the firewood and headed back. A black and orange butterfly flitted about ahead of him as he walked along the path that took him through the vegetable patch and to the back of his mother's cottage. He grabbed the t-shirt he'd left on the nail by the door.

'Dima, just in time. I've just taken the bread out of the oven, and there's tongue and horseradish. And some salad,' she said as he walked into the small kitchen. Dimitri wasn't really hungry, his mother had made him eat a healthy second breakfast before he went out, but he just smiled, went over to kiss her on the head and sat down on the chair she had pulled out for him. The smell of fresh bread was too good to forgo anyway.

'Thank you, mama.'

The horseradish sauce was just as spicy as it used to be, and made his eyes tear up a little. His mother sat down opposite him with a cup of tea. He had brought her a bag of fresh lemons, but could see that she was still using the slice she'd cut this morning.

'How are the tomato plants growing this year?' he asked.

His mother blushed. The tomatoes were a contentious subject. Last year his mother's neighbour, Darya, had had the first ripe one. And she'd had the longest cucumbers. This year, Dmitri had picked up a bag of special tomato fertiliser for his mum, just in case she wanted to experiment, as he'd said. He'd never seen the bottle again, but thought she might have decanted the contents into something else.

'Oh, they're nothing special. Same as always,' she said with a smile. Then she squeezed his hand.

The rest of the meal was spent in silence. There wasn't much to talk about. He'd done most of the things that needed doing, including fixing the roof on the banya, and there wasn't much to say about his job. And neither of them wanted to break the peace and talk about Darya and her rich, successful son. It seemed like his mother had given up on the battle for 'best son' in the village. It pained him, but he couldn't well explain that Darya's paper-shuffling, bribe-taking son was the lowest of the low. That all Darya's son did was steal from the state, the people. People like his mother and Darya.

————

AFTER THE MEAL, Dmitri's mother took the plates away, and he went to the banya to clean up. There was no bathroom in the cottage, and the only two taps were in the kitchen and the banya, which was a separate building to the side of the vegetable patch. He had suggested getting a hot water tank, but his mother had brushed him off. Too much of a luxury. And anyway her kettle worked just fine on the wood burning stove. It was only after Darya had had water installed that he'd managed to convince his mother to have running water at all. There was no need to light up the fire and heat the banya itself, he just wanted to clean up a bit.

The door opened to a small room with a stove, a stack of dry wood on the side, and a small door into the banya. There were makeshift hooks on the wall, a couple of wooden buckets and a small dish with some old soap pieces glued together. Dmitri wrung off his sweaty t-shirt, and put a bucket under the tap. He took off his jeans and boxers, and put them up on the hooks on the wall. The scar on his calf was healing nicely; in a year or two it wouldn't be visible any more. It wasn't often anyone managed to get close enough to injure him these days. Most of his scars were from the years after the coup, when he had been struggling to find a job as a bodyguard or enforcer. A reminder of how brutal the fight for wealth and positions had been. The finger he lost to a bullet, the broken vodka bottle that had cut dangerously close to his spine. It was a lot more orderly these days. More about playing the political game, building alliances, paying kickbacks. There was still violence among the low level gangsters and the fulltimers, but the bankers, politicians and ex-KGB men didn't try to kill each other anymore. Why use a car bomb when you can get someone sent to a prison camp in Siberia? Or committed to a mental hospital?

He grabbed the full bucket and poured it over himself, relishing the cool water washing away sweat, dirt and city. He put the bucket back under the tap again and grabbed a piece of soap. Then he heard sounds of rumbling, as if a heavy diesel engine was starting up. He shook his head, trying to get rid of the water that had lodged itself in his left ear canal. His mother hadn't mentioned anyone having building works. He grabbed a sponge and scrubbed his neck and shoulders. Then he heard it again. Not just one engine, but several. And shouting and yelling as well. It came from the main road, the opposite end of the little village. He grabbed his jeans and jumped into them, and ran to his mother's cottage.

'What's going on, mama? Do you know what's happening?'

But his mother was in the front garden, talking to Darya, the neighbour. She was on her mobile phone, walking back and forth. An older man came running over.

'They're going to tear everything down, say they have documents to prove they own this land,' he said and looked at Darya.

She walked away from him, still talking on the phone.

Dmitri opened the window a bit more to hear what was being said. He could see the outline of heavy machinery in between the trees at the far end of the village. And the roaring engine sound came from a huge, yellow bulldozer that was making its way down from the back of a trailer.

'But Misha, they are here, now, with a bulldozer. They're about to tear down Sidorov's cottage,' Darya said into the phone, hands wringing. Then she walked over to the others. 'He's a bit busy right now, he can't throw everything else aside,' she explained to the others.

'But you said he had sorted it out, the papers, that he had a judge certifying our deeds?' Sidorov said, before he went back to his cottage. A loud argument followed from the old man's front garden. Dmitri's mother came running back in.

'What's going on, mama?'

'Oh, it's all such mess. I don't know how this happened,' she replied.

'What happened?'

'They came a few weeks back, some important men with papers claiming they owned the land and were going to build here. But we have our own deeds, and Darya's son was going to get it all sorted. He was sure there was just some administrative error, that they had the wrong coordinates. He went to see a judge, apparently it was quite a costly process as we all had to chip in, something about our deeds being outdated.'

'You paid a judge?'

'Yes, Darya said that was what one had to do. But something must have gone wrong.'

I know exactly what's gone wrong. Raiders. Taking what they want, because they think they can get away with it. Low level crooks.

Darya's son was far too low down the food chain to make any difference, bribe or no bribe. There were more raised voices from outside, and from the window Dmitri saw

Sidorov appear from his house with an old shotgun, but before he'd even raised it to his shoulder, one of the men with the bulldozer grabbed it out of his hands and hit him on the head with the stock. The man collapsed in a heap on the ground, and Dmitri's mother would have collapsed herself if Dmitri hadn't led her to a chair. Dmitri reached up to the top of the kitchen cabinet and found dust and his father's old rifle. There were a few boxes of ammunition there as well. He just hoped the gunpowder was still usable. He sniffed the boxes and left the one with the acidic smell.

'Mama, stay here. Do not go over there, these are not people you can reason with.'

Dmitri ran out the back door, rifle in hand, and headed for the trees. He ran through the undergrowth, not noticing the butterflies or the flowers. He'd always known Darya's son was useless, but this was even worse than useless. A couple of deer ran away as he rounded the corner of the village and found the hilltop he had been looking for. He lay down on the ground, resting the rifle on a tree stump. The rifle hadn't been used in decades. Not since he'd tried, and failed, to shoot some rabbits as a boy.

Sidorov had been pulled aside by his neighbours, and the bulldozer driver had climbed into the cab. The roar of the engine as it fired up made the songbirds scatter and disappear into the trees. The bulldozer was moving forwards, driving over the well kept, but old, fence. The picket pales broke like matches, snapped and disappeared under the tracks. Dmitri took aim, but the rifle jumped off his shoulder as the bullet left the barrel. The bullet hit the blade, but no one seemed to notice through the deafening sound.

At least Dmitri knew in what direction the aim was off. He fired again, hitting the mirror to the left of the cab. The driver paused, the dozer was halfway across the fence already, and he shouted to someone on the ground. Then he pushed forward again. Dmitri leaned over the rifle, his right cheek top of the stock and slowed his breathing. Then he gently pulled the trigger. The bullet went right through the cab, and shattered the rear window. The driver flung himself out of the cab and onto the ground, running behind the heavy machinery. The other builders around him were shouting, and Dmitri fired off another shot, this time aimed at the car that looked most expensive, bursting its front right tyre.

The men were looking around them, yelling, and one of them walked towards Sidorov's cottage, where the old man was trying to protect his home with his own body. Dmitri could see the stranger clenching his fists as he trampled across the vegetable patch, and then he fired another shot. The bullet went straight in front of the man's face, and he fell to the ground, screaming, trying to crawl back to the bulldozer and the other guys. The cars revving their engines, the men scrambling to fit into the ones that hadn't been shot at and spun away. Leaving the truck with a digger and the bulldozer behind.

Dmitri spat out a fly that had found his way into his mouth, and walked back to his mother's cottage. These guys would be back. And they wouldn't come empty-handed. As he re-entered his mother's cottage, he could feel her eyes following him around the room, mouth half open. He put the rifle and the last box of ammunition back on top of the kitchen cabinet, and grabbed a glass of water that he downed in one go. Then he looked at his mother. She tilted her head, as if asking a question, but then gave a little smile instead. Her eyes welled up. Not sadness, but pride. Dmitri had seen the same look when his brother had left for the army.

She knew. Of course she knew. Mothers always did. How could he not have noticed it before? And how long had she known that his pretend bureaucrat job was just that, pretend?

'I need to make a call,' he said.

'Of course. I'll go and make sure Mr. Sidorov is okay,' she said and made herself scarce. She picked up the little box she'd always had plasters and other first aid things in when he was a kid, and closed the door behind her. Dmitri grabbed his phone and turned it on, before dialling Sorokin's number.

'Hello?'

'It's me. I need some help,' Dmitri said. 'Urgently,' he added. These guys could be back with guns in twenty minutes, maybe less.

'I'm listening.'

'There's a group of raiders trying to take over my mother's village. Want to build a new mansion for some fucking minigarch.'

'Ok, I'll see if I can find out who they're working for.'

'They only left because I chased them away. They'll be back with guns any minute now.'

'Ah. That complicates it a bit. There's a lot of uh, minigarchs, about these days. Any idea who they're working for?'

'Name on the bulldozer says Pichugin.'

'I'll see what I can do,' Sorokin said and hung up.

Dmitri paced around the room, and realised he'd brought half the forest back into the house with him. He went out the back and brushed off the worst before he looked in his old drawers for another t-shirt. Metallica, it said on the front. That t-shirt was almost as old as his career. The month after the coup he had gone to the concert Metallica and other heavy metal bands had in Moscow. He, and a million and a half other young Russians. Those were the days. The days of hope, opportunity. But it had ended up as always. The people on top taking what they wanted, the rest being left to fend for themselves. Dmitri wondered what to do next. He could try to block the road, perhaps, but there weren't enough bullets left to mount a proper defence if the guys came back with automatic weapons, as he expected they would. He could try to overtake one of them, steal a gun and take them out that way. But there were too many innocents, too much risk that his mother and the others would be caught in the crossfire.

And he didn't want to out himself either, that would put his mother at risk for the foreseeable future. He just had to put his faith in Sorokin and his connections.

Dmitri sat tapping his left knee when his mother came back.

'He'll be fine,' she said. 'Just a nasty bruise, nothing broken.' She looked at Dmitri, at his phone, and back to his face again and bit her lips. 'I've always known this couldn't last. Us old people living out here, just outside the big city, in a world of our own. I do know what goes on, you know. But I would so like to get to see the garden flourish once more. The smell of the air after it has rained, the little family of sparrows that come back to me every year.' A tear ran down her cheek, and she wiped it away with a corner of her apron.

'Mama, no one is going to take this away from you. Not now. Not ever,' he said. But they both knew they were empty words. It wasn't up to them any more.

Darya poked her head inside the door. 'Lena, they're coming back. The boy down at the petrol station says they are on their way back. And there's more of them. If only your boy hadn't made them so angry, we could have reasoned with them, got them to wait until my Misha could sort this all out,' Darya said.

Dmitri didn't even bother looking at her as he sat hunched over the table.

Dmitri's mother shooed her neighbour out of the doorway. 'If your very important son had done what he said he'd do, this would have never happened in the first place, thank you very much. I think you will find that Mr Sidorov is quite relieved he hasn't been beaten to a pulp and still has a house to go to!' she said, and slammed the door in Darya's face.

He could see her shaking, and he reached out to her and grabbed her hand. For a minute or two they were both motionless, all they could hear was steady breathing. Then the phone rang.

7

'Yes?'

'You really put me to the test there, Dima. Really put me to the test.'

'And?'

'You know how many minigarchs and raiders there are in Moscow these days? Everyone is trying to get one up on everyone else. Everyone has a contact who's a judge, knows a man in the FSB. It's a complete labyrinth,' Sorokin continued.

Dmitri could see his mother pretending not to listen in. 'Are we okay?' he hissed at the phone.

'Yes, yes. Of course you are. The contractor, Pichugin's, has a KGB-shnik on their board. Someone who used to work with me in the old days. An okay guy. He's got a very profitable seat on the board of the company, but I explained the matter. That there were some national security interests involved here, that it would be a distraction from the important assignments ahead, and he immediately offered to withdraw his support. No questions asked.'

Dmitri could hear that Sorokin was smiling to himself, pleased with himself and how he had played the system he so often complained about.

'We've been told they're on their way here, just a few minutes away?'

'Oh, that shouldn't be a problem. If they do turn up, just ask them to call Pichugin himself. You might not want to reveal your involvement though. These are,' he paused. 'sensitive situations, as you know. Wouldn't want to embarrass anyone.'

Dmitri had just put the phone on the table when he spotted the first black Hummers between the trees. They weren't joking around. He looked at his mother.

'Shall I go over?' she asked. 'And tell them Pichugin wants a word? They're not going to shoot an old lady just like that.'

Dmitri didn't like it, but was probably the best option. He watched as his mother took her apron off, hung it on the back of the door, patted down her dress and walked towards the road and the approaching cars. Darya, the neighbour, was looking from her window, phone at her ear, but the handset slipped out of her hand as Dmitri's mother passed her. On old clogs, with a dress that she had worn and mended hundreds of time, and with a faded headscarf on her head, his mother walked towards the first car. The automatic guns were out of the windows already, aiming straight at her, but she kept going. She said something that Dmitri couldn't hear, and they waved her on to a car further back. Dmitri wished he'd been closer. He could only see his mother through the trees now. She was leaning into a car window, gesturing towards the bulldozer. One minute passed. Then another. The sparrows were singing from the rooftops, and the only other sound was the slow idling of the car engines. Then the car window rolled up again, and the convoy backed out again, back towards the main road. Dmitri let out a sigh of relief.

He left the house and walked towards Sidorov's house, where he found the old man and his mother picking up the pieces of the broken fence. Dmitri didn't say anything, but helped them put the wood in two piles, one for the smaller pieces, another for the picket pales that could be reused. One neighbour came and restrung the frames for the peas and beans, another had brought some early seedlings to replace the trampled ones. Darya came over as well, with a trowel and a selection of her own seedlings. Everyone worked in silence, and Dmitri could feel them looking at him, but he never caught anyone's eyes. He went around what was left of the fence and climbed into the bulldozer. The engine roared as he started it up. It only took a second or two before the neighbours had all gathered around his mother, demanding to hear what had happened.

Dmitri backed the bulldozer away from Sidorov's garden, and parked it at the end of the track and didn't hear what his mother was saying. As he went back to the others, he could see his mother beaming at him, patting down her dress in the way she always had done when she didn't know what to do with her hands.

Sidorov turned towards him. 'Your mother says to thank a former colleague of yours at the ministry. I would appreciate it if you could pass on my sincere gratitude. For everything,' he said.

Dmitri nodded. 'Of course, Leonid Ilyich.'

They both got back to their silent work, digging up the picket pales that had got stuck in the soil under the bulldozer.

The only one who couldn't let it go was Darya. 'But they will be back, they wouldn't have left their equipment here just like that. What do we do then? Call Dima's mystery friend?'

'Oh, I think we can consider that compensation for the damage caused,' Dmitri's mother said and turned to a gawking Darya. 'I told the man I thought it was only fair that we get to keep the machinery as compensation. We need to build a new fence for Sidorov.'

8

CENTRAL MOSCOW

RORY GOT off the metro at Kievsky. It was midday and not too busy, and people were giving her plenty of space to move around. She stood on the escalator, closing her eyes, but found herself beginning to sway with the rocking motion it made, and opened them again to avoid losing her balance. Only one more place, and she could rest. At the metro's entrance to the fancy Evropeisky shopping centre, she noticed a group of girls, or more like young women, shrinking away to leave as much space as possible between them and her. Perfect.

Back out on the street Rory got out a CSKA Moskva cap and tucked her hair into a messy ponytail. The traffic outside the shopping centre was crazy, as always. Cabs, minibuses and regular cars vying for space, each driver trying to outsmart the other. The already dented minibuses, the marshrutkas, seemed to have a clear advantage. They didn't have anything to lose by forcing their way through. An old woman with a headscarf and three furry bundles in a box in front of her sat leaning against the traffic lights. She looked at Rory with disgust, and pulled the box closer to her. Rory was in work mode, but couldn't keep herself from sneaking a peek at the puppies anyway.

Maybe she could smuggle one home with her once the job was done? If she had enough time, she could travel by train all the way back to England. She loved the trains in Russia. The random conversations with whoever happened to share your compartment, the bottomless samovar and the bossy train attendants.

A group of young men shouldered into her, and brought her back to present day. She'd missed her light. Damn. That last beer had really got to her. The last people hurried across the eight lane road, in front of a row of cars revving their engines. Rory took a deep breath, and rubbed her sweaty palms on her jeans. She closed her eyes again, this time visualising every facial feature of the two men she was looking for. Pavel's straight nose, the strong jaw and the now rounder cheeks. Ivan was thinner, gaunt even, with high cheekbones. His eyes not as deeply set, the nose had a bulbous tip. Both had blue/grey eyes, thin eyebrows and mousy grey hair. Nothing that would stand out in Russia.

If Pavel or Ivan were in there, she would spot them. No doubt. Then she pictured the tattoo Pavel had on his arm. The elaborate design with the helicopter, guns at the side. The parachute suspended over the rotors. Below there was the banner with the years, 86 and 88, and the location, Logar, Baraki region. And the initials of their unit; D-SH-B. Desantno Shturmovaya Brigada 56. The top of the tattoo had been obscured, but it was pretty obvious that it said Afghanistan, in Cyrillic lettering. The first and last letters had been visible.

The lights turned again, and as Rory reached the other side of the road, she could see the entrance to the stolovaya. The yellow and blue circuslike roof had patches of black tape to cover up holes, and a stream of greyed Russian flags draped towards the opening in the tent. Two portaloos, with an attendant waiting inside one of them, stood to the left. Five rubles only, half the price of the ones outside the Kievsky station. Rory walked through the archway, into the faded canvas dome. The stench of beer and piss made her nostrils flare, and she paused for a second by the entrance to get used to both the smell and the dim lighting.

There were five long rows of picnic tables lined up next to each other, with people sitting in twos and threes. Towards the right there was one larger group, guys with military tattoos spelling out VDV on their hands and upper arms, and a few of them were wearing the telnyashka, the blue and white striped military shirt Pavel had been wearing in the photo. The signature shirt for the VDV, the airborne troops. There was a pair of crutches resting next to one of them, and a wheelchair on the opposite side. Veterans. Younger than the ones she was looking for, but the same branch, at least.

A waitress with too much makeup and greying hair tied back into a slick ponytail slalomed between the tables carrying three jugs of beer, getting a slap on her bum as she put them on the table with the veterans. It made Rory think of Dick again, but she put that thought away. Looking at the men, the waitress and the other people around her, Rory became painfully aware that her pretending to be one of them would only work as long as people didn't look too close. She could fake the clothes, the torn jeans with stains of beer, dog hair and dirt. She could fake the hair, dirty strands hidden under a faded cap. But she could never fake the skin. The faces filled with nooks and crannies, a map of years of alcohol abuse, sleeping in the streets, scars from having been beaten up by bored police officers or a boyfriend, the marks from a previous winter's frostbite. But no one seemed to have noticed her. Rory looked around, searching for the man in the picture, or the man he used to be. And looking for anyone else that might not belong there. Not that she thought this was anything other than a missing, presumed drunk, case, but paranoia had become a habit after years of working for Dick.

In a corner, under a faded picture of tropical flowers, a man sat hugging his beer. Nope. Not him. The right age, but not the right features. She had another look at the table with the veterans, and noticed the odd one out. An older man sat with a bit more space than seemed natural between himself and the others, but still he wasn't far enough away to be on his own. The features were right, the eyes and the arch of the nose, and when he emptied his beer in one swig, she could see what looked like a military tattoo on the edge of his left hand. VDV in cyrillic lettering. Ivan. Pavel's drinking buddy and old friend. Rory sat down on the next table along, on the opposite side from him. As the three pitchers were passed around the group of veterans, Ivan moved his glass over towards them.

'Go get your own beer, old man. I've had enough of your scrounging,' one of the veterans said as he pushed the glass away, knocking it over. Ivan looked as if he wanted to disappear into the woodwork, and shrank away, towards Rory. It was him all right. And he was drinking beer, not vodka. Rory relaxed a little. There was a good chance he would be clear headed enough to get some sense out of.

'I'm a friend of Masha,' she said and moved a little closer to him. 'Pavel Ivanovich's daughter?'

'Masha, oh, I didn't recognise you,' he said, his voice thick and groggy.

Rory didn't correct him. Things might be easier this way. When the waitress came over, they both looked up at the woman with the pursed lips.

'Beer, please,' Rory said, in her best Russian accent, but realising she couldn't quite pull it off.

'100 grams,' the man said.

The waitress looked at Rory, lifting her eyebrows as if to

ask if she was paying. Rory nodded back and added some salted meats and pickled vegetables to the order.

'150 rubles,' the waitress said.

This was a payment upfront kind of place.

Rory put her hand in her left pocket, the one with the money that matched her outfit. Her hand came out with a few crumpled notes that she handed to the waitress.

'Is he bothering you?' one of the younger veterans asked her after the waitress had left the table.

'No, not at all. Family friend,' she replied.

Rory turned back to the man in front of her. His face looked swollen and discoloured, with what looked like a frostbite not quite healed yet on his right cheek. His chin was wet with beer.

'Yeah, daughter of my friend, she is. Mashenka.'

'How are you, uncle Vanya?' Rory asked, using the name Masha had used for her father's close friend.

Ivan muttered something, and pushed his empty glass away from him, eyes fixed on the table. The nails on his fingers were deformed, and he was missing half a ring finger on his left hand. He seemed to be looking at Rory's hands. They were dirty, but well kept. Long fingers. Short, sensible nails. She moved one of her hands to her face, pulling aside a strand of hair, to get him to lift his gaze a little, and his eyes followed. He'd clearly already forgotten that he thought she was Masha, and looked at her as if trying to figure out who the hand belonged to.

'I was wondering if you could help me find him? Pavel? And his boy, Sasha?'

'Pasha? Oh, he's long gone. Haven't seen him in a long time.'

'But I thought you met him every week? That you went to the banya together?'

'Oh, yes. We do go to the banya. He takes me every Monday. Cleans me up, inside and out. Very good of him.'

'Did you go last Monday?'

'What day was that?

'Last Monday, a week ago?'

'What day is it today?'

'Today it's Monday.'

'No, we haven't been today. We always go on Mondays.'

'But you went last Monday?'

'Yes. '

'Are you going today?'

Ivan tilted his head a little, and his eyes dropped to the table again. The crease between his eyebrows narrowed to make his face look all crumpled up.

'No, Pasha is long gone. We don't go to the banya any more.'

The waitress came over with the beer and vodka, and tossed the plate of cold meats and pickles on the table between them. Ivan looked at the vodka, a milk glass full of clear liquid, and downed it before Rory had even had a chance to reach out for her beer. Then he grabbed a few pieces of tongue from the plate, shoved them into his mouth and closed his eyes whilst savouring it.

'Does he come here, to drink with you?'

'Pasha drinking?' A big smile spread across Ivan's face. 'Oh, those were the days. We used to be drinking and fighting and drinking some more. No. Pasha doesn't drink any more. Something happened, and he just stopped. Nothing happened to me though, so I kept drinking.'

'He didn't start again?'

'Pasha? Oh no, that isn't like him. Once he decides on something, he doesn't change his mind.'

The conversation went on, in circles, for the next half hour or so. Rory wanted to scream at the man in front of her, 'Where the fuck is Pasha?' but she knew that would get her nowhere. Ivan seemed so confused, or was he afraid? Whatever it was, she didn't want to frighten him any more.

'Which banya is it you usually go to? You should be going there today, no?'

'Yes. No. He always cleans me up a bit first, Pasha does. Doesn't want me to be drunk when we go. But I can't go like this,' he said and nodded to the empty glass in front of him. 'Pasha wouldn't approve.'

'But Pasha isn't here. Maybe he is there waiting for you? We could go there together?'

'I don't know, I. Pasha always comes to pick me up. Gets me sober.'

'Maybe you can show me where the banya is? I could see if Pasha is there?'

The man withdrew into himself, his shoulders dropping forward and his chin reaching for his chest.

'Or you could tell me how to find it? Or the name of the place? You don't have to go there.'

'No, we don't go to the banya any more,' he said.

Rory gestured with a hundred ruble bill to the waitress to get another vodka, and it came swiftly this time. Then she motioned for the waitress to leave without returning the change, and saw the first sign of a smile that day. Ivan reached out for the glass, but Rory got to it first.

'What banya was it again?' she said, feeling slightly guilty about using vodka to get information out of an alcoholic.

Ivan looked at her hand and the glass, and the furrow between his brows got deeper again.

'Presne …. ,' he muttered, 'Too hot. The smell. The stench.'

'The one by street 1905? Krasno …,'

'Yes, yes,' he said, interrupting her. 'But the smell,' Ivan said, shaking his head, and his hands started to follow.

Rory pushed the glass towards him and into his hand. He quickly lifted it to his lips and emptied it, spilling some on his already stained jumper. But the shaking stopped. She sat for a while, sipping her stale beer, whilst Ivan calmed down again. She ate some of the pickled cucumber, and tried to start a conversation again, but Ivan had descended into a world of his own.

'Stinky, stinky,' was all he said. Or at least that was what it sounded like.

After a little while she said her goodbyes and got up, leaving the rest of her beer behind, only to see him pour it down his throat. The veteran who had asked if Ivan had bothered her, nodded as she left. She gave him a tired but resigned smile. As if that had all been a waste of time. The banya near the 1905 metro station was one she'd heard about before, an expat friend had hired it for a birthday once. It was a proper Russian style one, not a place that attracted all the tourists or the super rich, like the famous Sanduny baths downtown. She could do with a cleanup, and decided to go straight away.

Back by the entrance to the circus tent, Rory gave twenty rubles to the lady by the portaloos, who promptly offered up the heated one she used to sit in with her knitting. There was toilet roll and wet wipes inside, and Rory scrubbed off the worst of the grime and rearranged her hair to hide the stickiest strands of it under a woollen beret. Then she went and got some new clothes from the small market outside the train station, emptied half a pack of Tic Tacs and went back down to the metro, gradually changing her appearance as she went. Different hair style, change of clothing, a bit of coloured lip gloss on her lips and a bit of it on her cheeks. The escalator at the Ulitsa 1905 station was busy, and the space she had been given while looking her scruffiest, was replaced by people trying to push past her to get up and out on the streets.

Rory had to ask a few people for directions to the banya, but found the right street after a lady lugging her shopping home from the market said she was heading the same way.

The grey building was the kind you could walk past every day and never notice - render peeling off bricks, the windows covered with dust and specks of paint. It had two entrances, one for men and one for women, although inside they both led to the same counter where a grey haired lady with a leopard print top one size too small and glasses with leopard print frames sat playing solitaire on an ageing desktop computer. There was a price list on the wall behind here, alongside a garish calendar featuring a pink sun rising over the horizon and pink flamingos playing in the lake below a waterfall. The logo of Mosgosstrakh, an insurance company, in the corner. Most of the prices had been crossed out and edited several times.

'Standard session, please,' Rory said, not knowing what that meant. But it sounded like the obvious option, and it was the first one on the price list.

Rory enjoyed going to Russian banyas, but had never quite understood the fascination with the more painful aspects of it. The whipping with the birch branches, the not just cold but actual ice water they plunged themselves into after spending time in the banya itself. Worst of all was the soap scrub she had once signed up to by mistake. She had felt like they were scrubbing all her skin off, and had to look twice to check that she didn't have bleeding patches afterwards. But she loved the rituals; the careful preparation of the banya, the herbs or whatever they were that were added to the fire, that filled her nostrils as she inhaled the hot air. How the heat made staying in there almost unbearable, and the shower afterwards that made you feel so alive.

The leopard lady took her money, and smiled, before she wrote everything down neatly on a notepad, underlining the amount paid.

'Do you want tea as well? And sandwiches? You have to pay extra for that,' the lady said.

'Yes, please.'

'Before or after?'

'After, please,' Rory replied, not quite sure exactly what it would be after.

The lady wrote a new line with details and an amount, gave her a pink ticket along with the change, and a token for the small lockers, where Rory could leave any valuables. Not that she carried anything of value. But she left most of the cash, and the burner phone she had yet to turn on. A couple of men came in as she was locking it, and put their money on the counter, not even stating what option they wanted. They seemed to be paying less - maybe she had paid for extras after all. They asked the leopard lady if the stink was gone, and she lowered her voice so Rory couldn't hear the answer. Rory sniffed the air, but all she could smell was chlorine and soap. Ivan had mentioned the smell. Or had he said stench?

Rory went into the women's section and put the bag with clothes she had bought from the market, and the stack the leopard lady had given her, down on the fake leather bench.

A big and a small towel, a pair of single use slippers and the funny felt hat she was supposed to wear in the banya itself. There weren't many visitors on a Monday afternoon but she could see some curly grey hair appearing and reappearing behind a bench a few seats down, and a few younger women, students by the look of it, in the far corner. There weren't enough women there to make striking up a casual conversation easy. She would have to start asking questions at some point. Looking at herself in the small, round mirror hanging from the hook at the top of the leather seat made her wince. No wonder the lady at the counter had smiled so kindly at her, probably thought she was in dire need of a proper clean up. Her skin was grey, there were dark circles under her eyes after nights with no sleep. The lipgloss she'd put on looked comic more than anything. And her hair. Her long, thick hair clung to the side of her head, lumped together in thick strands that made her look like she had bald patches. She quickly replaced the beret with the felt hat she'd been given to wear in the banya.

Beyond the changing area there were big, wooden buckets, the size of half barrels, high up on the wall. There was a big clunk as a young woman tugged at the chain hanging from one of them and received a bucket full of cold water over her head in return. The sight sent shivers down Rory's spine, but the woman showed no reaction. There was also a blue and white tiled plunge pool, with mosaic just above the cold water, depicting some image from Greek mythology. Poseidon, she thought. The pool was big enough for three strokes across and three back. That is if you could make it that far before cramping up. There were tables and wicker chairs, upturned dainty cups on saucers and a small counter with perspex glass by the entrance, where the sandwiches and the samovar were.

Rory hung up the threadbare dressing gown and a towel before getting out of her smelly clothes. She had a long shower to clean off any dirt and grime from the preceding 48 hours of going from watering hole to watering hole, and could feel the smell of beer being washed away. But when she went towards the banya, the steam room, with the felt hat now covering her newly washed hair, she was turned away by the stern bath attendant.

'You have to wait. The *parilka* is not ready yet,' she said.

The woman reminded Rory of the discus throwers from the era of Eastern bloc doping scandals - face and body looking like one building block put on top of the other. Two women came out of the parilka, the steam room, and went straight for a swim with Poseidon. The room need to be prepared for the next session to establish the right steam and level of heat and humidity before they would let anyone in again. That was probably why some of the other women were having a break. Drinking tea, shaving their legs in the shower.

Rory pottered around, nicked some shampoo from a left behind bottle in one of the showers and washed her hair a third time, and listened to the other people's conversations. Not much of interest. The students were talking about university politics, the elder women about their health. Hip operations, achy joints. That was all she was able to hear, without the eavesdropping becoming too obvious. When the banya was ready again, she approached once more, felt hat on her head.

'You're second,' the bath attendant said.

'Oh, ok.' That was when Rory noticed the bucket full of birch branches soaking in water.

The bath attendant grabbed a set of branches from the bucket, went into the banya and started whipping one of the older ladies lying on the bench. So that was clearly included in the standard price then. Oh well. Rory allowed herself to relax, enjoy the warmth. She could feel the alcohol coming from her pores, forced out by sweat and steam. When it was

her turn she took her bathrobe off and lay down on the
bench, face down. She almost enjoyed it as the birch branches
got the blood rushing to her skin and the wet leaves brushed
away the sweat and dirt.

Rory left the banya just after the students, hoping to
eavesdrop on a conversation about the stench, or had they
used the word smell? The young women jumped into the ice
cold pool and Rory braced herself, got under the bucket of
water thinking it would be easier to do than to immerse
herself in the plunge pool. She pulled the handle, trying to
look like it was the most obvious thing in the world, but the
shock of the ice cold water hitting her head, shoulders, back
made her gasp for air. Any feeling of drunkenness got
replaced by a good old headache.

The discus thrower was standing by a curtained off area
and stared at her, then beckoned her over. There were three
massage tables in there; two were already taken by the
elderly ladies, so Rory climbed up on the middle one. Great.
A soap scrub. She should've enquired what the standard
package included. Then she heard snatches of conversation.
'The smell, the stench'. 'So good that it's gone'. The lady with
the bad hip asked how it happened, was it really true that a
man had died, one of the regulars? And had they fixed the
slippery floor since then? In the midst of a buckwheat
massage, the sloshing of water and skin being scrubbed to
pig pinkness, Rory got several variations of what had
happened the week before.

'They were drunks, shameful drunks. Shouldn't let people
like that in here,' said one.

'No, it was all an accident, the man just slipped and hit his
head. I've seen him here lots of times before, his friend might
be a drunk but not the guy who fell.'

'I heard they had invited prostitutes in, that they were in
the VIP room. Isn't that so?'

'I've heard it wasn't an accident at all. That the drunk had hit his friend, and then put him head first in the oven to cover it up.'

The discus thrower was the only one who didn't provide a version of the story, and the others were nagging at her. 'Lyuba, you were there, weren't you? Didn't you have to go clear up the mess?'

'I'm no gossip, but I can tell you this, it was not a pretty sight. That smell has stuck with me all week. And the gunk that was left in the oven after they had taken the body away? Horrid. Charred pieces of meat. The male attendants on the other side all had excuses for not dealing with it. Pathetic creatures. So I had to, once the police were done. Didn't take the police long though, they were certain it was an accident. I feel sorry for his son though, that poor boy. He's been here with him a few times. Never when he's taken the drunk here, of course.'

Rory had tried to remain still throughout the conversation, but could feel herself tensing up, and she noticed that she had been holding her breath. And now her tense muscles were getting the full force of the discus throwers feeling of injustice. She winced as she got a particularly rough scrubbing of her left arm. It felt like she had got burn marks above her elbow.

'Poor family, getting that back. I wonder if they still had an open casket at the funeral?' said one of the other women.

'Oh, I don't think there's been one. My friend who works as a cleaner at morgue number 10 said he's still there, at Botkin. The son must be too young to deal with it all, and I don't know if they had anyone else. A travesty, really. For a God fearing-man to die alone like that.'

The naked bodies next to Rory both made the sign of the cross before they got up and continued their conversations back in the changing rooms. A pat on the shoulder indicated that Rory was done as well, and she found a cup of tea and a sandwich, thick slices of cold meat and a layer of butter between dry bread, was waiting for her. It would do. Actually, anything would do food wise at this stage.

She tried to process the snippets of conversation. Ivan and Pavel had been here. It had to have been them. But not the boy. Not Sasha. The letter she had seen in their letterbox had been from Botkin morgue. Not the hospital. Why hadn't Ivan said something? And where was Sasha?

After getting dressed, she went looking for an internet cafe to look up morgue number 10 on the map. She had walked around the banya building when she noticed the sign.

Internet. Computer games.

Rory went in and found the morgue on Google Maps. It was next to Botkin hospital. Walking distance, at least for Moscow. She couldn't risk searching online for the accident at the morgue, but scanned through the website of the tabloid Krasnaya Zvezda. There. A short mention of a veteran dying in a gory accident at the banya she'd just been too. Relatives not yet informed, a police man was quoted as saying.

Rory logged on to Signal. There was a message from Tom. Asking if she was doing okay. Someone must have told him about Morocco. Why did he imply that she might not be okay? Rory felt herself getting worked up. About Richard, the reaction from her all male colleagues. She didn't need them. And she didn't need Tom's pity either. A nagging thought crept into her head. It was out of the ordinary for Tom to be able to communicate when he was on tour, on a mission. Maybe something had happened. He could have got injured. She shrugged it off. She had more pressing things to think about. Like a dad who might be dead, and a boy who'd gone missing. Her love life, or lack of one, could wait. Then another message appeared.

Finally.

The last known location of Sasha. There just a company name and an address. Rory had to look twice. First to the name of the internet cafe in the window, then back to her screen, then back to the window.

Could it be?

Rory took her time logging off and putting her coat back on. There were only a group of older kids and an adult man in the cafe.

'How much do I owe you?' Rory asked the stone faced girl behind the café counter. The girl had large, neon pink expansion rings in her ears and there was a unicorn on the right index finger that tapped the keyboard.

'*Крума*. I love your tattoo,' Rory said.

The girl gave a little smile, and Rory went for it.

'You haven't seen Sasha lately, have you? My nephew. Young kid, blond, plays *CS:GO* here on Mondays?'

The girl grinned, her eyes lighting up.

'Sasha, yes, he was here last Monday. Sweet kid. Always leaves the change,' she said. 'Oh, of course. You're here for his bag? We were meaning to get it to him, I think he left his homework and everything, but the phone was in the bag, so we couldn't reach him. Don't have his home number.'

'Yes, I'm here for the bag. He was going to take it with him on holiday,' Rory replied. She surprised herself sometimes, with how easy it came to her to lie. 'Did you see him leaving on Monday?'

'No, he was here one minute and gone the next. He's not in trouble, is he? For gaming? I know his dad didn't like him playing *CS*.'

Rory wasn't sure how much to tell. Not until she knew what kind of people she might be dealing with.

'No, not at all. He must have just run for the bus and then forgot about it. Typical boys. Thanks!'

Better to be on the safe side.

Rory took the bag and walked out of the building. She walked a few blocks in the wrong direction before she found a bench and sat down to open the backpack. Some school books, a half eaten chocolate bar. Bose headphones and a phone. The phone was dead, probably out of battery. Rory pondered for a while. It might have some useful information about where Sasha could be, messages or emails. But it was a modern smartphone, there was no way of taking out the battery and the phone could be traced if she charged it. She should have taken some prints at the apartment, that would have enabled her to unlock it with the fingerprint reader. But the more she thought about it, the more worried she got. The Americans had tracked switched off phones in Iraq, so the Russians could probably do the same. Until she knew what, or who, she was dealing with, the risk was too high.

Rory went back towards the banya, to where she'd noticed a dilapidated brick wall. She'd grabbed an empty crisp bag from a bin on the way, put the phone in it and tied it up with an unused hair tie. The gap in the wall was just big enough for the phone.

THE MORGUE WAS in a beige stone building, next to a church. Two tall towers, chimneys perhaps, stood next to a parking lot filled with blue vans. The building itself looked like a fortress, the beige stone only broken up by one row of windows on what looked like the third floor. Rory went to the entrance, around the side, and found the hallway deserted. 'Registration' it said on one door. 'Morgue' it said on another. She knocked on the latter, but only heard a radio from inside, and pushed the door open. A man with skin the colour of the white walls around him stood by a filing cabinet. When he saw her, he came to the counter.

'Yes? Can I help you?' he said in a whisper of a voice.

'I'm looking for someone. A man, uh, body, that was brought here last week, Monday I believe. He'd had an accident in the banya?'

'And you are?'

'I'm a friend of the family.'

'We really only allow access to closest family,' he said, with his hands resting on a thick book labelled register.

'I know, it's just, my friend isn't able to come herself, so she asked me to. She's not very well, and, uh, she didn't think she would be able to do it. It would be too much for her, poor thing. I could call her and get her to confirm if you like? And I'd be happy to pay for the phone call, of course,' Rory said and put a few hundred rubles on the counter. The man stared at the bills, giving no indication that he was the kind that could be bribed. Rory reached for her pocket for another few notes, and got a curt smile in return.

'I don't think that would be necessary. We can make an exception, I am sure,' he said and opened the book. His finger went up and down the list of dates, before it landed on the previous Monday. 'Number thirty six, Abramov. Awaiting formal identification. Yes, I remember that one. Please write your name and sign here,' he said, pushing a visitors' book towards her.

Rory put Masha's name down, making sure to make her writing close to illegible, her signature just a random scribble.

The man shuffled around the counter and led her into a larger room with white walls and flickering lights in the ceiling. Along the left side there was a stainless steel worktop with a sink at each end. A long hose was attached to one of the taps, long enough to hose down the entire room. The drawers below the worktop had labels with acronyms Rory didn't recognise. She'd never really had any need to know the Russian names for medical equipment. Nor had they featured in conversations with her mother or grandmother. At the opposite end of the room was a big grey door with two small window panes, and that's where the man led her. The fridge. Not individual ones, as in the American crime shows on TV, but one giant fridge with lots of dead people on the shelves, in grey body bags. He motioned for her to wait, and she watched as he entered and pulled one of the shelves out onto a trolley. The trolley hit the steel door on the way out, making the sheet and the body under it shake. The attendant opened the zipper, revealing the whole of the upper body.

The smell of burnt skin and flesh was overpowering, even though the body had been kept in close to freezing temperature. Like a barbecue gone wrong. Rory had to make herself ignore the face, or what was left of it. Focus on what she could use, what she could see. There was a VDV tattoo on the right upper arm. Afghanistan, 1986. She recognised the parachute, the inscription and the helicopter gunship. The picture she had wasn't detailed enough to identify Pavel by the tattoo though, she had to find some other way. Rory forced herself to take another look at the burnt face, or what was left of it. The left side was almost fleshless, and she could see through to the teeth underneath. Where the nose should have been was just a gaping hole, a mix of charred skin and dried blood. She closed her eyes, tried to see Pavel's picture in front of her, to compare.

The attendant touched her arm. 'Are you okay?'

Rory opened her eyes again. 'I'm okay, thank you. It's just, a bit much.'

Then she leaned over the body to see the face straight on. That's when she noticed that the eyes were too close together. Or, the eye sockets were. The angles of the triangle making up the nose and eyes were all wrong. This wasn't Pavel's body.

But both the banya staff and the attendant here thought it was, and there was no doubt it was meant to look like him. She looked again at the tattoo and wondered how long it had taken to find someone with the same one. She wanted to touch it, to check that it was a real tattoo, not something painted on after death. What had Pavel got himself into that was worth doing all this for? Where was he now, and where was Sasha? For the first time Rory got worried. Worried she might have walked into something far too big for her. This wasn't just a case of a missing child. Someone had been killed to make it look like Pavel was dead. She looked up at the attendant. Was he in on it? Was the dead body a bait? Had he told someone she was here? But his eyes were full of concern, and worry. She could see no malice. And he hadn't been out of her sight since she arrived, no phone calls had been made.

'I'm sorry for your loss,' he said.

Rory did the orthodox sign of the cross on herself, from right to left, and bowed her head whilst whispering a blessing before she stood up straight again. The smell stayed in her nostrils and intensified when she inhaled. The tears in her eyes weren't fake, nor was the lump in her throat. She had to get out of there before she was sick. Perhaps the attendant spotted her distress because he pointed to an unmarked door in the corner. There was no loo, but a utility sink that seemed to have served a similar purpose before. She didn't want to leave her DNA behind, but used the opportunity to steady her guts before she went back out to the attendant. He had already pulled the zipper back up, and was about to roll the trolley back into the fridge.

'Thank you for your help,' Rory said.

'Not at all. And I am very sorry for your loss,' he said again as she hurried to the exit and the fresh air. 'If you could just sign out ...' Rory heard, as the door closed behind her.

She took a quick look at the visitor's log, and changed the number for which body she had been to see from 36 to 38 before she scribbled in the sign out box. There was no need to leave a trace behind if she could avoid it. And knowing that someone had gone to great lengths to make the dead man look like Pavel was both reassuring and worrying. If he was dead, he'd be the one on the table.

Rory paused, and heard the attendant working on something in the other room. She stepped back towards the visitor's log. She scanned the previous pages to see if anyone else had come to look at body 36. There were two entries. She recognised the name of the policeman she had seen quoted in the article about the 'accidental death' at the banya, but she couldn't make out the name on the second entry. Then she heard the attendant closing the fridge door, and quickly took out her phone and photographed the name and signature.

11

THE FIGURE on the floor had stopped begging for water. When Dmitri pushed him into the next stress position, sat on the cold concrete floor, legs straight forward, arms behind the head, there was not a sound from the hooded head. Dmitri was pleased. This was how it was supposed to be. The hours in isolation had softened his target. The figure tried to fold the hands behind his head, but a quick whip from the cane stopped him. It didn't take long before the man started shaking again, his elbows drooping towards the floor. Another whip from the cane and the elbows were pointing straight out again. Dmitri let the feeling of power flood through him. The emperor of life and death. It was odd to think that this was the same man he'd narrowly avoided in 1991.

Dmitri adjusted his headphones and caught a few strokes of the white noise he was subjecting his prisoner to. He quickly turned his own music up again. Rachmaninov's third piano concerto. Not the second one. It wasn't right for this kind of work. It had to be the third one. Made him feel like he was separate from this situation, even if he was the creator of it. He went over to the table and chugged half the can of energy drink. This would have been a lot easier if he could have shared the job with someone, but Sorokin was too busy covering up what they were doing, and anyway. Sorokin would have been rubbish at this. And they couldn't trust anyone else.

The stench of the urine and faeces managed to get past the barrier of menthol gel under Dmitri's nose, so he added a bit to keep the worst away. He'd grown up with a long drop as the only toilet, so it wasn't too bad. But where the outside loo had had natural ventilation because of the poorly put together timber frame, this room was hermetically sealed. An old radio studio that had stood empty since the crackdown on independent media begun after Putin came to power. The man on the floor had slumped sideways, and Dmitri went over to prod him with the cane again. It didn't take much. His prisoner straightened up again, if only for a few minutes. It was time.

Dmitri lifted him up on the chair and angled the lamp to shine straight in the prisoner's face before he took the hood off.

'Name?'

'Pavel Ivanovich Abramov,' the man said, squinting towards the bright light between him and Dmitri.

'Profession?'

'Retired.'

'Previous profession?'

'Driver. Soldier.' The prisoner looked down towards his hands. The blood had dried up, and he peeled at a flake that was coming loose.

This was as far as Dmitri had got every time, before the man in front of him had started getting difficult. The standard soldier replies. Name, rank and serial number. As if the Geneva convention was at all relevant for the situation they both found themselves in. Dmitri blamed Sorkin's goon for creating the antagonist attitude. He favoured persuasion himself, it was a lot easier than forcing information out of anyone. And Dmitri's attempts at torture seemed to just harden the prisoner's stance. Make him even less cooperative. But he had to get him talking, and fast. Sorokin's rival, Volkov, had started asking questions, too many questions.

'Can I have some water, please?'

Dmitri threw some water on the table between them, and the prisoner leaned forward and lapped it up. No pride. None whatsoever. How could Dmitri break a man who didn't seem to mind if he was broken or not? If only they'd found his son. It would all have been over in half an hour if they'd had the boy. But Sorokin's goon hadn't thought to wait until he could get both of them. That goon had 'accidentally' fallen into the river at night.

Good riddance, Dmitri thought. But he'd rather have the boy.

12

THE WOMAN GUARDING the two portaloos was still sitting inside the heated one, the needlework in her hands now a one-armed jumper. There were less people this time around, a couple of smaller groups of men and women nursing their glasses. A single empty beer glass, dried white foam stuck to its side, was the only evidence of anyone ever having sat where the group of army veterans had been just two days earlier. Ivan was nowhere to be seen. The waitress was the same sour faced one as last time. She had pink eyeshadow today, not blue like last time.

'Have you seen Ivan, he was here a couple of days ago, the veteran, maybe in his 60s?' Rory asked her.

'What, do I look like an enquiry service to you? Are you buying drinks or not?'

'I was going to meet him here, and buy him one.'

The waitress turned and walked away, back to the bar, making herself busy stacking glasses. It was obvious she didn't want to waste her time on anything that didn't earn her money. Rory followed after her.

'Maybe I can leave some money behind the bar for him?

And a note?' she said, and started unfurling some five hundred rouble notes.

The waitress looked at her hands, before she lifted her stare. 'He doesn't come in this late in the week. Spends his pension in the first few days, then goes elsewhere until the next lot arrives.'

'Where could I find him though? And is it ok if I leave these here?' Rory replied, putting the ruble notes on the counter. The waitress nodded. A week's salary, maybe two, laid out in front of her was too tempting a prospect.

'He's got a shack down at the market, does the cleaning around there in exchange for a roof over his head. At least that's what they say.'

'Thank you,' Rory said and took her hand away from the money.

'Hope you like dogs, though,' the waitress said, quickly pocketing the money before any of the other staff saw it.

Rory walked back across the main street, into the throng of people on their way home from work. The market was a few blocks away, behind the shopping centre, as far as she could remember. The two places so close to each other demonstrated the speed at which different versions of Russia were moving apart. The western style capitalist haven with its indoor ice rink, cinema and luxury spa stood in stark contrast to the gritty traders and hagglers in the rundown market, evidence that not all Muscovites had benefited from the improved economic situation. It hadn't changed much since the last time she'd been there – years before, but there were signs stating it would soon be replaced by new blocks of flats. She remembered the labyrinth of stalls and booths, babushkas with massive shopping bags with a week's worth of shopping on each arm pushing people from side to side. In the dusk she could see the rickety shacks, one after another, lining the little walkways. The babushkas had left for the day, and so had most of the traders. A young boy with raven black hair, was sweeping up the rotten vegetables, broken cardboard boxes

'Is there an old man who lives here?' Rory asked. The boy just stared at her, then went back to his sweeping.

'He was a friend of my father,' she continued. 'It's very important that I find him. His name is Ivan Nikolayevich.' She searched her pocket for some change, swearing to herself about having given the waitress far too much of it. She pulled out what was left, a few fifties and hundred rouble note.

'I need to find him,' she added, holding out the money.

The boy grabbed it, then went back to sweeping again. She hesitated. Had he just taken her money, and wasn't going to give anything in return? Then she spotted the guard coming up from the alley, two German shepherd crosses following him.

'We're closing up now, girl. Time to go,' the guard said.

'Yes, of course. I was just heading out.' She turned to walk away, the guard looking at her as she disappeared towards the entrance.

Shit. She could always come back tomorrow, but something was telling her that time was not on her side. Or Sasha's. Or Pavel's. As she rounded the corner and was out of the guard's sight she slowed down, wondering what her next move should be. Maybe she could hide behind the pile of rubbish? The dogs would notice though. Then she heard running steps behind her.

'That way, he's down at the other end,' the young boy whispered to her and pointed to the far side of the market. There was a thin stream of smoke dancing upwards above the tin roofs. 'Stick close to the outer fence, that's where the guard walks last.'

'Thank you.'

'He's always nice to me, the old man. We play football in the mornings, before the others get here. And now that his friend is gone, I feel sorry for him.'

'Has he told you about his friend going missing?'

The boy looked away, realising he might have said too much, and ran back towards his broom. Rory turned and jogged towards the perimeter fence, in the opposite direction of where the guard had gone. She paused when crossing any of the pathways, checking he was out of sight before she sprinted to the next crossing. It was bigger than she remembered, and having to stick to the outer fence took longer than she would have wanted.

She was only two more labyrinthine blocks away from the stream of smoke when one of the guard dogs spotted her from the other side of the last alleyway. The barking dog came running after her, the other dog joined in the chase, and she knew that they would catch up with her. If only she could get into the building where the smoke was coming from, she'd be safe. The barking came closer and closer, and she tasted blood in her mouth, her throat burning with the sudden need for oxygen to fuel her muscles. The shack was hidden from view, but Rory could still see its roof and corroded chimney. She wasn't going to make it. The dogs in pursuit were too fast.

She tried to find a way to climb the fence, but there was too much razor wire on the top. Though it might be preferable to crawl through that than be torn apart by dogs. She turned the corner and saw the shack in front of her, a building that looked like it might fall down any minute, with windows and a door rescued from someone else's fallen down shack. There was no way that could keep the dogs out. Rory paused, turned around so she had a second to face the dogs before they jumped her.

From behind her, where the shed was, a deep growl filled the air. Great. Surrounded. As the guard dogs turned the corner, she could see them hesitating, slowing down, looking at what was behind her. It was as if she had become invisible. As the growl behind her came closer and closer, they folded their ears back, lowered their heads and shoulders down towards the ground, tails tucked between their legs. Making themselves as small as they could, they turned and ran back to where they came from, and disappeared from sight.

Rory tried to settle her breath, cold and hot sweat mixing at the nape of her neck, running down between her shoulder blades. The growling continued, but didn't get closer. Closing her eyes for a brief second, she took a deep breath, and turned towards the sound, resisting the urge to put her hands up to protect herself from whatever it was that was behind her. An enormous wolf-like creature, but with the eyes of a dog, took in her every move. Teeth on display and with saliva running from its mouth, Rory wondered if she wouldn't have had a better chance with the German Shepherds after all. At the corner of her eyes, she picked up a small movement from behind the plastic covers where a window once had been.

'Laika, it's ok. She's a friend,' a slurred voice said from inside, over the slow hiss of music playing on a radio.

Laika folded her ears back, lapped up the saliva dripping from her jaws and approached the visitor, tail gently wagging. Rory tried to relax, and held her hand out to let the dog smell her. Laika hesitated at the movement, but moved closer and sniffed Rory's outstretched hand before she turned and walked back towards the shack.

'Ivan, is that you? I really need to talk to you,' Rory said.

'I'm busy, just leave me alone. I don't have anything to say to you.'

'I went to the banya, the one you told me about? They said a man had died the day you were there with Pavel. Hit his head on the oven and burnt his face?'

The radio was turned off, and an eerie silence lay over them.

'It wasn't Pavel. But you knew that, didn't you?' Rory paused. She wanted to go closer to the shack, to look Ivan in the eyes when she told him these things, but she was worried the giant dog might not approve. 'Please. I need to find out what's going on. To find Sasha, and Pavel. You're the only one who can help.'

Ivan appeared in the doorway, and scratched the dog behind the ears as she leaned against him. 'There's nothing I can do to help. Pavel always did things his way. He can look after himself.'

'And Sasha? Can he take care of himself as well? You know Masha will come looking for them, if I don't succeed. Is that what you want?'

Ivan looked out into nothingness, his bloodshot eyes turning glassy. 'You better come in then. But don't walk on the left side of the steps, Laika has her puppies under there and doesn't like anyone getting too close to them.'

Puppies. Of course. Even trained guard dogs would know better than to challenge a bitch protecting a litter of puppies. At least one that was a head taller than them. Rory exaggerated her detour to avoid the left side of the steps, making it clear to Laika that she had no intention of interfering with her little ones. As she stepped into the shack, she could hear little squeaks from under the floorboards.

Inside the shack it looked almost homely. Dirty, but cosy, in a weird way. A thin mattress with floral sheets with large drawers underneath took up most of the opposite side, there was a kitchen cabinet next to the stove in a corner, and a radio hanging from a hook on the wall. Three pictures and a laminated icon hung in the corner, above the bed. One of the pictures looked like it might be Pavel and Ivan, all young and fresh faced, in crisp new uniforms, in front of a Soviet military helicopter.

'What happened at the banya? Did Pavel have anything to do with the man who died? Is he on the run?' Realising she was asking too many questions, and rushing it, Rory stopped herself, and just looked at Ivan, waiting. A minute passed, in which he looked at everything in the room, except her. Then he cleared his throat.

'Tea? I don't have sugar, but there's lemon,' he said.

'Yes, please.'

Ivan placed a blackened pot on top of the stove, and rummaged around in a box of used tea bags, as if he was trying to find the one with the most life left in it. His mouth was opening and closing several times, as if he was getting ready to say something, before changing his mind. With the tea brewing in the mug, he sat down on the mattress next to her.

'I – uh – I don't really know what happened. We were in the private room, as usual, but Pasha had just sent me to get something from reception when it happened. I don't know how he knew, but somehow he did. So I didn't see anything. Just heard the scream. And the smell. That awful smell.'

13

THE STINK of charred skin and flesh was still fresh in Rory's mind, and she was relieved that all she could smell now was smoke from the wood burning stove, dog and dirty clothes.

'Did you see the body afterwards?' she asked Ivan.

'No. One of the bath attendants got there first and then they closed it off. The staff thought it was a horrid accident. That I had got poor Pavel drunk, they knew about my drinking, you see, and that he'd fallen over after I left the room. They hadn't seen or heard anyone else coming in. I knew Pavel couldn't have fallen, he hadn't had a drink in over a decade. But no one believes a drunk like me. There was a back door entrance to the private room. Some use it for getting prostitutes in. On my rough days, Pavel had used to get me in. But there was no sign of anyone else,' Ivan said.

Rory wondered why Ivan had been left to tell the tale. A pro wouldn't have left a loose end like that. Or maybe they had, as she had, thought Ivan was beyond saving. That he was always drunk and incomprehensible.

'The only reason I'm not in jail for murder is that I was talking to the receptionist when it happened. I'm sure I was meant to go down for it.'

'Any idea who could have done it? Could Pavel have staged his own death, maybe he wanted to disappear?'

'It's not impossible. He's always had money, Pavel. I never knew where from, but he was always doing ok. And I know someone had come to see him. A complete stranger had knocked on his door, when Sasha was at home. The boy couldn't explain what he looked like. But he recognised the car. The kid is good with cars, less good with people. It was a car he'd seen before, some specially modified one.'

'What kind of car?'

'It looked like a regular BMW, but Sasha noticed it was the one they had shown at a car show a year or two ago. A BMW X5 that was armoured to withstand bullets from an AK-47. Pavel knew someone who'd done the odd job for the guy who bought the display model. Sorokin, I think his name is. The Magpie. He's a politician. They're all politicians now. Gives them immunity from police investigations. Not that Sorokin would need that. He used to work for the KGB. Probably still does.'

'How do you know he's KGB?'

'One of the guys I see in the stolovaya has done some jobs for him, was bragging about it. Guess you didn't think I noticed anything around me there, let alone remembered? You're right. I often don't. It depends on the time of week. I don't always drink because I have to. Sometimes it's because I want to. I want to forget.' He looked into his own half-empty mug. 'Did you know how Pavel and I met? We served together in Afghanistan. We were in the airborne troops, we were,' he said proudly. 'The elite. The professionals. These days a lot of the vets you see in the striped shirt are crooks and murderers. But not us.'

Rory was about to ask a question, to bring the conversation back to the politician, Sorokin, but paused to see what Ivan would bring up next. Experience had taught her that sometimes the most important questions were the ones you didn't know to ask.

'We had a few months left of our tour when the mujahideen got our helicopter. Pavel and I were the only survivors, and when the mujahideen poured over the crash site, we had no way of getting away. We got a good dozen of them before they got us though. But they didn't like that much. There was no Geneva convention there. Just plain misery, abuse and torture. The stuff they did to Pavel,' he said, shaking his head. 'They seemed to take great pleasure in watching him, he just wouldn't crack. I gave up after the first few hours, a fractured knee cap and this,' he said, and showed a hand full of nailless fingers. 'But Pavel. I can still see it, you know. They made me watch. How they tore out his fingernails, electrocuted him. Crucified him to the door with rusty nails and threw knives at him, like some sick circus act. And then, one night as the mujahideen had tired of their games and left a few guards to look after us, somehow Pavel found the strength to get us out. Killed the guards with the same nails they had used on him.'

Ivan rubbed his knee, as if the memory had brought the pain back.

'Anyway. Pavel saved me that day. Half carried me to the nearest camp. That whole experience is why we started drinking, both him and me. The nightmares, the memories. After Afghanistan we both carried on normal lives for a while, he got his job as a driver, I got a nice pension as my knee stopped me from doing much. Then the Soviet Union fell apart. I think it was seeing fellow Russians turning on each other like they did in the early 90s, all for money, that did it for him. Had he really fought, and gone through what he did, for that? When my pension stopped coming, and I no longer had anything distracting me from my nightmares, I replaced the occasional vodka with home brew. And then with ethanol. And then with whatever type of alcohol I could get my hands on. Shoe polish. Perfumes. Pavel always seemed to have money, but he got hooked all the same. Almost lost his daughter because of it. Then, later on, when his son was born, his wife refused to let him see his boy unless he sobered up. So he stopped. And never drank again.'

Rory realised her tea had gone cold, but took a sip anyway. She'd had long conversations with Tom about his war zone assignments and PTSD. About how, even if he did come home alive, it might not be to a life he would think worth living. They'd had massive arguments over it too, it was what had torn them apart. Rory just couldn't bear to sit at home, waiting for news, good or bad. Losing her mother so early had scarred her. But the risk of PTSD was as frightening as actual death on the battlefield. Tom had said it was worth any risk, that there was a higher purpose. She couldn't help but wonder, would he end up like Ivan? For a little while the two of them, Rory and Ivan, sat there looking at each other. Then Ivan cleared his throat.

'He's my only friend, my only family. If there's anything you can do to help him and Sasha, then please. Do it,' Ivan said.

'I will try my best. It's why I'm here,' she replied. 'You're sure that the man who came looking for Pavel the first time was working for this guy, Sorokin?'

'Yes. Pavel was, and I believed him. It certainly wasn't an official matter, the man didn't want to be seen, and there were little things that Pavel couldn't quite put his finger on, but that his army instincts picked up on. Probably some private project Sorokin and his ilk are up to, scheming one way or another to get richer and richer.' A wave of fresh air flew into the shack as Laika pushed the door open with her nose. The dog sat by Ivan's sore knee, and his hand automatically moved from the knee to her head.

'You think this is about money?' Rory asked.

'It seemed to be more complicated than that, but everything here is about money these days. Pavel was a bit cagey about it. He's had some sort of income over the years that has been a bit mysterious. Said he'd done well in the voucher auctions in the 90s. He must have done very well though. Sent his daughter to the UK to get her education.'

'Do you think Masha would know about this, how he could afford to pay for her education abroad?'

'I'd be surprised if she didn't, she is one clever girl. Didn't she tell you about it?' Ivan asked.

Rory leaned back to the wall, with a slight shake of the head. If Masha knew about her father's money, and how it could be the reason for his disappearance, why had she not mentioned it? And what else had Masha not told her?

14

THE CARS ARRIVED IN PAIRS. A shiny sports car, maybe a Porsche or a Ferrari with a rich man and his beautiful companion leading the way, followed by a black 4x4 carrying men with short cropped hair, the barrels of submachine guns visible in the windows. Oligarchs. Or corrupt politicians and bureaucrats. They were often one and the same these days. The two doormen standing outside Casino Mitrofan looked as though they were hewn from granite, their suits taut at the shoulders. This was, according to her research, Sorokin's favourite nightspot. 'Guns not allowed' it said on the sign by the door. There were enough in the parking lot to start a small war. It made Rory think of Tom again, wondering if he was even still alive. She shrugged the thought away, and focused her attention on the doormen, walking between the parked sports cars so the bouncers wouldn't know that she had arrived in a Renault. They watched her as she approached, glancing towards her hands. She had put on a fake sapphire and diamond ring, wanting to give the impression of being a rich man's wife, not someone who was looking for one. As she walked towards the door in her red soled Louboutins, confidence fragile as an eggshell, the door was opened from inside.

'Are you a member?' the woman in an elegant black evening gown just inside asked her in Russian, knowing the answer already.

'No, just visiting for the evening.' Rory replied in the Queen's English English, as she reached into her purse and found her platinum credit card, making sure that the room key to the Golden Ring hotel was out of sight.

'I see.' The woman looked Rory up and down, paused a little at her bling ring and again at her shoes. At least one of them were real.

'This way, madam.'

The woman led her to a small room to the side where an almost identical looking woman sat behind thick bulletproof glass. Rory saw her precious platinum card, the one card Dick had let her have her own name on (he didn't have much choice on that one) put through an old fashioned manual credit card imprint machine. With perfectly manicured fingers the cashier wrote $50 000 in the amount box and slid the imprint through the slot for Rory to sign it. The minimum buy-in. Rory felt a cold sweat breaking out. That was a year's salary for her. When she'd had a job. She forced a smile and signed the paper, thanking god that they hadn't become so modern that they did an online credit check.

'Tatyana will take you to the cash desk for your chips.'

Rory followed the first woman up the marble staircase and into a red hallway where a gold plated icon hung at the end. Before the revolution this had been a nobleman's house, and it was one of the few that had been restored to perfection after the end of the Soviet Union. Only the discreet metal detectors by the entrance to the main room detracted from the old-world atmosphere. As Rory made her way into the ballroom, trying to look graceful in her too-high heels, she scanned the room. The walls were covered with old mirrors, which made it look a lot bigger than it was. The ceiling was decorated with a beautiful fresco, depicting a pair of cupids firing their arrows at the people below.

There were blackjack, roulette and craps tables in the centre, already busy and stacked with chips, but the poker tables were at the far end. Two had male card dealers, the other two had female. Rory would have to make a quick decision, as Tatyana had already made it to the cash desk in the room next door and was about to get her tray of chips. One of the female dealers was around forty and was standing in front of a huge pile of chips, the outcome of a big hand. The other dealer was younger, blonder, and with more cleavage on display. Her. The Sorokin Rory had got to know through her hours of research would choose her.

'Madam? Which table would you like to start at? The Roulette, perhaps?'

'No, I think I'd like to try my luck at the poker table. The third one from the left. Three is my lucky number,' Rory replied.

They walked towards the table with the young dealer. There were five men there already. The third seat was available, and Tatyana set her chips down at it. The mirrors high up on the walls, with greying corners and a slight distortion, gave Rory the perfect view of the entrance to the room, without anyone being able to look at others' cards. A short, stocky man in his forties, built like a wrestler, was sitting to her right. Could have been from the Caucasus. On her left were two Americans, sharply tailored suits, tired eyes that looked like they'd been working day and night for a week. They were flirting with the card dealer, a magnum of Dom Perignon standing askew in the ice bucket behind them. The wrestler was flipping a $1000 chip between the fingers on his left hand. Opposite her were what looked like a couple of athletes, ice hockey, judging by their build.

Good – this table shouldn't leave me bankrupt.

She threw in her cards on the first few hands she was dealt, a mix of both real and faked nerves. Fake because she could do the stats in her sleep after having played her way through university, and her opponents seemed to be playing with their egos rather than their cards, or were too busy flirting with the card dealer. Real, because she didn't really know how to get close to Sorokin. It resulted in her losing to one of the hockey players who made three of a kind in sevens as the final card was put on the table. He leered at her, displaying a gap in his teeth, and said something to his friend that made them both roar with laughter as he raked in the chips.

As Rory was dealt a better hand, she noticed Sorokin coming through the hallway, flanked by two beautiful women who were all legs and short skirts. A ditzy blonde in a red dress that looked right off the runway, and a dark haired woman in a silver dress with metal studs enhancing her already ample cleavage. They got to the metal detector, and Sorokin let the blonde go through first, before following himself. A small red light flickered, resulting in a security guard giving him a quick pat down, with Sorokin gesturing towards his wristwatch. It looked expensive even at a distance. When the brunette followed, the red light flickered again, and she stepped aside as Sorokin had. The security guard seemed to hesitate, as he was given an 'I dare you' stare. Nowhere to hide anything there. Both women took Sorokin's arms again, and walked through the room with him, an eager Tatyana following with two trays of chips in her hands. Rory noticed the dealer looking at her, wanting to know if she was still in the game or not.

'Got a hangover from the last hand?' said one of the Americans with an overbearing smile.

'Oh, I don't know. I think maybe. Um.' Rory tried to make a decision, whilst observing the new arrivals, but had lost track of both the cards and the money. Shit. 'No, I'm out.'

Rory saw her chips being raked into the pot. At least she could keep an eye on Sorokin now. He had stopped to shake the hands of a few people, but was, as expected, headed for the poker tables. The furthest American, who was also out of the game, leant back to ask if Rory wanted another Mojito. She'd been nursing the first one for the last ten minutes, drinking melted ice water.

'Sure, that would be lovely, thank you for asking.' Nodding to their now empty bottle of champagne, she added, 'Are you celebrating something?'

'Yeah, just secured a big merger. Can't say who, but you'll see it all over the news tomorrow. Two years of hard work. But we nailed it in the end.'

'Congratulations,' Rory said, and lifted her glass to his. The conversation had given her the opportunity to look directly at Sorokin as he approached. He was taller than in the pictures, but the two women at his side, in their stilettos, were even taller. All three headed straight for their table. Rory's research had paid off.

'Tanya, krasavitsa,' Sorokin said as he went over to kiss the card dealer's hand. Both the Americans and the wrestler at Rory's right seemed to stiffen up at his arrival.

'One bottle of Putinka, the limited edition. Unopened, please. And a bottle of champagne,' whispered the brunette to the waitress.

The vodka arrived at the table, its neck extending from a block of ice. As the waitress moved to open it, the brunette stopped her with a discreet hand gesture, before she took it herself. The sound of the metal seal breaking seemed to satisfy her, and the waitress went on to pour the vodka into Sorokin's glass. The women had a glass of champagne each. Rory swallowed hard. That metal studded dress was hiding more than it was revealing. Female bodyguards. She had heard rumours that they were popular in Russia, in particular for protecting rich men's wives and kids. They could play the part of friends and nannies, and provide protection without attracting attention. But she hadn't pictured them looking like catwalk models. There hadn't been many, or any, with the stick thin look in the army. Rory's heart sank in her chest. How would she get to Sorokin now?

'How have you been, my little bird, have you missed me?' Sorokin asked the dealer, who giggled in response. Having been discarded for a more desirable man, the two Americans turned their attention to the cards instead. Not what Rory needed right now. Having to concentrate on not going bank-rupt as well as trying to find a way to talk to Sorokin wasn't going to be easy. She'd lost too much money already, and was getting worried she might fail at both. The wrestler seemed to have got a new intensity in his game, and the Americans were no longer distracted.

She discreetly counted her own chips and found herself more than $20,000 down. That's when she realised that the black chips with the silver rim the wrestler was flipping between his fingers weren't even in her stack. $10,000 chips. There was barely enough to play a few more hands the way these guys kept increasing the stakes. Why did she ever think playing poker with money she didn't have was a good idea? There must've been other ways to solve this case. Or she could've just given up, admitted that she didn't have what it took to work on her own. Stupid, stupid ego. Too busy noticing others' giant ones to see how my own is becoming my downfall. Several hands were dealt where she folded straight away, and her second Mojito became a third and a fourth.

Then her luck turned. Pocket queens, two beautiful red ladies, looked up at her as she lifted the corners of her cards. Sorokin would have to wait. It was one of the best hands to start out with, and she wanted to eliminate some of the competition before the cards on the table were dealt. The hockey player was the first to bet, and called the blinds. But the wrestler raised it with $500. Rory flicked two $1000 into the centre of the table with a red fingernail. The American next to her was thinking hard, trying to crunch the numbers, and decided to stay in the game.

The second American folded, and Sorokin stayed in, but the hockey player next to him threw his cards down. Four men were still in the game. It didn't make sense. Could they all have great cards? The wrestler clenched his jaw as the remaining American sipped and sipped at his whiskey. He must have something worth playing. Sorokin could be showing off, and the hockey player was probably bluffing again, but the wrestler? He'd been fidgeting ever since the last hand was dealt.

The first three cards hit the table, two tens and a five, all different suits. Little chance of a flush or a straight then. The hockey player smirked at Rory as he threw in a $5000 chip and eyebrows shot up all around the table. Please say he's bluffing. After a little hesitation, the wrestler called, so did Rory. The American stared at the hockey player as he slid two $5000 chips forward. Sorokin had a bejewelled hand slung over his shoulder and smiled as he added his money to the pot. How could five people be willing to bet over 10 grand that they had the best hand? The hockey player stared at the American, his tongue protruding from the gap in his teeth.

'Fuck, I'm out,' he said in Russian and threw his cards on the table. The wrestler added $5000 to stay in the game. Rory knew what cards she had but glanced down at her pair of queens anyway. Hearts and diamonds. This had to be it. She called the $5000, and swallowed, her throat feeling thick. The dealer put down a jack, and the American leant in even more. Someone could have a full house, or even four of a kind, and she still only had two pairs. They couldn't all have good cards at this stage, someone must bow out now. But the wrestler, now the first to bet, threw in another $5000.

Rory took a wild guess and, with a small prayer that the

tens were not all on one hand, put in her last $5000 chip, leaving her with a small, colourful pile of lower value chips in front of her. The American and Sorokin followed suit, the blonde and the bodyguard brunette following the game as intently as the players. The dealer took a deep breath, and for once her hands were the centre of attention. She discarded the top card from the deck and placed a fifth card on the table before turning it over. A queen. Rory almost had to pinch herself. A full house. And enough money on the table to bring her well out of the red. If only no one has a pair of tens. She glanced around. The wrestler had got even more fidgety. He put two of the black $10 000 chips on the table. Rory counted up hers - she had about $7000 left - but pushed it all away from her.

The American nodded at her, and let out a whistle. 'You might be out of money, lady, but you've sure got guts.' His colleague leant back and glanced at her hand resting on top of her cards.

'OK. Let's do this,' the American said and added his $20000 to the pot. 'You've got the bar tab covered, right?' he said to his colleague, who was shaking his head. Now they were all looking at Sorokin. He looked like he might be tempted to pull out, but in front of his dates and everyone else he counted out twenty $1000 chips and pushed them into the pot.

The wrestler threw his cards face up on the table. A nine and a jack. Rory leant forward in amazement. He had nothing.

As the whole table stared at his cards, Rory caught a glimpse of something shiny in the wrestler's right hand and he sent a knife hurtling towards Sorokin's head. Sorokin froze, mouth half open, his macho grin turning into a grimace as the brunette pushed him off his chair, the knife thunking into her studded leather handbag. The wrestler leapt out of his seat, another knife in his hand, knocked Rory off her chair and barged past the ice bucket standing behind the Americans and toward the man on the floor. There was screaming and the sound of glass shattering, half melted ice cubes skittering across the floor. The blonde sought refuge in the arms of one of the Americans, who was trying to hide under the table.

The dealer was running away as fast as she could. The wrestler lunged at Sorokin on the floor but the brunette kicked the knife out of his hand and as she tried to land a punch he dodged, grabbed her wrist and threw her onto the table. Poker chips scattered in all directions. The wrestler jumped on Sorokin, who was trying to get up and away. He wrapped an arm around the politician's neck and tried to put the other on the side of his head. The wrestler would break his neck in a second if he got a proper hold. And Sorokin was Rory's only lead.

Not noticing the broken glass under her, she grabbed what was left of the champagne bottle and lashed out. She struck the wrestler's left shoulder, causing enough of a surprise for Sorokin to wrangle out of the choke hold. Out of the corner of her eye Rory could see the brunette drawing a small pistol from her bra, before her vision was filled with an arm headed straight for her head.

15

DMITRI LOOKED at the people sat on chairs and sofas in Sergey
Aronovich's office. Dmitri had always liked these pre-Revolu-
tion buildings, and was pleased to see that Aronovich, the
director and owner of the legendary Casino Mitrofan, had
had this one refurbished to perfection. The ceiling was a piece
of art by itself, and the icon in the little nook opposite the fire-
place looked ancient. Sorokin was, as Dmitri had expected,
leaning on the bar cabinet that had a silver plate with two
carafes with brown liquor on top of it. A large ice cube was
floating around in a glass next to his elbow, and he held an
ice pack to the back of his neck. Dmitri kept his back to the
room. The bodyguard, Elena, was busy attending to the
others who'd been involved in the fracas.

Two men in suits sat on one sofa, and seemed to recount
the events in more and more dramatic fashion. Americans.
Dmitri had recognised the hockey players in the corridor
outside, top league players. Sorokin's girlfriend of the
moment was lying on the sofa opposite the Americans.
Dmitri was seething. This was exactly the kind of situation
they were supposed to avoid right now. Headline-grabbing
bust-ups in places with lots of foreigners. In particular Amer-

icans. Blabbermouth Americans. Dmitri motioned to get Sorokin into a darker corner of the room, away from the bar. He had no intention of anyone seeing them together.

'You're attracting too much attention, flashing cash you don't even have yet. People are not just asking questions any more. This is the second assassination attempt this year. Any idea who's behind it? He was Chechen, by the look of it?' Dmitri said. He'd seen the body on his way here, on a trolley outside the kitchen freezers. There was bruising to the face, and the bullet hole in his head. Elena had done well.

'Relax, we're all fine. Elena was on top of it, just as you said she would be. Not bad looking either, that one. Shame about the bruises, though. Not a pretty sight on a woman,' Sorokin said.

Dmitri couldn't believe his ears. Sorokin had to get his priorities straight, and fast. His fists tensed up, and he took a deep breath of air.

Sorokin continued. 'And yes, he was Chechen. A pro, but not top range. Worked for one of the brothers, the younger one. Seems they got a cleaner to hide the knives in the loos.'

'Are you sure which brother he was working for? I'm not interested in starting a blood feud here,' Dmitri said, knowing that the drink Sorokin held in his hands was not the first this evening.

'Yes, certain. No doubt about it. The younger brother. He's been trying to set up in Moscow for a while now. Wants in on the tax reclaim schemes,' Sorokin said.

'Then I'll deal with them in the morning,' Dmitri said and nodded in the direction of the room. 'Who are these people, anyone we need to worry about?'

'Mostly regulars, according to Aronovich. Not as regular as me, but they've pretty much all been here before. Apart from the Chechen, and the woman on the sofa over by the wall.'

'Who is she?' Dmitri said, and looked at a pair of long,

slender legs stretched out on the arm rest. Elena was tending to the woman in question, and there was an ice pack on her forehead, so he couldn't see her face.

'Some foreign dignitary's wife. Possible gambling addict, maybe on some sort of prescription drugs? She had a variable game, was on and off. The Americans know her, I think. Got knocked out, so Elena is looking after her. Will be quite the surprise when she realises she won the hand.'

Apart from Sorokin, it was Elena and this woman who had the most visible injuries. Bruising and some cuts and grazes. Elena's movements were slow, cautious. The movements of someone who'd been in a fight, and was only just beginning to feel the effects of it. Dmitri knew the feeling only too well. He wanted to go over and ask what really had happened, he didn't trust Sorokin's version of events. The snippets he caught from the Americans' conversation made it sound like the woman on the sofa had played a part. But he didn't like to be seen with Sorokin.

Dmitri looked towards Elena again. The legs she was tending too twitched when she put some Iodine on a graze on the woman's thigh, making the skirt reveal even more of the legs. He cast a quick glance around the room, there were no mirrors but he found he could just about make out the woman's face in a reflection on the giant computer screen on the desk. Caucasian girl, in her twenties, perhaps. Then he saw her eyes opening, looking around the room. Dmitri looked away, before she would notice him staring at her. She tugged at her skirt, and Elena offered up a man's jacket to cover her bare legs. He'd have to talk to Elena later. If Sorokin had his sights on his colleague, he had to warn her. Not that she couldn't look after herself, but he knew only too well what Sorokin's combination of charm and wealth could do to a person. Dmitri had to get out though. He'd stayed too long already.

'Did you manage to open the package?' Sorokin said as Dmitri walked away.

Not here, not in front of strangers, Dmitri thought. 'Let's talk in the car. Are you going home?'

'Home? The night is still young, Dima,' Sorokin said and winked at his date for the evening, the young model sat next to the Americans.

'Then we'll talk tomorrow,' Dmitri said and walked away. He noticed that the woman on the sofa was gone, only a crumpled jacket where she'd been. He gave a slight nod to Elena, and left through the door he'd come in, without anyone noticing. At least he thought no one had noticed.

16

RORY WOKE UP, the neon lights still flashing on the other side of the curtains, casting a sickly green and yellow glow around the dank room. She rubbed the sleep out of her eyes, and had to think for a second to remember why she was feeling so sore and groggy. A knock to the head could do that. One of the cuts on her hand had opened up again, and she quickly ran to the bathroom to stop the blood from dripping onto the bedlinen. She could do with some time to think now. Having seen Sorokin talking to the tall guy, the one with half a finger, she knew that she was up against worse than she had hoped.

Sorokin's friend was a pro, if she'd ever seen one. Rory wouldn't have noticed him if he hadn't looked at her just a fraction too long. He was good looking, but in such a bland way he'd just seemed part of the interior. A true chameleon. Better than anyone she'd ever worked with. She'd got herself out of the casino as fast as she could afterwards, only pausing to collect her winnings, and had taken hours getting back to make sure she wasn't followed. She didn't want anyone connecting her real identity, the one that had been at the casino the night before, to Jelena, the Polish hotel guest.

Out on the street she headed for the metro, and took it to Vorobyovy Gorystation and headed for the entrance on the south bank of the river. Running had always been her way of meditating, the best way to clear her head and make sense of what was going on around her. She had used it to digest and find out how to deal with the cliques of an all girl boarding school, and she found it to be equally useful for work conundrums. And it was an easy way to get rid of a tail, or see if she'd gained one. She set off into the park along the river, warming up on the flat bits before she'd start climbing the hills to the ski jump to get her heartbeat up. She'd always been a bit wary of running in parks in Moscow; there were stories of runners never coming out again after having been chased down by packs of feral dogs. But as it was coming towards summer and barbecue time, there would be plenty of leftovers for the dogs to eat from the nearby cafes.

'Not a bad day for a run, is it?' Rory suddenly heard, in an unmistakable American accent, from a man coming from a different path to hers.

'Ah, no, not bad,' was all she could muster in reply.

'You come here often? I don't think I've seen you before?' he continued.

Rory looked at him. A forty something man judging by the wrinkles around his eyes and on his neck, but he looked younger, or at least fitter, than his age. Sand coloured hair, dark blue eyes. And barely sweating at all even though they were climbing the hills up to the ski jump.

'I'm sorry, that must have sounded like the worst chat up line ever,' he continued.

'And yet not bad enough to be funny,' she replied.

'Ah. My apologies. British?'

'Yes. American, Midwest, perhaps?'

'Yes. Have you been?' he replied.

'Nope,' Rory replied and set off on a path too narrow for them to run side by side.

'You're not going to make it easy for me are you?' he asked.

'Make what easy?'

'How's your head?'

'Excuse me?'

'I mean, you didn't get a concussion last night? It could be dangerous to go running,' he said.

'And you know about me getting hit on the head because?'

'The man whose life you saved, Sorokin, is a rather well known entity. Let's just say news travels fast when people like that are involved.'

'No, let's not say that. Let's say why you have been following me on my morning run.'

'That obvious?'

'Yep.' Rory was forcing her legs to move faster up the hill, though she'd known from the beginning he wasn't someone she could outrun. But she was pleased to see that the American had to put in some effort to keep up with her. Not easy to move that amount of muscle around. She paused at the top, and looked at him.

'Um, if you don't mind, could we take a different route down, through the forest?' he asked.

'Really? Go through the most deserted area with a stranger who knows more about me than I'd like?'

'Yes, really, Rory. I think it would be in both of our interests.'

At hearing her name, and seeing the size of his upper arms, she conceded that if he'd had malicious intent, then he could have just attacked her before she saw him in the first place. She started a slow descent on one of the lesser used paths in between the trees. 'So, what do you want from me? How did you find me and why do you care what I'm up to?'

'We think …'

'We?'

'Yes. We think we might have some mutual interests with you. And wondered if you might be interested in sharing information?'

'Information about what?'

'Things you might hear, might come across, in your investigations. People you might meet?'

'What do you know about my investigations?'

'A fair amount. That you're a seasoned people finder, and that you came here looking for someone. And that your search has led you to cross paths with people we happen to be interested in.'

'Sorokin?'

'Yes, him as well. But also people he may or may not be working with.'

I would love to know all about who Sorokin may or may not be working with, she thought. 'And what information would you give me?'

'We might be able to share some information on the people we are interested in, things you can't look up on Google, or Yandex.'

Rory bit her lip. She thought she'd been really careful, only searching when she was using her encrypted connection. It was usually safe, very few people would have the means to break into it. But this guy was probably from an organisation that did have that ability. CIA perhaps? NSA? No, they didn't have agents, did they? She wondered if they had been able to track her phones as well. No, impossible. She only had burner phones and only put the batteries in when using them. But then how did they know she was going to the park this morning? Did they have someone keeping tabs on her at the hotel?

'I realise this might all be a bit sudden, and perhaps surprising. But I think you'll agree that we could help each other.'

'I'm not sure if I need your help, but thanks for asking. I'll think about it.'

'I sincerely hope you will do more than that. It would be better for everyone involved.'

'That doesn't sound like an invitation to cooperate? You're not threatening me, are you?'

'No, no, of course not. But I would have preferred an answer now.'

'Well, that may be, but you can't always get what you want. Have a nice day,' Rory said and turned off the path to the right, back in the direction of the bridge across the river. The man ran after her to catch up.

'Rory, please. Take my card at least. I apologise if I came across too harshly. I just think you might be able to help us with some pretty important stuff. Serious stuff.'

Rory glanced at his card. Simon Chandler, deputy cultural attaché, US Embassy. She couldn't stop a little chuckle escaping from her lips. 'Deputy cultural attaché, eh? A little bit obvious, no? Looks like you prefer protein drinks to champagne.'

'Well, we can't all blend in as easily as you do,' he said, with a tight smile.

'Okay, Mr. Chandler. I have your details, and I promise I will be in touch,' she said, memorising the details before handing the card back.

She could see that he took the return of the card as a rejection, and was about to start another spiel trying to persuade her. Then he stopped himself, and gave a faint nod of approval. He looked around them, and took a carefully folded sheet of paper out of his pocket. It had four different drawings on them. Four artist's impressions of varying detail and quality.

'And this is?' she asked.

'We were hoping you might tell us. If you'd seen any of

them. We believe they're the team of agents that Sorokin is managing.'

Rory looked at each of them, mapping the faces and the distinguishable features. She noticed Chandler staring at her, looking for any sign of recognition.

'No, I haven't seen any of these men,' she said. 'Sorry.'

Then she turned and ran on, back towards the river, and up and down some smaller paths to get the most distance possible between her and the CIA man before she reappeared at the river again. She hummed a tune as she went, the first that popped into her head, incorporating both Chandler's email and phone numbers in its new lyrics. Then she realised that she'd used the Captain America theme song.

She wished she knew how they had identified her as someone of interest, and even someone of use, to them. But realised it probably had a lot less to do with her than it had to do with Sorokin. The American lawyers at her table in the casino had probably had friendly chats after the events of last night, and she hadn't done anything to hide her identity there. She could never have got in without a real credit card.

Running back to the metro station she let herself relax again, and started planning her next move. There was no reason to worry about Chandler catching her in a lie. She hadn't seen the four men he had shown her.

But she had recognised *him*.

17

THE MAN on the floor stared at him, eyes wide open, dragging himself towards the other side of the room. The blood from the hole in his abdomen was dark red and came out in spurts as he tried to reach the Vityaz submachine gun next to his lifeless comrade. Dmitri lifted his gun, and started squeezing the trigger. Then his pocket began vibrating. He could feel his shoulders tensing up, and let his arm drop a little before he raised it again. Poof. Perfect. Right between the eyes. He smiled to himself as he fished his phone out of his pocket. Mother. Again. What is she going to badger him about this time? He'd taken her to church only last Sunday, and she hadn't stopped talking about how her neighbour Darya had been on holiday in Egypt with her son and his family.

'What?' Dmitri said as he pressed the button on his ear piece. He could feel his shoulders tensing up again as he remembered their previous conversation. Egypt! Imagine that. She would probably never have any grandchildren herself, she was resigned to that now. But a holiday in an exotic place like Egypt sounded terribly nice. Dmitri hated Egypt. He'd been there for work a few times, and couldn't stand the place. Too noisy, too chaotic. The only good thing about the place was how easy it was to kill someone.

'Hello?'

'Dima, it's just me.'

'Yes, I know it's you. What's this about? I told you I have meetings all this week.' Dmitri looked down at his shoes. Devil take! There were a few drops of blood that had made it all the way over.

'Yes, yes, I'm sorry to interrupt. You must be very busy. It's just.'

'Yes, mama?' he said, trying to sound more conciliatory, so she would get to the point.

'Well. You know that light I was asking you about, the one just inside the backdoor, that hasn't been working for a while?'

Oh, he knew the one. The light above the door she never used, that she constantly asked him to change, but that had a different bulb fitting from the others and he'd never got around to buying the correct bulb.

'Yes?' he said again, getting his handkerchief out to soak up the red droplets from his leather shoes. One of the men in the corner let out a groan. Why would those fuckers never die?

'Just a minute, mama,' he said and muted the call before he walked over and put another bullet in the groaning man's head. The sound of the single shot bounced from wall to wall. He unmated the call again.

'Sorry, just had to deal with a request, mama. So, what's this about?' he asked, taking out the clip to see how many bullets he had left. He always counted, never lost track, but this conversation had derailed him. And he didn't even know what it was about yet. It better not be about Egypt.

'Well, I thought maybe I should just change it myself, you know. To save you the trouble. And I know you're so busy, I didn't want to …'

'So you changed it yourself?'

'Yes. But that's not why I'm calling. The thing is, I sort of had a little tumble as I was getting down from the chair.'

'You fell off it?'

'Yes. It was one of those old ones, from your dad's brother. You know, the ones your uncle had made himself?'

Who the fuck cares which chair it was! 'Yes, I know the ones,' Dmitri said through gritted teeth. 'Did you hurt yourself, mama?'

'I think I might have. I, uh. I can't seem to get up again. My hip is all funny, and, well, it hurts rather a lot.'

'Where are you now?'

'Oh, I'm still here. By the chair.'

'You mean on the floor? Oh, mama. How long have you been there?' he said as a wave of bad conscience and logistics flew through his mind. Getting his mother to hospital, getting the cleaner in to sort out the dead guys.

'Oh, just an hour or so. I tried calling you, but I guess you were busy with your important meetings.'

Busy, yes. But for the two guys lying in a heap in the corner, it had been a rather involuntary meeting. And this whole charade about him having a regular office job having been broken after he chased the raiders away from her village. So she probably knew, or had some idea, what he was up to. It wouldn't have bothered him so much if he'd been on an official assignment, but this was Sorokin's dirty work. It made Dmitri feel dirty too. Tainted.

'Mama, why didn't you call the ambulance? Or one of your neighbours?'

'Oh, I don't like ambulances and doctors much. And I don't have any cash around. And Darya would just gloat if she heard I tried changing the lightbulb myself. Her son always sorts out those things for her.'

Dmitri had to give it to her. For a woman who probably

had a broken hip, and had been lying alone in pain for the last hour, she still had what it took to make him feel guilty for not changing a light bulb. In a room she never even used.

'Mama, I will send for a private ambulance, and it will take you to the best doctor. Don't worry about it. I will come and meet you when you get to hospital, ok?'

'But, I'm still in my night clothes Dima. I can't go to the hospital dressed like this. And everyone will be asking questions if an ambulance shows up here. Couldn't you just come over after work?'

'You need to see a doctor straight away, mama. Not when I can get to you. I'm too far away,' he said and put his gun back in the shoulder holster. He knew his mother well enough to know that she'd be mortified to let anyone see her in her night clothes. 'Okay, this is what we'll do. I will send a good friend, Serge, and his girlfriend, who's a nurse. She can help you get dressed, and they will drive you to the hospital. Okay? Mama?'

'If you really think that is the only way,' she said and trailed off.

'It is. I will see you at the hospital. Now I have to get off the phone to make the arrangements, but do call me straight away if you get any worse.'

Dmitri felt like throwing the phone into the wall, or hitting something. He considered kicking the bodies to get release from the frustration, but knew that would just damage his shoes. He thought back to that yoga teacher he had gone out with for a few months. Took a few deep breaths and started typing to find Sergey's number. His fingers kept mistyping the letters on the small screen, but it was the only phone they had managed to install the right kind of encryption on, so he had to stick with it. Sergey replied straight away. He'd take care of his mother. Then Dmitri called the cleaner.

'Yes?'

'I've got a pickup for you. And transport, return to sender. Two packages'

'Where?'

'Grid 5, section 27. How long?'

'Ten minutes.'

'Perfect.'

Dmitri hung up and walked around the room to pick up the casings and any stray bullets. It was the cleaner's job, but there was no point in just hanging around. There were a few red holes in the concrete walls, where the bullets had gone through and through. He counted five strays. The other three must still be in the bodies. He went outside, and called Sorokin.

'Yes?'

'All done, but I will have to take the rest of the day off. My mother is on her way to hospital, and I'll need to go with her. Looks like a broken hip.'

'Oh, dear. That's not good. You're taking her to Botkin hospital, I assume? Have you called Dr. Tkachenko? He's the only man for the job.'

'I got Serge on it, I hope he's sorted it out.'

'I'll get Irina to make a call anyway, just in case. You wouldn't want anyone else to do it, not after lunch,' Sorokin said, sounding more concerned than annoyed that things weren't going to plan. 'What about our friend, have you managed to …?'

'No, not yet. I want to let him stew for a bit. Soften his resolve. But I'll go there tonight. Should be nice and quiet around there then. Is there anything new? The wolf?'

'No, no. Just a little anxious to get those documents. It's a little tense around here these days, what with that oligarch falling out of favour and getting arrested a couple of days ago. I think there might be a few who are looking for ways out, or the money to buy out.'

Dmitri wondered what it was like, when things were tense in the Kremlin. Or what it was like when it wasn't tense, if that ever happened.

'Is anyone on to us?'

18

RORY HEARD the hotel phone just as she turned off the shower. She wrapped herself in a towel and ran into the bedroom.

'Hello?' she said in Russian.

There was no sound at the other end, then the sobs of someone trying to stop herself from crying. 'I need to know how it's going, have you found Sasha or my dad?' Masha said in between the sobs.

Rory tried to be reassuring. 'I don't have anything to tell you yet, I'm afraid. I found Ivan, as I told you before, but he doesn't know much. I need more time,' she said.

'But what did Vanya say? Has he seen them? Or heard anything? Is my father drinking again?'

'Please, Masha, one thing at a time, ok. I haven't been in touch because I don't have anything new to tell you.' The sounds in the background made her hesitate. 'Are you on a train?'

'Yes, sorry, the connection is pretty bad. I'll just call back if I lose reception though.'

'You're calling from your mobile?' Rory's heart skipped a beat.

'Yes, I was just sitting here, thinking about Sasha and...'

'You do not call me from your mobile, ever. Ok? Never. I gave you a very clear set of rules.'

'But I need to know what's going on,' Masha tried.

'I'm going to hang up now. I will contact you via the first option on your list. Do you understand?'

'Is that the—'

'Do not talk about this on the phone!' Rory yelled at her. 'You are putting us all in danger. Stick to the rules, and we'll talk later on today ok?' Rory slammed the receiver down before Masha had had a chance to reply.

If whoever was responsible for Pavel and Sasha's disappearances had Masha's phone bugged, then her client had just blown Rory's cover. And Rory had used her fake Polish passport to book the room, the only fake identity she had access to. This could barely be any worse. Rory threw on some clean underwear and clothes at the same time as she threw the rest of her stuff into her bag. Her handbag was ready for a swift departure anyway, but it still took her a good two minutes before she was out of the room. She pondered taking the lift, but decided it'd be faster to run down the stairs. She leapt two steps at a time, skipping the whole bottom section of each flight before hurling herself around the corner for the next.

Three minutes. She took a left at the bottom, and went through the bin areas to leave the hotel.

Four minutes and she was out.

Sitting in the little triangular park across the road from the hotel, sharing a six pack of beers with a couple of local drunks and trying to catch her breath. She wanted to run, get away, as far away as she could. But she wasn't here to run. She was here to find.

Ten minutes had gone. The first beer cans lay empty on the grass.

Fifteen. A couple of cars had arrived at the hotel, but nothing that stood out. Then she spotted him. On foot. It was difficult to tell at this distance, but she was pretty confident she was right. It was him. He leisurely went into the reception area and chatted with the receptionist for a while. Then he went over to the lifts. Rory looked over to where he had come from and saw the car. The bullet proof car. She gave her beer to the woman next to her, and ran across the street, towards the BMW. Just as she passed it she leant down to take her shoe off, and shook out an invisible stone. The little click of the magnet on the tracker attaching to the chassis was impossible for anyone but her to hear.

19

RORY ADJUSTED the headset and microphone so she wouldn't have to raise her voice to be heard at the other end. The boys playing computer games next to her did a good job at drowning out anything but themselves. Then she pressed dial. She could hear the odd ringing sound of the Morrison's payphone at the other end.

'Hello?' Rory asked.

Masha's voice was calmer now. 'Hi. I'm sorry about earlier.'

'It's ok. I know you're worried. And I am sorry I haven't had anything to tell you. But until we know what we're dealing with, we have to be careful. Now more than ever. Make sure you stay off social media. Can you take time off work? No? Okay. But keep your eyes open. Only eat and drink what you have prepared yourself, or what has been prepared in front of you. Never eat twice in the same place. Never order the same dish twice. Don't stand too close to the platform edge, those kinds of things.' Rory knew she was making her client panic now, but better to be scared than careless. And she needed her to understand that now was not the time to be holding back information.

'Now. There are certain things I need to know if I am to get any further. Where did your father get his money from.'

'Pension. From an old job. For the Soviet communist party.'

Rory could hear the shopping trolleys going past in the background. Then an announcement on the tannoy: More staff needed at checkouts. 'The Soviet Communist Party? The one that doesn't exist any more?'

'Yes, I know it sounds mad. But he said his boss had set up a private pension for my father, and himself.'

'Who was his boss, and where is he now? Why didn't you tell me about him?' Rory fired off the questions, but knew she should have asked on at a time.

'I think his name was Lebedev? He's dead though. Died on the first day of the attempted coup in 1991. The one where they put Gorbachev in house arrest, but left Yeltsin to fight back?'

'How did he die, was it related to the coup?'

'I don't know. I don't think anyone knows. It was said to be a suicide. He jumped out of a window. But my father said that wasn't true, he'd driven him to work that day, and there was no way he was suicidal.'

'And he wouldn't have jumped because he realised the coup was failing?'

'I don't know. I don't think so. My dad never said much, didn't want to betray the trust shown to him. But I think his boss was the one managing the Soviet foreign investments. He took my dad with him to all sorts of places, countries I'd never heard about then but that I now know are international financial centres and tax havens. They went to the Caribbean several times.'

'What happened to the investments after the coup, when the boss died?'

'I'm not sure. I've heard talk about the money coming back under Yeltsin, that he hired some foreign forensic accountants, and that Yeltsin's 'family' and oligarchs stole most of it. But I don't know.'

Rory looked at her watch. They had talked too long already. She'd have to hang up. She wanted to know more, but it would have to do for now.

'Ok, I need to go. I will call again, in two or three days' time, if not before. Okay? I had to leave the hotel, so you won't be able to reach me. But if there is anything, you can send an email to the address I told you. I check it a few times a day.'

———

AFTERWARDS, Rory walked down the street and found a coffee shop with free internet. She got out a phone with no sim card and logged on. There was one new message. From her father.

Hi Rory, I was sorry to miss you last Sunday, but glad to hear you are keeping busy. I'm going on another research trip from next week, and will be away for the best part of a month, so it would be great to see you before I leave if at all possible. Lots of love, dad.

Rory felt a pang of guilt at having forgotten about his upcoming trip. He was going to spend a month in Iceland, trekking up Eyjafjallajokull or some other active volcanoes looking at biodiversity in the ashes left behind on the snow and ice. He'd even suggested that she join him for parts of it, as a father/daughter bonding time. She'd never really replied. If her mum was watching she'd be ashamed of her daughter. Of how Rory, more than ten years on, was still punishing her father for her mum's death and for his way of dealing with it. He had tried to apologise for sending her away to a boarding school. Tried to explain that he was so heartbroken, so depressed, that he couldn't possibly look after a teenage daughter on his own. And that he knew now that it was the wrong thing to do. She couldn't forgive him. Didn't want to forgive him. If she had, her last defence against the grief of losing her mum, a wall of anger, would come down. She wasn't ready for that. Not yet. Maybe never.

It was why she had broken it off with Tom in the end. Knowing that he was going to be in a war zone for six months at a time, putting his life on the line every day, was unbearable. It was the first real relationship she'd had, the first time she'd ever told anyone, apart from Priya, all about her mother's illness and death. Priya was still treading carefully around the subject, never bringing it up unless Rory did first. But Tom had been different. He'd challenged her to reconcile with her father. Start again. Tom was the reason they had their monthly Sunday lunches. But it just got too much in the end. The fear of losing Tom, spending every day, one hundred and eighty days in a row, wondering if he was still alive. If he was coming back to her in one piece. And it wasn't just the physical injuries she was worried about, the mental damage scared her more. Post-traumatic stress was just the beginning of it.

He was a difficult person to leave behind though. For a long time he'd refused to accept that she was breaking it off. First with stubbornness. Then came the anger. Then he seemed to have resigned himself to it. He couldn't just walk away from the army, even if he'd wanted to. He'd signed up with the SAS for six years. And he had two more to do. She knew that she'd hurt him, badly, and the last message from him, full of anger and spite, had felt thoroughly deserved. But she had to do what was best for her.

20

DMITRI PULLED up to the barriers. New guards again. Excellent. There wasn't much chance he would be remembered if he didn't see the same people more than once. He showed a parking permit, and slowly moved forward when the gate opened.

Straight ahead was a gap in the massive block of buildings that led to the inner courtyard of what had once been a thriving Soviet factory complex. This was where all the light bulbs for the entire Soviet Union had been made. When the country fell apart, and the market and the subsidies had disappeared, it had soon been closed and the equipment sold off. A fabric factory had survived for a bit longer, but couldn't compete against cheap Chinese imports. Today the factory complex was occupied by a very new, but in some ways not so different Russia. The main office building was home to one of the so-called troll factories, where youngsters were fighting an online war to protect Russia's interests – not so much change there. But the fact that the troll factory needed super-fast broadband, had filled the other buildings with internet start-ups while some of the smaller buildings provided studios for artists and photographers and practice rooms for bands. It was a strange mix.

The building they had hired was set apart from the others. It had, in the 90s, been a television studio for an independent channel that only lasted a few years. Since then it had been left unused, and unchanged. A sound proofed facility was perfect for their purposes.

As Dmitri pulled up behind the small building, where his car would be almost out of sight, he could hear a heavy metal band practicing nearby. He unlocked the rusty gate to his building, and closed it behind him. Behind the rickety wooden door that was visible from the outside, he came to the door he had installed himself. A thick, metal door, with security worth almost as much as the building. No one knew what was in here, and even if they had, they wouldn't care. That was what his country had become. A place where everyone looked after themselves first, and where putting your nose in anyone else's business could prove fatal. When he unlocked and opened the door, he could hear the music still going. Or the sound at least. It was really a recording of white noise, with the irregular addition of some atonal modern stuff Dmitri had always found deeply unsettling. He'd considered asking for a demo of the band practising next door to add to his collection, but thought they might not be quite bad enough to achieve the desired effect. Inside the room, his prisoner was slumped sideways, half leaning on the chair he had been tied to. Dmitri threw a stick at the body, and it jerked at the impact. A slow groan indicating that the man had managed to fall asleep, even in such an uncomfortable position.

Dmitri put his hand to his mouth, his stubby finger tapping his upper lip, as it often did when he had to figure something out. He had been sure that the solution would come to him as soon as he returned here, but no such luck.

He'd tried asking persistently, firmly, deceitfully, harshly, brutally and horribly. But nothing had worked. Maybe he should have tried the rock band next door.

Still, he shouldn't be surprised. He'd seen the target's body when he stripped him. The man had clearly seen worse than anything Dmitri could ever think of. It had been covered with scars from beatings and lashing, burn marks from a war gone by: even his fingernails had been missing. After the first few attempts at getting Pavel to talk had failed, Dmitri had looked up his service record from Afghanistan. And as he expected, Pavel wasn't new to being a prisoner. He had been captured by the mujahideen along with a fellow soldier, the drunk who now lived near Kievskaya. Both had been elite airborne troops back then, the sole survivors from a Soviet helicopter the mujahideen had shot down. Dmitri felt conflicted about having to treat a war hero like this, to submit him to this degrading treatment. But this man was his ticket out. So here he was, sitting in his own faeces and urine - disoriented, thirsty and hungry. Every time Dmitri had tried to interrogate him, Pavel had kept his wits about him. Hopefully, the last few days of isolation had softened his resolve a bit.

Dmitri undid the plasticuffs that tied the body to the chair legs, and sat him up on the seat, fastening Pavel's wrists to the armrests. Dmitri was a lot bigger, and a lot fitter than Pavel, but he wasn't taking any chances. He'd read in his army records about the daring escape from the mujahideen cave in Afghanistan. Pavel had killed the guards with his bare hands, and carried his fellow soldier, who had a broken leg, to safety in a town several days' walk away. He took the hood off, stiff from the blood that had soaked through from the man's broken nose.

'Name', Dmitri said.

Pavel looked up at Dmitri, his eyes trying to get used to

the sharp light after having spent the last 48 hours in complete darkness.

'Name.' Dmitri kicked the chair.

'Pavel Ivanovich Abramov,' Pavel said, the words only just managing to make their way through his dried up mouth.

Dmitri threw some water in the Pavel's face, and the prisoner licked up every drop that went near enough to his mouth.

'Where are the files?'

'I don't know what files you're talking about. Please, can I have some water?'

'If you tell me where the files are.'

'I don't have any files. Please, water,' Pavel said, the last words being followed by a violent cough, that brought a mix of blood and phlegm onto his chapped lips.

Dmitri saw this was going the wrong direction, again. Pavel was managing to get to him – he felt guilty. But if he gave him water before Pavel gave him something in exchange, the balance between them would be all wrong. Still, it wasn't as if anything else had worked. On the spur of the moment, Dmitri decided to change the rules of the game. He took out a new bottle of water, the one he had brought for himself, unscrewed the cap and put it to Pavel's lips. The man swallowed it like a thirsty animal. Halfway through the bottle the water went the wrong way and a cough brought some of it up again.

'Easy there, don't want to drown you. Let's slow down a little,' Dmitri's voice said, and he caught himself talking to Pavel as he did with his own mother.

'Thanks,' Pavel said, his voice clearing up a little.

It was the first time they'd made eye contact.

'What was your first job after the military?' Dmitri asked, not expecting a reply.

His jaw almost dropped when he got one.

'I worked for an Army general for a while. After Afghanistan. Then I started driving Communist Party officials. Bureaucrats.' The prisoner coughed again.

'Can I have their names, please?' Dmitri asked and held the bottle to Pavels lips again.

The prisoner took a smaller sip, and after it came a long list of names. Regional party secretaries, committee members, ministers. Then Lebedev.

'Why did you stop working for the Party?'

'My boss died. On the day of the coup in 1991. And when the whole country fell apart at the end of the year, there was no party left to work for.'

'How did he die? Was he part of the coup?'

'No, not that I know. He said he wasn't. That he'd tried to stay out of it. But I don't think he managed.'

'What do you mean?'

'Well, someone must have been unhappy about the decisions he'd made. Why else would someone have killed him?'

'Killed him?'

'Yes. They said it was suicide, but he could never have killed himself. He had no reason to kill himself. And he would never have done it like that. He was terrified of heights. Would never have climbed onto a window ledge unless someone made him do it. I don't understand how they did it though. The KGB were sure he had jumped.'

'Were you ever suspected of being the cause of his death?'

'Me? Why would I have done that? Lebedev was good to me. Probably the best boss I had.'

'So you weren't just his driver?'

'I was supposed to be his bodyguard as well, but he said he didn't need one. Said he had no enemies. That no one knew anything that could give them reason to want him dead.'

Dmitri wondered what was going on. Why his prisoner had decided to talk. Was it a plot? Or had he softened his resilience enough? The white noise was gruesome, Dmitri himself couldn't bear to listen to it for more than a few minutes at a time. But was this too good to be true?

'What did he do then, your last boss?'

The prisoner got a twitch at the side of his left eye. Telling a lie, perhaps? Dmitri thought not. More like he was preparing himself to tell a selective truth.

'He was one of the Party's financial managers. A genius with numbers. So he travelled around the world investing some of the Soviet Union's great wealth. The West thought they were winning the cold war. They didn't realise that we'd bought up a lot of their imperial ventures.'

Dmitri recognised the patriotic pride. His prisoner wasn't too different from himself.

'What happened to these investments after Lebedev died?'

'I don't know. How would I know? I was only the driver.'

'You didn't go back to the office?'

'Only to get my personal things. A picture of my wife. A spare jacket to wear when I had to take Lebedev somewhere fancy. There wasn't much. And the building caretaker locked up the office straight away. Wanted to see what the outcome was of the coup before she would let anyone in.'

'Could she have taken anything from the office?'

'The caretaker? How would I know? If this is about not being there when he was killed, then please, I have felt bad about that for the last 25 years. Drove me to drinking, it did.'

Dmitri was almost amazed, maybe his treatment of the prisoner had worked after all?

'So what do you think happened to him?'

Pavel coughed again, the raspiness of his voice gradually disappearing. 'I don't know, I shouldn't be speculating. But I noticed that there were things missing, papers lying around the place in a way he would never have done. He was always very neat and tidy. Kept things in order, he did. Maybe he had upset someone with what he was doing.'

'And what was it exactly that he was doing?' Dmitri asked.

'Could I have some water please?'

Dmitri went through his bag to find another bottle.

'The West thought they were all so clever with their technology boycotts, and undermining us by forcing the oil price down, but they didn't know that we had invested in, and profited from, everything they invented. From their arm sales, their cars, their fancy new computers, their silly Star Wars scenarios. There wasn't an American factory we didn't own a share of, if it was over a certain size. And Lebedev was the mastermind of it all. It was a shame to see his great work being torn apart in the 90s, the money lining those western 'accountants' pockets, and going into the great drain that was Yeltsin's entourage and oligarchs. A shame, and a great betrayal of the people.'

'What happened to the paperwork from these investments?'

'The KGB, the new KGB guys who took over after those pathetic coup makers were imprisoned, took control of whatever was there. They didn't seem to have a clue about what they were looking at though, kept asking me, but I didn't know. I was just the driver. But I assume someone figured it out, and got those accountants to sort things out.'

'And why were you not with your boss that day?'

'I was. I drove him to his office, as usual, and went upstairs with him. It was the day of the attempted coup, so things were quite chaotic. Lebedev had insisted he didn't want any part in it, so he didn't really know what was going on. And on TV they were just showing *Swan Lake* all day. I wanted to stay close, that day more than ever, but he sent me to see what was going on at the Red Square. When I came back, a cleaner had found him in the backyard. She was screaming, the body was a complete mess of broken bones and blood. There was a window open in his office.'

'Did you go with him abroad?'

'Of course, I was his bodyguard as well, not just his driver.'

'To meetings?'

'Yes.'

'What happened at these meetings?'

'I was never in the room. I waited outside, with the secretaries.'

'The last trip, where did you go to? Did anything different happen there?'

'I think it was sme Caribbean island, don't remember which one. Not Cuba. I had to sign some papers, but that wasn't out of the ordinary.'

'Papers? What kind of papers?'

'I don't know. I didn't read Latin letters. Just signed when asked. Lebedev said it had to do with deceiving the Americans, using different names, unknown names like mine. But I never quite understood. I didn't need to, Lebedev was the smartest man I have ever worked for.'

'Where are the papers from this trip?'

'I don't know, with the others, I expect.'

'Could he have left them at home?

'He didn't keep anything work related there. He did once, it didn't work out too well.'

'What do you mean?'

'He. He met this girl. Pretty, Ukrainian girl. Katya, I think. Daughter of some exiled dissident. She sometimes came on the trips. Labedev's wife found photos of her. Not easy to explain. So he never kept anything at home after that.'

'Could this girl have the papers?'

'Maybe, I don't know. He always sent me away when she

was around. I knew his wife you see, liked her. I didn't think it was right, and said as much.'

'Do you remember her full name?'

'No.'

Dmitri got out the pictures he'd taken from Lebedev's office in 1991. 'Is this her?'

'Well, yes, I believe so. Where did you get that from?'

'The KGB listed everything in the office. I believe Lebedev used to have a briefcase, but there is no record of it anywhere?'

'Oh, that old thing. Yes, a gift from his late father. He never went anywhere without it. It was a beautiful briefcase. I think his father bought it abroad. He had been a diplomat. Lebedev spoke English and French fluently after growing up abroad.'

'But if it wasn't in the office. Where do you think he would have kept it?'

'Oh, he left that in the car. I only found it afterwards, on my way home.'

'And where is it now?'

'I don't know, not sure. I didn't really know what to do with it, or the car, afterwards. Everything was so chaotic, no one was in charge it seemed. So I waited to find out who would end up on top.'

'Maybe you gave it to someone? His wife, perhaps? The KGB guys?'

'No, I, uh. I went through it. There wasn't much there, some papers in a foreign language. And a few letters he had asked me to send. I sent those off, thought that was what he would have wanted. Business as usual, you know.'

'Who were the letters to?'

'One was for his, uh, girlfriend. The others I don't know. Companies he was working with, I think.'

'And where did his girlfriend live?' Dmitri unwrapped a paper bag with a sandwich he had picked up on the way, slowly, pretending not to notice that Pavel was staring at the food. Pavel's jaw dropped a little. It had been almost a week since he'd last eaten.

'France I think, or that little country, Monaco. Yes, somewhere near there. On the coast, by the sea. He showed me pictures once, beautiful blue water.'

'And the briefcase itself? What did you do with it?'

'I was meaning to take it to his wife, but couldn't find her. And I didn't really want to get involved with those KGB guys. The girl. I think her name was Katya. It was a big envelope he sent her. Not what you would normally send to a girlfriend. You know. Little love letters. This was different.'

Dmitri tore the sandwich in two, cut off the plasticuff on Pavel's left hand and gave him half of the sandwich. Pavel grabbed it, but managed, with the same self control that had got him through the torture all those years ago, to eat it slowly.

'I'm sorry I don't remember her full name. I started drinking, you see. After the coup. The memories were too much. From Afghanistan,' Pavel said, swallowing down the first bite of bread.

Dmitri looked at Pavel, and followed his eyes to the remaining sandwich. He smiled to himself, thinking he could now add master interrogator to his CV. Invisible assassin and master interrogator. Not that he'd ever have to do anything like it again, after he'd found that girl. He was pondering whether or not he should kill off Pavel right away, but decided to talk to Sorokin first. There was a chance his prisoner had more useful information. Not likely, but not impossible either.

Dmitri could burn Pavel's face, like he'd done with the guy at the banya. And then swap the bodies. That'd tie things up nicely. Though it'd be easier to feed the real Pavel to the dogs, Dmitri didn't want to leave any loose ends. Dmitri gave Pavel the last piece of bread. No reason not to show some generosity at this stage. He was a war hero after all. There was something that didn't quite make sense though. Why would Pavel talk so freely now? Surely it couldn't just be the food and water? Dmitri pondered this, and decided to double check the info about the girl with Sorokin straight away.

21

DMITRI PARKED his car in the first parking bay he found and ran to the lifts. As the lift shot up through the building, he couldn't stop snapping his fingers. There wasn't much of a sound, he'd never been any good at it. It made him feel like he was still actively doing something, and not just waiting to get to Sorokin's top floor suite. He had changed out of the clothes he used in the interrogation room, but he could still catch a whiff of the stench of bodily fluids.

The lift stopped and Dmitri walked out to the solid steel door opposite. He put his palm on the scanner and looked into the facial recognition camera before the locks clicked open. He could hear the slight buzzing of the electronic jammer as he walked into Sorokin's office. There were floor to ceiling glass windows, but they had that greyish tint that indicated they were covered in the thin film that would prevent electronic signals from going in or out.

Dmitri didn't even bother turning his phone off, let alone take out the battery.

'I got through to him. Finally.'

Sorokin turned off the TV and closed his laptop. 'And? Did you get the documents?'

'No, but he as good as told me where the papers are. Turns out the old Lebedev had a little lady on the side. You remember the photos I took from his drawer? That was his mistress. And he sent her a letter on the day he died.' Dmitri slowed down as he noticed Sorokin's mouth going from a smile to a frown.

'Girlfriend? You think the girlfriend has the papers?'

'Sure sounds like she's our best bet.'

'You fool. That 'girlfriend' was working for me. She's the one who told me about the papers in the first place.'

Dmitri felt like he'd been slapped. He could feel the blood rushing to his ears. Then he hit the wall. His knuckles felt like they shattered as he made contact with the concrete behind the plasterboard. 'That bastard. He thinks he's so smart. When I'm done with him ...'

'Calm down,' Sorokin went over to the bar and put a few cubes of ice in a towel and gave it to Dmitri. 'What else did he say? He might not have known she was a plant, so he could be telling the truth as he knew it. Did he mention anything else Lebedev left behind? Letters, papers, the briefcase?'

'Yes, but when he mentioned the letter to the girl, I didn't quiz him more about it. I got a description of where she lived, but I guess you know that already. '

'Has he got it? The briefcase?'

'I think so. But I don't know where. It's not in his flat or at his dacha. And he's not going to tell me now. He knows he's fooled me once, and will just try again. If only we had his son.'

'Well, we don't have him. And apart from waiting for him to show up at the morgue to identify the body we put there, there's not much we can do to find him. We can't exactly put him on the wanted list, Volkov or one of the others would find out and start digging.'

Sorokin looked towards the windows, towards the centre

of Moscow. He had a panoramic view from the top floor of one of the modern skyscrapers in Moscow City. 'There is another person he might be willing to reveal all to protect. There's a daughter. In London.'

Dmitri forgot about his fist for a second. 'He has a daughter? Are you kidding me? And you didn't think to tell me this before because?' Dmitri said, trying his best to not get as close up to Sorokin's face as possible.

'I didn't tell you because it should have been irrelevant. I assumed you would be able to get the necessary information out of pretty much anyone, let alone a recovering alcoholic. But I guess I was wrong. You're not very good at getting information at all, are you?'

'I could have got him to say anything if I had some leverage. I can't fucking believe this. First you 'forget' to tell me he is a war hero, a man who managed to survive and then break out after months of captivity at the hands of the Afghan mujahideen. Then you 'forget' to tell me he has a daughter. It's as if you wanted me to fail.'

'None of this would have been necessary if you had just got the right documents 25 years ago, remember?'

'Oh, on the day you happened to get yourself imprisoned for three years? Yeah, that's all my fault.'

The two men stared at each other, nostrils flaring and jaws clenched so tight the tension reverberated through the room. Finally Sorokin took a deep breath, and unclenched his fists.

'I didn't tell you about the daughter, because she is not to be touched.'

'Oh, another girlfriend of yours?'

'I take your point, but no. Not mine. But someone else's. Or at least she was, I'm not sure if they're romantically linked any more.'

'Who?'

'Someone we wouldn't want to mess with. Not now. Probably never.'

'Who is it? I'm not going in blind again, you'd better be upfront from now on.'

'It's Demidov. The steel magnate.'

Dmitri let out a whistle. 'Okay, I can see how that would cause complications. But we've still kidnapped her father?'

'Yes, but I don't think there has been much contact between father and daughter. He pretty much abandoned her and her mother when he started drinking. And as long as she can be convinced that her father died in an accident, we don't have anything to worry about. The body in the morgue should do that trick, right?'

'Yeah, it's a close enough match. Wouldn't pass a DNA test, of course, but no one ever gets those done over here. But you said there was some doubt as to whether she was still with Demidov. If it's over, surely he's moved on and forgotten her already?'

'That's the complicated bit. Masha is not just a pretty face. She's a bit of a mathematical genius, so Demidov made her the manager of his UK investment fund. It would certainly be noticed if she disappeared.' Sorokin went through some files in his desk and got out a paper cutting. The picture showed a gorgeous young woman, who looked a lot like her father, standing next to one of Russia's most powerful oligarchs.

'But the father doesn't know that would stop us though, does he?' Dmitri frowned as he tried to make sense of things. Why didn't Sorokin trust him enough to tell him this from the beginning? And why, after thirty years of working for Sorokin, had Dmitri not realised that he should do his own digging?

Dmitri looked at the Moscow river, winding its way through the city below. At the church spires dwarfed by the modern, surrounding buildings. Dmitri knew why he didn't do any digging. He was afraid of what he might find. It had been his way of coping with his work, of keeping a clear conscience. Pretending it was all part of defending the motherland. But with this last job there was no pretending. The hooded figure hidden inside the old warehouse complex on the other side of the river was no enemy. Not to him, not to Mother Russia.

'Was it the daughter who tipped you off about the person staying at the Golden Ring hotel? I guess you have her under surveillance?'

'Yes. Only electronic surveillance, I don't want to risk anything else given her job and connections. But she lives her life through her gadgets, as most of her generation, so there's no need to follow her around. Google maps does that for us. And Instagram.'

'Any recent pictures I can use on her father?'

'Good thinking. Yes, I'll print some off. She's been offline the last week, but her friends aren't.'

Sorokin opened another laptop and printed two pictures of a slightly older version of the woman from the newspaper cutting. She was still stunning, but the first lines were beginning to show around her eyes. Her warm smile almost made Dmitri smile as well. Then he stopped himself. He had to stay professional. Cold. Detached. The fact that he never hurt women and children could not impact on his ability to look like he could, and would, when he was facing the prisoner again.

22

RORY'S TEETH CHATTERED. The bus shelter she stood next to was on the opposite side of the road from the big industrial complex, and if she wanted a clear line of sight to the barrier, the cool breeze coming from the Moscow river came straight at her. She got some sleepy dust out of the corner of her right eye. She hadn't wanted to sleep in the bed at the rent-by-the-hour, no ID necessary, hotel she'd found, even to touch the covers, so she'd slept on the cold floor, bag under her head, coat on top. Now it felt like the cold had wedged its way into her spine, and there was no sign of it moving out.

The cafe opposite, on the corner of the former industrial complex, didn't open till ten. Fifteen more minutes to wait out in the cold. Or until he emerged again. The man from the CIA guy's drawings. The man with half a finger missing. The man Sorokin had talked to at the casino and sent to her hotel after Masha blew her cover. Dima. Dmitri. Rory had spent the last two days tracking his car, trying to figure out where he could be keeping Pavel. And if he was working alone. She prayed to God he was the kind of guy who worked alone. Not just because one opponent was better than multiple, but

because it revealed something about him, his nature, his pref-
erences.

Of all the places Dmitri had been, this was the one that
seemed most likely. It was the third time he'd gone here since
she'd seen him at the hotel. The whole structure looked like a
gigantic Soviet fortress in red brick, five or six floors high,
several blocks wide. She'd walked around it, hoping to find
another way in, but there was none. Some of the building, in
particular the section furthest from the entrance that backed
onto a pot-holed one-way street, was dilapidated. The
windows were boarded up and doors covered in metal shutters. She had tried, but decided it would be impossible to
break in without being seen from the main road. The front
part of the 'fortress', which had the one sole gateway to the
interiors in it, had all been done up. Judging by the people
coming and going, it housed a variety of businesses now.
Young men in skinny jeans and women with oversized
glasses or ombre hair, some carrying camera bags or portfolio
cases. A few workmen and women in dirty overalls and
greasy fingers. Musicians with guitar cases.

Her fingers were stiff with cold, her body longing for a
cup of tea. A warm cup to hold and a bit of caffeine to kick
start the day. She needed to pee, but didn't want to risk
leaving her spot in case he left while she was doing it. But
there was no helping it. Thinking about that cup of tea had
sent the wrong signals to her bladder. And it would make her
warmer. It was one of the things her mother had taught her,
on one of many hiking trips in the Lake District. How
holding the pee in wasted energy that was better used to stay
warm. Not to mention how distracting it was when her body
kept focusing on one thing and her brain tried to do something else.

She had a look at the tracker app. No movement
detected. Then she ran around the corner, to the porch of a
closed up shop, and huddled down in the darkest nook by

the door. The paint was peeling off the bricks and the smell made it clear she wasn't the first one to do this. A mother with a pram passing on the opposite side of the street pretended not to see her. There was no time to feel embarrassed, and the relief from emptying her bladder was instant. A door slammed shut close by, and Rory tried to force the last bit out before the person walked past and found her mid-stream.

Rory pulled her pants and trousers back up, then jogged away as she did up her zipper. As she turned the corner, a muffled woman's voice let out some invocation of God as she stepped into the little puddle Rory had left.

Oh well. There were worse things.

Then Rory was back at her post, by the bus stop, checking what looked like the average smartphone but only had one purpose; tracking. A bus came and went. Some people got on, others off. And two teenage boys were entertaining themselves and the others with tales of the weekend past. It was the perfect spot, she had a direct line of sight both to the gate and the barriers, but would disappear into the busy streetscape for anyone leaving the 'fortress'.

She didn't have to wait long.

Her phone vibrated. Movement detected, and approaching. The black BMW was gliding through the opening between the buildings, before it paused while the guard lifted the barrier. She looked at rear tyres and the boot, tried to look for any sign there was something heavy in there, say, the weight of a boy and an adult male, but got no indication either way.

She couldn't make out the driver. Was it him? The man she'd heard Sorokin call Dima? Or maybe there were others involved?

As the car pulled up to the main road, it came out from the shade of the buildings. It was him. No doubt. And he was alone. But there was still a chance he had an accomplice inside. She followed him with her eyes, to the end of the street where he turned towards the river and out of sight.

Rory felt her pulse racing. This was it. She had to wait for a group of hip young things heading to work before she could blend in and get past the gate unnoticed. When they all piled into an entrance with a bright reception area and walls plastered with glossy magazine covers, she paused at an ashtray, pretending to fiddle with her phone. Then she turned and walked further into the courtyard.

It took a little while to find the car tracks, his car tracks, disappearing into flattened bramble and weeds behind a container full of rubbish. The building they led to was the most worn down in the entire complex, a low brick building with a corrugated roof, metal bars in front of the windows and a door that looked like it had been working its way free of its hinges for a decade. There was half a sign to the left of the door, but the writing on it was faded and impossible to read. Hiding in plain sight. It was risky, but amazing when it worked. If this was where Sasha and Pavel were kept, then this was all a small scale operation. Something only a few people knew about, and Sorokin and his man clearly wanted to keep it that way. It reduced the chances of there being anyone else inside.

A couple of the neighbouring buildings were almost as ramshackle, and she sneaked into one of them, where a heavy metal band was playing the same section of a tune again and again. An attempted guitar solo. She found a grimy window that faced the low brick building. No activity. Sorokin's man was probably working alone. If this had been one of Richard's gigs, they would have kept it under surveillance for at least 48 hours. But Richard wasn't here. And this was the first case Rory had had where people were getting killed. The first one since the army. The smell of the charred human flesh came back to her. There was no time to evaluate and plan for 'scenarios'. This was a time to act.

Rory ran over to the building and opened the first door. The lock was a joke, all she had to do was to lift the door by the handle, and the catch was free. She had a quick look at the old sign. TV something or other. She slipped inside and closed the door behind her. The window was dirty, but let in enough light to see what was around. The small lobby had an old desk and a metal chair with no seat, and another sign saying Studio, Telekanal Monster.

There was a noise of some sort, but she couldn't place it. Like a radio that was stuck between stations. Then she felt the chill going down her back. She'd heard this noise before. And the memories it brought back weren't of the good kind.

White noise.

The noise of hell.

The sound of interrogations, disoriented prisoners and torture. One of the reasons she'd left the army.

The inside door was a recent addition. A metal door with a padlock half the size of her hand. She checked her tracker. Signal lost. Rory took out a nail manicure set, and started fiddling with the lock.

Ten seconds.

She paused and listened for the sound. The radio noise was there, the heavy metal band had moved on from the guitar solo, the singer giving his vocal cords some exercise.

Twenty.

Thirty.

Click.

The white noise flooded her senses as she opened the door. And the stench. She had sat on both sides of the table in the middle of the room. As the prisoner, when being trained in resistance to interrogation, and later as the interrogator, when she was deployed in northern Iraq. It was a world she thought she had closed the door on, for good. For her own good, too.

There was a man sitting on a chair with a canvas bag on

his head, in front of a backdrop of the Kremlin. No sign of the boy, just a table, a stereo and a bag in the corner. The man sat up as she came in, following her movements. His arms were bare, his singlet torn.

The tattoo.

The Mi-8 helicopter, the parachute. Logar, Baraki, 86 88.

She'd found Pavel.

She ran over and tore the hood off, the stench of urine and faeces overpowering. His nose had gone almost black with dried blood and bruising, his eyes looked up at her, trying to focus on her face.

'Is your son here? Where's Sasha?'

No reply.

Pavel stared at her, and she wasn't sure if he was unable or unwilling to talk. His trousers were stiff with blood and urine, and her fingers got sticky as she cut the cable ties tying him to the chair with her pocket knife.

'Pavel, your daughter Masha sent me to find you. You and your son, Sasha. Can you stand up?'

Pavel nodded, and pulled himself up, holding on to her hand.

He took a step forward.

Then another one.

'Pavel, do you know where Sasha is? Please, is he somewhere nearby? Has your captors got him?'

'Masha hired you to find me?'

Rory could hear the incredulity in his voice. 'No. She didn't. She hired me to find her brother. Your son. She thought you might have started drinking again.'

'Ah.' Pavel's voice was quiet as a whisper, so Rory had to lean in to hear what he said. 'That's more like her. He's not here. I don't know where he is.'

Still holding him up, Rory pulled the bag over with her foot, and leaned down to fish out what looked like a not too dirty t-shirt. She pulled it over his head. It gave him a semblance of normality.

They had reached the door when the tracker in Rory's pocket started buzzing. Dmitri's car was on the move again. Probably Dmitri too.

Rory looked around her, trying to find something Pavel could use as support. She reached over to the door, and had to let go of his arm to pull it open. Pavel collapsed in a heap before she could stop it. She lifted him back up again, sweat beginning to appear on her temples. The cold she had felt just minutes ago had vanished. They moved out of the building, into the daylight, and Pavel winced. Was it the bright daylight or the cold air? She couldn't risk taking him out the main entrance.

Pavel leaned on her shoulder, struggling to support his own weight as they walked around a corner of the building, away from the metal band, away from the approaching Dmitri. And towards what looked like a deserted part of the main factory complex. She recognised the facade, there was an identical looking one backing onto a dead end street she had seen on her recce.

Rory forced through the bramble, tearing her clothes on the way, but neither she nor Pavel seemed to feel the pain. The building in front of them was four stories high and with broken windows on the raised ground floor.

It would be easy to follow their tracks as far as the building, but the darkness inside would make it more difficult to find them. They walked up the steps to one of the steel doors, but it had an old padlock with cyrillic letters on it. So had the others. There was no time to pick the locks either, they looked so rusty they wouldn't even open with the right key. They had to climb through a broken window.

That window. It was high up on the wall and Rory had to tiptoe when she put her hand inside and felt the ledge, and found the fastener. Hoping it wouldn't have rusted in place, she forced it open, one inch at a time, until it let out a creak and swung freely towards them. Pavel's breath was rasping next to her. A broken rib might have pierced a lung. Or maybe it was just him not having had anything to drink in ages. She grabbed his wrists, lifted them up to the ledge and held onto them with one hand, as if she was doing a lifesaver manoeuvre in a swimming pool. With all the broken glass around, she couldn't risk pushing him in first.

The tracker started vibrating in her pocket again. Three long bursts this time. He was getting closer. He might be stuck at traffic lights nearby, or on the thoroughfare running along the Moskva river. Or he could also be approaching the gates.

It would take five seconds to check. But she might need those to pull Pavel out of sight. Rory took a deep breath. Then another one. Holding Pavel's hands on the window ledge with her left hand, she put all power in her legs into jumping up to the window. But she couldn't get high enough to use her right arm as support to get over the ledge.

The scanner vibrated again. Object was closing in. The half finger man must have passed the gates by now. How long did she have? Thirty seconds before he came to the building, and another twenty before he realised Pavel was gone?

She cursed herself for not having spent some time covering their tracks inside. She could have cut the power, left the bag on Pavel's chair and made it look like he was still there.

Pavel groaned next to her, and his body had started sagging towards the ground. Her left hand had to grip on tightly to his wrists on the ledge to stop him from collapsing into the weeds outside the window. His nose was bleeding again, and Rory used her arm to wipe it off, to stop them from leaving a trail of blood everywhere.

Second attempt. And the last one, judging by the buzzing in her pocket. Only one deep breath this time.

This was her only opportunity to save Pavel's life. Failure was no option. She knelt a little, then pushed up towards the window sill again, kicked into the brick wall on the way up and forced herself up high enough to rest her weight on her straight right arm. Pavel let out a small groan as the pressure of her weight split between her hands, but in the next second she had swung herself through the window.

Most of the glass was on the outside, not the inside, and she pulled Pavel up and in. First his arms, then his torso, and then she pulled his legs through the gap and closed the window behind them.

She could hear Pavel's wheezing breath was getting worse, but couldn't stop to think about what, if any, injury she might have caused him. At least he was still alive. She could just hear the car, as her scanner went on a vibrating frenzy. Closing her eyes to get used to the dim lights inside the building, she counted the seconds before the car engine stopped running.

Five. Ten. Twenty. He was clearly not in a hurry. Thirty. That wouldn't be enough for her eyes, but she opened them anyway to survey what she could see of the room. As she pulled Pavel up again, she could hear the engine being turned off, and the car door open and shut. They might have a minute's head start, at most.

The room, or, hall, they were in, was filled with old machinery of some sort, large metal structures two metres wide and at least as tall. Like brutalist robots. They looked small with the double height ceiling. The beige and brown chequered floor was covered with dust and debris fallen from broken lights, and whatever was falling down from the ceiling high above them. And bird poo. Lots of bird poo. There was a mezzanine level at the far end, that they might be able to get to if the wooden staircase hadn't rotted through completely. The few machines left seemed like they had been used for some sort of textile making, there were stains of colour around a few of them, giant rollers and a flurry of cotton dancing around the room like tumbleweed whenever a breeze came through. The windows facing the street in the opposite wall were all boarded up with old planks. She didn't think Pavel would be able to make the jump from the window to the brick wall on the other side. She remembered a door towards the corner of the building, closer to the main road. A door with a lock she could pick, if they didn't get lucky and it could be opened from the inside.

'Please, water. I need water,' Pavel managed to let out next to her, before he succumbed to a coughing fit.

There was no time for that, but his coughing reverberated through the room. Dmitri would find them in no time at all if she couldn't get Pavel quiet.

'One second. Here, just take a small sip. You'll just get sick if you have too much.' Rory was amazed at how this man who looked half dead, still managed to move at all, even if she did have to carry most of his weight.

Pavel took a small sip, then another, and just as Rory was ready to wrestle the bottle from his hands, looked up at her through his bloodshot eyes. 'Thank you,' he said and gave the bottle back. His breathing was barely audible again.

The sound of someone trying to open the metal door behind them tore into the quiet like thunder, and Pavel started shaking uncontrollably at hearing the swearing outside. The staircase. They must get to the stairs and out of the massive hall before he makes it inside.

They slalomed across the hall, keeping to the darker patches of the room, avoiding any source of light from the outside. Rory had to drag Pavel half the time, and progress was slow. But she couldn't carry him. She'd almost done her back in pulling him up through the window.

Out of the corner of her eye, Rory could see a head

peering in one of the broken windows. The one they'd just crawled through. She ducked, pulling Pavel down with her. Dmitri wouldn't be able to see much, and Rory got on her feet again, moving away from the windows and towards the staircase.

Another sound.

Rory paused, motioned for Pavel to be quiet, to be still, but to no avail. His wheezing was coming back, and he couldn't suppress a small cough that escaped between his lips.

Fuck.

The head popped up again, and the light from a mobile phone shone towards them. Another cough followed, and Rory tried to pull Pavel behind the nearest machine.

Before she could get them to safety, she heard the shattering of glass.

She wasn't sure which came first, the flashing muzzle, the sound of a whole chamber being unloaded, or the pain in her arm.

23

WHEN THE SHOOTING STOPPED, Rory looked over towards the window. Her ears were ringing.

The gun was gone. So was the man. A bullet was stuck in the leg of the machine they had tried to hide behind.

She looked at her arm, and at Pavel. She wasn't sure if the blood was his or hers.

Pavel looked at her. 'You've got to get out of here.'

'We've got to get out of here.'

'I'm not going anywhere. He got me. In the shoulder.'

It was only then she paused to notice the pain in her upper arm, the one she'd used to pull Pavel backwards, behind the machine. Dull, aching pain. Their blood was mixing on Pavel's top, hers more of a trickle, his a deep dark red. The bullet had gone through her arm before it struck Pavel. The bullet hole was too high to have killed him, but the amount of blood coming out of it was terrifying. Rory put her hand on it to stop the flow, whilst looking for something to make a compress with.

'I wasn't sure if I could trust you. Thought you might be some decoy, a ploy to get me to reveal where my son is. But I don't have much choice any more. And you could've easily got killed by that bullet.'

Pavel coughed again, and she gave him the water bottle. He took a small sip. 'There's an old briefcase, in my garage. It belonged to Lebedev, a Party official who was killed in 1991. He was my boss. There are some keys in there, I'm not sure what to, but I think that is what these men are after. But my son is hiding out there, in the garage, I'm sure of it. It is our secret hideaway, only the two of us know about it. You have to get him away from there before they find him. If they find out I have a daughter, I won't be able to stay quiet any more. It's only a question of time before they do.'

'I'm not leaving you here.'

'You have to. Or he will catch us both and you will make me have to choose which of my two children to save. Please don't make me do that. Go. Save Sasha.'

Rory knew there was no time to argue. And that Pavel was right. She wanted to say that she would be back for him. But the look in his eyes said it all. She had to leave and find the boy, before Sorokin's man got inside the building and had them both trapped. His voice was faltering, but she managed to catch the directions he was giving her.

'When you find my boy, please run. As fast and as far away as you can. These men won't leave any loose ends. They will hunt you down.'

Rory didn't know what to say. She'd been threatened with all sorts of things before. This was different. But there was no time to panic. Not now.

She crawled across the floor, her left arm wanting to give way a few times but the adrenalin kept her going. The blood trickled down her arm and was disappearing between her fingers. The checkered linoleum had come unstuck in places, revealing the old floorboards underneath and leaving sharp edges hidden in the dust and dirt, and it slowed her down. She kept looking over her shoulder to see where the gun was.

No sign of either gun or hand. She pushed herself under one of the old machines and found there was no direct line of sight to the windows on the opposite side any more and ran the last bit to the boarded up windows facing the road.

She could hear Pavel coughing, trying to prop himself up against the weaving machine so he could breathe better. She wanted to run back, to pick him up, carry him out, to safety.

I have to get the boy. Have to get the boy.

Then she gathered all her strength and kicked the old planks as hard as she could. Her foot broke two of them, but the hole wasn't big enough. She tore at a few pieces of the splintered wood, but it was too slow and her left arm wasn't cooperating. She backed up, kicked at the planks above. Once. Twice. They splintered, sending wood flying into a gap between the building and a brick wall running along the pavement. Just about big enough. Rory had to resist the urge to run back to Pavel, to try to get him out, to safety. There was no time. A door slammed shut on the courtyard side of the building.

She wriggled through the gap, head and arms first. Splinters of wood clung to her clothes and hair. There was a small ledge on the outside, big enough to balance on as she hung on to the remaining planks with her right arm. Then she leapt over to the brick wall and half fell, half jumped onto the pavement of a pot-holed dead-end street. The building on the other side was boarded up as well, a tall brick wall dotted with metal shutters. She squinted, the daylight seemed so bright and even the Moscow air felt fresh.

To the right Rory could see cars driving past on the road where she'd waited at the bus stop only half an hour earlier. A trolleybus went past, a little girl looked at her through the windows. Rory's arm thudded and the blood had started dripping from her hand. She walked as fast as she could without looking too suspicious, trying to get some distance between herself and the kidnapper. Not pausing, she tore off the right hand sleeve of her top and wound it around her arm. She had to hold onto one end of the fabric with her teeth, tightening it till it hurt. Then she slung her jacket over her shoulder, wiping the blood on her hand away with the sleeve.

She had to remind herself to keep breathing, to keep walking. A police car drove past on the main road ahead, and for a second she wished she could just flag it down, get them to rescue Pavel. And the boy. But corruption was so rife in Moscow, there was no guarantee they'd not arrest her instead.

If she'd had the time, she would have hit her head against a wall in frustration at having had to leave Pavel behind.

She'd failed.

She'd left him behind to be tortured once more.

But Pavel's voice echoed in her head.

Get Sasha. Save my boy, please, please save my boy.

Rory clenched her jaw, ran up to the main road and looked around. There were a couple of cabs, but not the one she needed. Modern cars and drivers had GPS.

Then she spotted it. A tatty old Lada, once upon a time it had probably been dark red, now it was a maroon/rust colour combination. She turned around and lifted her right arm. Some luck, at last. There weren't many Ladas around any more. Muscovites tended to use licensed, pre-booked cabs these days. Modern, western cars.

The driver, a young man, tufts of black hair poking out from under his cap and thick brows over hooded eyes, looked like he wasn't more than 20 years old. Rory guessed he'd come over from Tajikistan or Kyrgyzstan to earn some hard cash for the family back home. He leaned over and rolled down the passenger side window.

'Where to?' he asked.

Rory just opened the door and got in. She got her wallet

out, displaying a thick wedge of euros, and the driver pulled away from the kerb.

'Towards Krasnopresnenskoy naberezhnoy. I would like to borrow your car. No. To buy your car,' she said.

'I don't understand, buy the car?' His accent revealed he wasn't a native speaker. Too young to have experienced going to pre-collapse Soviet schools where everyone learnt Russian.

'Yes. Buy the car.' Rory started peeling off and counting fifty-euro notes. 'Two, four, six, eight, ten. Here's five hundred euros. More than the car is worth.'

The driver looked at her, and the money. Then back to the road.

'Five hundred euros. Now.'

The young man crossed two lanes of traffic without indicating, provoking a chorus of beeping, and stopped at a bus stop. 'Five hundred?' He counted the notes twice, his eyes getting bigger each time.

'I'll need your cap as well,' Rory continued.

The driver pocketed the money and opened his door. 'The clutch is a little stiff. And the battery is not good. You should drive it for a few hours to charge it,' he said as he got out.

Rory jumped across into the driver's seat. 'Thanks, I'll remember that. Do you want to take this?' she said and pointed to the prayer beads hanging from the rear view mirror.

The driver shook his head. 'No. You might need them more than me,' he said before he took his cap off, brushed off some dust and handed it to her.

24

DMITRI RELEASED the clip and put a full one in as he sat hunched down outside the window, waiting for Pavel's new kidnappers to return fire. But nothing came. Maybe they were waiting for him to show himself in the window again.

Volkov's men. It had to be Volkov's men. How had they found out? How much did they know? And would they be able to get Pavel to talk?

Dmitri had to get him back. But he had no intention of giving these thieves target practice by silhouetting himself in the window. The old, disused textile factory had seemed like the perfect barrier between his sound proofed prison and the outside world. Now it had turned into an escape route. Dmitri ran for the doors to the right, the ones that led into the main factory hall. The steel doors were padlocked, but nothing a bullet couldn't fix.

Volkov must be operating on his own. If this had been sanctioned by the Kremlin, they would have just taken Pavel and driven out the main gate.

Dmitri looked around, no one in sight. Not a single person peering out from behind a curtain in the few windows that faced his way. Some things never changed. People still kept out of trouble.

Then he shot one of the rusty padlocks to pieces. The body shattered and left the shackle hanging on the staple. It was an easy shot, but even with the silencer on, the report - and the bullet ricocheting off the steel door - was loud enough to tell Volkov's men exactly where he was entering the building. No time to worry about that though. Dmitri leapt through the doorway. He knew there was a hallway inside, and from peering in the window before, he knew the door between it and the main hall was closed.

He went through every swear word he could think of.

This was not how it was supposed to go.

An easy job, babysitting.

He had to stop the prisoner from getting away. Crouching behind the door to the main hall, Dmitri listened. Quiet, except for the cooing of pigeons. Whoever was in there was lying low. Then a rattling cough - unmistakably Pavel.

Dmitri pushed the door open with his gun and retreated. Nothing. No burst of gunfire. They must be waiting for a clean shot. The kill shot.

He steadied his breathing. Then he heard clanking metal and wood splintering. They might be heading for the wooden platform. He knew the bottom steps were rotten through, but if they got past those they could disappear in the offices upstairs. Dmitri's eyes still weren't used to the dark, but he had to stop them.

Dmitri ran into the hall, throwing himself on the floor under one of the fabric dyeing machines. No one had shot at him. He peered around the corner of the metal leg. All he could see was the enormous dark shapes of the machinery. The light came in from the courtyard side and a hole in the planks on one of the windows at the far end, facing the street. Then there was another cough. There he was. His prisoner. Leaning against one of the big cloth dyeing machines.

Breathing heavily. Where were the others? Dmitri scanned the mezzanine level. He saw something move, but couldn't tell if it was human or just another pigeon, and fired at it before he dropped behind the metal legs of the machine again. Nothing. No return fire. A few more feathers in the air was all.

There was a hole in the boarding of a window facing the dead end street outside, but no sign of anyone else. Dmitri moved across toward the opposite wall, giving Pavel a wide berth and keeping several of the big machines between them, in case he'd been left with a gun. Then he made his way to the window facing the street, where the boards had been kicked in. Drops of blood on the floor. No sound from outside, apart from the cars driving by on the main road. He stuck his pocket mirror out of the window and used it to scan the street.

There. A black clad figure running for the corner, back to him. He leaned out of the window, gun in hand, took aim. The figure was gone. And there was too much traffic on the main road to chase after him. Another cough came from the void behind him.

Dmitri looked around the hall, checked the other entrances, and went over to Pavel. One hand had held onto an improvised compress, but it had slumped down from the hole at his shoulder. The other hand lay limp at his side.

Pavel looked up at him with a faint smile, then his eyelids dropped. It was the same smile Dmitri had just seen in the pictures in Sorokin's office. There was a pool of blood spreading where Pavel sat, and some drops leading towards the window. Dmitri smiled to himself. He'd got them both. The other guy must have thought Pavel was too badly injured to get him out. Bad enough for the enemy to try to save himself first. Dmitri pushed the prisoner's shirt aside with the suppressor and looked at the blood oozing out of his chest. It was a thick, dark red. The bullet had gone through just above the heart. The compress had stopped the worst bleeding, but he wouldn't last long like this.

Dmitri ran to the car and grabbed his survival kit. Back at Pavel's side he opened the bag and moved a box of epipens aside. Then he poured some water over Pavel's face. The eyelids flickered.

'I think it's time we talk. No more games. You tell me where the briefcase is, and maybe, just maybe, you will get to see your lovely children again. And yes, I said children. Your beautiful Masha, who's got your smile, isn't smiling right now.' Dmitri moved the prisoner forward and checked for an exit wound. There. Through the shoulder blade. No need to extract a bullet. Pavel groaned as Dmitri leaned him back towards the machine again.

Dmitri held Masha's picture in front of his prisoner's face. Pavel's eyes opened wide, and followed the piece of paper as Dmitri left it on Pavel's legs.

Dmitri got a compress out and pressed it hard onto the entry wound.

'I've got morphine for your pain.' Dmitri paused, his gaze steady on Pavel's face. He lifted a syringe from the case and flicked it expertly. 'But first I need some answers.' Dmitri put the syringe next to the photo of Masha.

The prisoner nodded, eyelids heavy with tiredness and blood loss. Dmitri had to keep the man awake to get his answers. He got out a bag of IV fluids. He'd never used his medical kit on anyone else before. Just himself. It was awkward working upside down, and he couldn't get the needle in at first. He put the bag on top of a ledge on the fabric dyeing vat. Then he started working on the wound itself. He flushed it out with sterile water before he covered it with a compress, then did the same with the exit wound, working as fast as he could.

The man in front of him was still awake, but only just.

'As you know only too well, death is final, but pain is not.

I'm sure you don't want Masha to learn that the hard way.' Dmitri crumpled up the photo, took his phone out and started writing a text message.

'Fingernails first, I think. Or what do you say? How painful was it when you lost yours?'

Pavel tried to unfold the paper with his mangled fingers, but only left streaks of blood.

'Please. Masha knows nothing. The briefcase - in a garage. Outside Moscow.' Then his eyelids gave up on staying open and his head fell sideways.

Dmitri swore through gritted teeth and poured some water over the man's head.

'The address. To the garage.' Dmitri picked up his phone again and started typing. 'For Masha's sake.'

It seemed to take forever before the prisoner opened his mouth to talk. Dmitri wasn't sure if it was an attempt at delaying him, or if it was the blood loss that left him unable to. But as soon as Pavel had finished, Dmitri ran out to get the car. Dmitri wasn't taking any chances this time. He had to take Pavel with him. The heavy metal band was still playing, and for once Dmitri was grateful to them. No one would have noticed the commotion at this end of the complex when they were used to that.

Pavel had passed out when he got back, no reaction at all. But he still had a pulse. Weak, but regular. Dmitri lifted him up in a fireman's grab and carried him to the car and laid him down in the back seat, legs higher than the head. He strapped him in and hung the IV fluids on the neck support, added some morphine to it, and put up the sun shading on both side windows.

Krasnogorsk. Near the Military hospital. Unit thirty seven. And it wasn't a document they were looking for. Sorokin had got it wrong all along.

25

RORY DROVE the battered Lada through Moscow traffic, snarling in the packed lanes on the embankment. Everything in a hurry, but moving too slowly. She had to get to Sasha before Pavel cracked. Before Dmitri found the boy and started torturing him as well. If she couldn't save the father, she had to get the boy.

Pavel's instructions rang loud in her head. And his last words.

They will hunt you down.

As she approached the third ring road, she found herself doing exactly what she had loathed in other drivers in Russia: she drove past the entire turning lane and swung round the front of the queue as the light changed. A couple of other cars did the same manoeuvre. The policeman standing on the other side waved them into the side of the road. Rory had to slam the brakes and they screeched as the SUV in front of her pulled into the side.

Under normal circumstances, she'd just pay the standard bribe and get on with her day. But a woman with a copy of a Polish passport, no driving licence and no proof of ownership of the car, driving around in an old Lada? She didn't think that would be an easy escape. She pulled her cap on tighter, to make sure her long hair stayed hidden. The police man waved at her, annoyed. What did he mean? He seemed to be telling her to pull out again. Away.

Then she noticed the car behind her. Another SUV. He had bigger fish to fry than a poor Lada driver. She'd heard before how being a traffic police man in central Moscow was so profitable that people had to pay tens of thousands of dollars just to get the job. She guessed this one was trying to recoup his investment.

Rory pulled into traffic again, and drove west on the road that turned into Marshal Zhukova. Her arm was aching, but the bleeding seemed to have stopped. She drove past the MKAD ring road, a right turn by the high rises after the river, west again on Volokolamskoe across the railway line, through Krasnogorsk, past another set of high rises.

This was it. She looped around what seemed like a suburban town centre, and turned left towards the forest. Away from the Soviet apartment blocks, away from the little kiosks selling cigarettes, beer and alcoholic bath tinctures. The road went past a parking lot and a small hospital before it disappeared into the forest.

There.

She could see them now, the garages.

A small dirt road turned left between two rows of garage doors that wound their way along the edge of the forest. She parked the car along the main road on a downwards slope. There were other Ladas there, as well as more modern cars. Then she pulled her cap down and walked as broad legged as she could towards garage number thirty-seven.

The brick and corrugated metal buildings had at some point been painted in different colours. Red, yellow, blue and green paint was peeling off. Most of the garages were single storey, but a few had more recent, ramshackle, additions on top. A couple of older men looked at her as she walked down the winding lane, and someone whistled a tune as she passed. She'd tucked her hair away, but it was still obvious that she was a woman. They probably didn't see many here. A few of the garages were open and she caught glimpses of the man-caves within: sofas, old fridges, stacks of beer cans. One trailed a thin wisp of steam; maybe the sign of a sauna inside. Number thirty-six had a greenhouse on the roof, bursting with planters. The door of number thirty-seven was down, but didn't seem to have closed properly.

Rory knocked on the frame before she lifted the door enough to crawl through the gap at the bottom.

'Sasha, Sash, are you in here? Your dad sent me, Sasha,' Rory whispered into the dark space. There was a bit of light coming in from outside, and she could just about make out the layout of the garage. There was a pit in the middle, for repairs, and work benches on each side. No car. She touched the light bulb hanging from a rafter. It was warm.

'Sasha, I know you're in here. Please, your sister in London hired me to come and find you, and your father told me to come here. But we need to get out, it's not safe here. Please, Sasha.'

There were opened tins of food, canned meat and sausages. Peach slices in syrup. Sasha hadn't had an opener, but had hammered a big knife through the lids to get the tins open. A six pack of beer was on the workbench, and a few cans had been opened but never finished. The boy hadn't acquired a taste for alcohol yet. A sound came from the back of the garage, like someone pushing a paint tin along the hard floor.

Rory reached for the light switch. 'Sasha, I'm going to put on the lights, okay?'

More shuffling, and more tins rattling. The light flickered

on, and Rory could see the shape of a boy hiding behind some shelves. Then he pelted her with screws.

Rory turned her back to him, but kept walking towards him. 'I'm not here to hurt you, Sasha. I'm here to help,' she said and turned to face him.

A shower of screws hit her chest before she grabbed him and held him close to her. 'I know you're waiting for your dad, but he can't come right now. The people who have him want something that's kept here, in the garage, so we have to get you out before they get here. Okay?'

At first Sasha tried to get free, but Rory just held on to him, hugging him, stroking his hair. Then his body relaxed, and Rory kept stroking his head. His clothes were dirty, and he smelled of shit and urine. Not easy going to the loo in amongst the trees at night.

'You've been such a brave boy, hiding out here on your own. But it's not safe any more.'

The boy had not yet said a single word. They stood there for a while, and Rory could feel the stream of tears through her top as the boy started to sob.

'It's okay, it'll be okay,' Rory said.

Then the whistling started again. The boy shuddered.

Rory looked around. 'Does that mean someone is coming, a stranger?'

'Yes.'

'Is there another way out of here, other than the main door?'

'No.'

'What about that hatch, in the side wall?' she said and pointed to a small opening under the workbench.

'That goes through to next door.'

'And the greenhouse, how does he get to the greenhouse?'

'There's a ladder, a rope ladder, up to a roof hatch.'

'Can you get through?'

'Yes, I think so. I used to do it all the time.' Sasha looked at her and let her wipe away the tears. 'But ... I don't think you will fit?'

'I'll find a way. Now go. Go through the hatch, and get up on that roof. As quick as you can, ok?'

Rory scoured the garage and her eyes found what they were looking for. The old briefcase, in between some gnawed at boots and a box of rusty fishing tackle. The boy was down on all fours, crawling through the hatch. He struggled a bit with his shoulders, but then slunk through the gap and was gone.

'Get up on that roof, ok, and stay low,' Rory said as she picked through the briefcase. She found the keys in the small inside pocket, and there was a tag too. Her heart skipped a beat when she read it.

She'd seen that name before. Somewhere. And not long ago. Mascherano.

Rory took one key off the ring and tried to make imprints of the other on a piece of old soap. It was too hard. She snapped a few pictures with her camera instead. Not ideal, but it was better than nothing. She pocketed the first key before she put the keyring back in the pocket and the brief-case back on the shelf. She grabbed a handful of dust from the floor and threw it on top of the case and the boots. Then the whistle sounded again. Closer this time.

Mascherano. She knew she had seen that name in connection with this case, but where?

Rory crushed the lightbulb with a brick before she knelt down and looked at the hatch. She'd have to get through, there was no other way. She might be able to outrun Dmitri with a head start, but not his gun.

Her head and shoulders passed easily enough, but her hips got stuck. She wiggled back a bit, pulled her jeans down to her knees and tried again. The wood scraped her hip, but with a little bit of easing and turning she got through the gap.

She pulled her trousers back on again as she saw Sasha disappear up the roof hatch. Just in time. Before Rory had managed to get on her feet she could hear someone tugging at the garage door to unit thirty-seven. Then it opened, and the light flooded into the space she had just left.

26

DMITRI SWUNG the big cantilevered door up and spun to one side, crouching next to the wide entrance as dust swirled and the oily air flowed out. A quick peek showed no one lying in wait and he made his way inside. Pavel hadn't worked on any cars here in a long time.

He'd called Sorokin on the way. Told him about the attempt at taking Pavel, and how he had finally extracted Pavel's secret. That the documents they had been looking for had never been in Moscow at all. But the key to the safety deposit box where they were kept would soon be in their possession.

A mouse scurried past him and disappeared under a box. It smelled of rotten food in there. Empty tins on the workbench, beer cans. The garage wasn't as deserted as he'd thought. Maybe the boy had been hiding out here, it would explain why Pavel hadn't talked before. The things people did for their children. Dmitri's own mother included.

Dmitri walked along the side of the workbench on the right, gun at the ready, suppressor on. Glass crunched under his feet and he scanned the space to look for any sign of movement. Nothing. It was a light bulb, the empty cord hanging from a nail attached to one of the rafters.

Dmitri reached for the cord to check whether it was warm from recent use, but thought better of it. The homemade wiring in some garages he knew came with danger of death attached. He knelt down instead, touched one of the larger shards of glass. It was still warm. Whoever had been there must have run away when the old bastards he'd seen at the entrance to the lane had started whistling to announce his arrival. He couldn't take long, what if the person who'd been there was getting help?

It was dark towards the back, where Pavel had said the briefcase was kept, and Dmitri had to move to see what was hidden in his own shadow. There, next to the boots. A dark brown leather briefcase, covered in dust and grit. Dmitri's pulse started racing. This could be it. His pension. Life sorted, for ever. For a second he let himself forget any notion that this might be a trap. He undid the buckles and flicked through the case. Some old, yellowed papers, a pen that had leaked all its ink. A moth eaten handkerchief. Then he saw the small pocket at the back.

The key. Had Pavel said key or keys? There was only one. No, he'd said key. Dmitri was sure of it. He phoned Sorokin.

'I've got it,' Dmitri said. He could hear Sorokin slamming his desk table.

'Fabulous. Fabulous. Any sign of the boy?'

Dmitri left the garage and pulled the door down again. 'Someone's been here. The boy, or a vagrant. They ran just before I got here.' He tried the doors of the garages either side. Number thirty-eight had a padlock on the outside and had weed growing up the front. Number thirty-six had a well-kempt integrated door in the garage door. Dmitri put his shoulder to it and the hinges gave way, leaving the door hanging on the hasp and staple. 'I'm checking the neighbouring garages, but it looks like the boy has done a runner. Do we need him?'

'No, don't bother with the boy, he's no threat. Pavel's talked now, anyway. We'll be gone by the morning, there's no time to lose.'

Dmitri walked around the neighbouring garage, but there wasn't much to see. Some shelves and drawers for tools at the back, stacks of plant pots on the right. An old bike leaning against a sofa on the left wall. Nowhere to hide. Dmitri paused. There was some loose soil on the ground, and marks on the hard floor indicated someone had crawled through the hatch from next door.

He didn't like loose ends. He paused, listening, but could only hear birds jumping on the corrugated iron roof, probably looking for flies warming themselves in the spring sun. If Volkov was on to them, Dmitri didn't have time to chase after a boy in the forest. He started walking back to the car; didn't want to leave it, and Pavel, for longer than necessary, then phoned Sorokin again.

'What did you do about the package?' Sorokin asked after detailing their travel plans for the following day.

'It's in the car. Injured and sedated.' Dmitri opened the door and got in. Pavel was lying in the backseat, unconscious. The colour was coming back to his face. 'Do you want me to get rid?'

'No, not yet. It might still come in handy.'

'Then it'll need some patching up.'

'Can you do it? I don't want to risk anyone else getting involved now. We need to get ready for Italy. Then the yacht is waiting for us.'

Dmitri sighed and drove back to the main road. 'Sure. Of course.' He didn't like either prospect. Having to care for the prisoner he had just broken, or spending time on a boat. But the prize at the end was in sight. More money than he could ever spend.

Dmitri let out a breath of stale air and rubbed his neck, cracking the joints by tilting his head from side to side.

'Go home, clean up, relax for a bit,' Sorokin said.

'What about the guy who got the prisoner out? Any idea who he is? No one was following me, but Volkov probably has people all over the place. He never fired back though, so I think he may be unarmed.' Dmitri drove back to the main road and headed to his own garage north of the city, where he kept both medical equipment, and the weapons he'd need for Italy. 'It doesn't make sense. Any chance he is someone Masha had hired?'

'I'm trying to find out. Volkov has suggested we meet for dinner this evening, with a Kremlin deputy chief of staff, to discuss some tax fraud scheme. I can't say no, not to the meeting, but I'll see if I can get Volkov to reveal himself. And throw him off the scent for long enough to get the documents. I have people monitoring Masha's phone and email, and apart from that one call to the Golden Ring, there's nothing to say she's looking for her father and brother. And the person at the Golden Ring? It was a female voice.'

'What? There's no way the person that took Pavel was a woman. I admit, it wasn't a big guy I saw, but a woman?' Dmitri shook his head. 'Nope. Can't have been. Not possible. A woman would never have managed to get him through that window. Unless we're talking about special forces. Have you made any new enemies lately? Could the CIA be after you? The Chinese?'

Dmitri noticed Sorokin's slight hesitation. Could there be something in the rumours that the old man had dealings with the Americans? That he was considering selling out, telling all in exchange for freedom to spend his money as he wanted? Dmitri had dismissed the rumours as a smear when he'd first heard them. The Sorokin he knew was a fervent Russian nationalist.

'No one knows about the papers and Pavel, apart from the

two of us. You said even he seemed confused when you started asking him,' Sorokin replied, having got his voice under control. 'Masha isn't short of cash though, nor stupid, so if she has hired someone, she must be paying for someone good.'

27

RORY HELD the boy close to stop him from shaking. The smell of the tomato plants tickled her nose. Rory had taken the ladder up with her, and closed the hatch as best she could, piling the bags of soil onto it to block out any light.

'Shshshshsh,' she repeated, over and over, into the boy's ear.

The voice from the garage below had gone, and they heard a car engine starting. His car.

Then it drove off.

Rory could only hear her own and the boy's breathing. He'd stopped sniffling, and had a wet sleeve instead. It was eerily quiet. Some sparrows landed on the roof outside the greenhouse, picking through the soil spilled from a torn bag of compost.

Rory counted the minutes. Two. Five. Her bad arm had started aching again, after going through that hatch and then climbing up the ladder. And the blood was beginning to soak through as well.

She thought about Pavel. About how a man, a strong man, could have carried him out of that building. Rescued him. Not left him behind, like she'd had to do. But she had to be strong, for the boy. She could hear Tom's voice in her head. Tom's reassuring, comforting voice. She knew what he would have said. That a man could have carried Pavel out, but he couldn't have got through that hatch.

Ten minutes gone.

'Let's go, Sasha,' she said and took his hand.

The boy tried to stand up but his legs gave way under him.

'Do you want me to carry you?'

'No. I can walk,' he said and straightened up again.

They walked hand in hand to the back of the garage rooftop and looked towards the forest. The leaves were just coming out on the deciduous trees, a few strands of grass in between the trunks were stretching towards the light. Rory jumped down to the ground first, before catching Sasha as he hoisted himself down. They walked, in silence, through the trees to where Rory had left the car.

It looked like any other car on this bit of road. Modern Moscow only stretched so far. She opened the door for Sasha and went around the car to get into the driver's seat. Sasha hesitated for a bit.

'I'm borrowing it from a friend,' she said when she saw his quizzical look.

'It's not that. It's just. My clothes, my trousers.' He looked away. 'They're … dirty.'

Rory found a fake Adidas bag with some clothes in the boot. A couple of fake Adidas tracksuit bottoms, some t-shirts, a pair of trainers. Lucky the Tajik was on the small side. She rolled up the legs on a pair of trousers, put a change of clothes on the passenger seat and walked back behind the open boot, to give the boy a semblance of privacy.

Rory went through the bag again, found a grey t-shirt with a red logo on it and tore it into strips. She took off her own jacket, undid the now bloodied rag and used the new one to tie around her arm. She would have to get it seen to, or at least stop using it, so it would stop bleeding.

She got in next to Sasha and turned the key. The starter just coughed. The Tajik boy knew his car all right. Rory released the brake, opened the door, and used one leg to push the car forwards, down the little slope. The engine coughed a bit, but started on the second attempt.

Rory swerved around the potholes. She had to make some quick decisions. Should they aim for the motorway, and hide in plain sight on Moscow city streets? Or should she get off the road and lay low until it got dark?

Not too long ago, it would have been easy to disappear on Moscow streets in an old, beat up Lada. But not any more. These days it would have been a lot easier to blend in with a black, shiny Mercedes. Or a licensed cab. The boy next to her was putting on a brave face, revealing no emotions, neither fear nor relief. After his quiet crying about his father in the greenhouse, he'd barely said a word.

'Sasha,' Rory tried. 'Sash. Your sister sent me to help you. To help you and your father.'

'No she didn't. She hates papa.'

'She doesn't hate him. She is just worried about you. And she sent me to find you both.'

'Where is he? Where's papa?'

'I don't know.'

'But you said he had sent you, told you where to find me?'

'Yes, and that was all true. But I don't know where he is now. He ...' Rory had a lump the size of a melon in her throat. 'I'm so, so sorry.'

'Is he dead?'

'No. He's not dead.' At least, not when she'd left him.

'Can we go and find him?'

'Not now. But I hope we will be able to later. We have to get you to safety first though, I promised him I would do that. Okay?'

'Okay,' Sasha replied, and looked into his lap. Rory could have cried at the look of him. He should never have been in this situation. He should have been at home, doing his homework, chatting about his day over dinner. Playing chess in the school gymnasium. Not in a stranger's car, running from an unknown danger, not knowing where his dad was or if he was even alive.

She drove around for a while, back towards the centre of Moscow. Around the MKAD, wiggling their way on back streets to the Third Ring road. They picked up some food from a drive-through, and the boy devoured his burger so fast she gave him half hers as well.

They were back at the embankment, heading south this time. Towards the University.

'Why don't you have a rest, Sasha? You can't have had much sleep in that cold garage. Just climb in the back and lie down, I think there's a blanket behind my seat.'

Rory pulled over and rummaged in her pocket to find all the parts of her phone. The boy looked like he hadn't slept in days, and was fast asleep in seconds. The network signal wasn't the best, but she managed to get online. It was time to call on her American friend.

28

THERE. Broad shoulders, tailored suit. Short hair. He had his arm out, hailing a taxi.

Ahead of her, a sleek, shiny taxi slowed down and its light blinked out. Damn. She couldn't get ahead of it in time - and he wasn't the type to prefer a cheap lift from a Lada. A Muscovite vision, all legs and blonde hair, came to Rory's rescue, striding to the pavement just as the man stepped toward the taxi. He conceded, opened the door for her and turned back toward the road.

Rory slowed down, and as the other car pulled away from the kerb, she stopped right in front of her target. He moved away from the Lada and put his hand out again. Rory backed up, placing the Lada straight in front of him again. He leaned in, and a few choice Russian swear words filled the car. Then, his eyes widened as he made out the face staring back at him from beneath the cap. He looked at the boy lying asleep in the back seat and got in next to her.

'I was beginning to think I wouldn't hear from you,' Simon Chandler said.

'Well, you wouldn't have. But it turns out we do have mutual interests.'

'You are aware I might have a tail, right?'

'Yes. Where would you normally go at this hour, if you weren't going home?'

Simon shifted uncomfortably.

'I couldn't care less if it's the worst brothel in town, I just want to stay undetected, okay? Somewhere they wouldn't bother following you.'

'Probably Mayak then. Evenings there tend to last till the morning.'

'Mayak it is. It's the place near the Estonian Embassy, right?'

'That's the one.'

'Ok, let me just get there, and I'll fill you in. Do you have anywhere safe we can go after?

'Yes. I'll show you the way.' Simon looked at her. 'How did you know where to find me?'

'Pretty good odds on a cultural attaché being around when a big profile singer comes to town. And also pretty good odds on you not being the kind that would hang around all night hoping a bit of stardust would fall on you.' Rory kept her eyes on the traffic, but thought she caught a little smile at the corner of his mouth.

The drive seemed like an eternity. Sasha was lying in the back, sleeping, unaware that the danger was no further away now than it had been. Pavel's hollow face haunted Rory. His crushed fingers, the blood gushing out of his shoulder. She had tried to pull him out of the way, and get herself in front of him, but the bullet had only gone through her on the way to him. Changing gears was becoming more difficult as her left arm stiffened up, and she had to use her knees to steady the wheel when she had her right hand on the stick. Simon was looking at her, narrowing his eyes.

'We need to get out of Russia,' she said. 'The boy and I.'

'How long have you been bleeding? Any idea how much blood you've lost?' he asked.

'It's been going on and off for six hours or so. I put a compress on straight after it happened, but it started again when I had to use the arm.' Rory could sense the mix of genuine concern and focus in his voice. 'I'm okay, though. My main priority is to get Sasha to safety.'

'You're not much good to him if you don't take care of yourself.'

Rory pulled into Bolshaya Nikitskaya and turned right onto Malyy Kislovskiy pereulok. They sat there in silence for a bit, looking at the entrance to the club. It was a nice place, Rory had been there a few times. It was a bit like walking into someone's living room and crashing on the couch, only bigger. An old piano on one wall, mismatched furniture, tumblers for wine. A bit hipster, but before that was a thing. They were both looking out for any cars that might have followed them, but none stopped within sight.

'Let me just leave my work phone with a friend from the Embassy, he's another regular here. It'll buy us a bit more time.'

Simon ran up the stairs and came back a few minutes later. Once they had parked at the safe house, Simon put the sleeping boy on a sofa in the living room before he showed her to the kitchen. Rory swallowed hard, her throat was dry and felt like sandpaper. Her arm was beginning to ache again. She looked up at the kitchen cabinets, originals from a bygone era. The well kept units could have fetched a small fortune at her favourite south London vintage shop.

Simon walked over to the fridge. 'Still or sparkling?'

'Still, please.'

He opened the bottle as he walked over to her. 'Ok, let's have a look at you.'

'What do you mean, look at me?'

'Sasha is not the only one in need of a bit of patching up. Or did you not notice that you got shot? Your jeans are full of blood as well?'

Rory tried to take off her top, to get a better look at her shoulder, but her left arm wouldn't obey her any more. Simon came over with a knife and sliced the sleeve up, and continued above the shoulder, leaving the fabric to fall to the floor. For a second Rory felt self conscious that she was standing there in her bra, but the pain in her arm made her forget about that again. At least she had followed her grandmother's advice. Always wear clean underwear; You never know when you might end up in hospital. Simon pulled her closer to the light, his hands feeling the skin around the wound.

'Do you know what you're doing?' she asked.

'Yeah. Done it before. Have you been shot before?' Simon flushed the wound with disinfectant, washing away the blood.

'No. Never.' The look of her own flesh, pink and pale, made her queasy, and she reached out to try to hold to something. The only thing she could get hold of was Simon's shoulder.

'No fan of open wounds, are we?'

'Nope. Pain I can take, blood is okay, but not human flesh. Looks too much like corned beef.'

He found a bottle of bourbon and poured her a double. 'Close your eyes then, I'll deal with this. It looks like you got lucky, and that there's just soft tissue damage. Pretty neat through and through.'

While he worked, Rory distracted herself recounting the last 12 hours, but didn't mention the key.

Simon stared at her. 'What were you thinking, going in blind like that? You could have got both of you killed. For all we know, Pavel might be dead already.'

'You didn't see the state of him. I had to try to get him out. Anyway, there's no reason for you to get upset. You'll get your information.'

'I didn't have you figured as a chancer, Rory.'

Rory had had enough of men telling her all the things she did that were wrong. She stared at him, could feel that the crease between her eyebrows was tensing up.

'You had to get him out - and then what? You can't just go in and start improvising. This is Russia. The country of seriously organised crime.' He sat her down on a chair, got out a syringe, and put the needle through her skin. The morphine numbed the pain, and she began to relax. She leaned into the back of the chair, whilst Simon continued whatever he was doing.

'Save the preaching for someone else, will you? I took the decision I thought best at the time. You weren't there. Thanks for your concern though,' she said, looking straight into his eyes. This wasn't the time to make enemies.

Simon stopped for a moment, strip plasters in hand, and looked at her.

'What? Anything else you'd like to berate me for?' she asked.

'Yes, there is. There is an assassin out there, on the streets of Moscow, that we could have stopped if you'd cooperated when I first approached you. But you were so firmly positioned on your moral high horse that you didn't care about the implications it could have for others.' Simon only paused for breath. 'And I'm also pissed off that you managed, in what, ten days, to get close to one of the men we have tried to identify for the last decade.'

'Firstly, I have my priorities, just as you have yours. And my job is to get the boy. And Dmitri, Dima? Why is he so special?'

'On first name terms, are we? You've just had a run in with one of the most lethal foreign policy tools Russia has. Defectors, activists, opposition politicians. This guy shows up and they die. Every new lead we get on the Kremlin inner circle: one of Sorokin's men flies in - our new informant dies. It's fucking uncanny. Fast acting cancers, sudden heart attacks in healthy 45-year-old men, car accidents, bar brawls that turn nasty. People that just vanish. We've never caught any of them in the act, but people just have a way of popping their clogs when they're around.'

'I didn't know you were looking for Dmitri on the day we met. The drawings you showed me, of the four different guys? I didn't know for sure until I saw him again, outside my hotel, after my client blew my cover. The drawings were all of him. The man I had seen for just a brief moment with Sorokin. One of the drawings had his lips, the other his eyes. A third had his chin. None got the nose right, but noses aren't easy.'

'You're telling me that those four guys are the same? No way. That can't be.' Simon put his hands through his hair, and stopped half way. 'Assuming you're right, that the drawings are of one man only. This super recogniser thing, it's real then? You can recognise a face you've only seen for a second in a different place, different time? I thought that part of your file was a bit dodgy, to be honest.'

'No, not quite like that. At least not for me. It's an innate skill, but enhanced with training. I remember the proportions of a face. Distances, angles, size of eyes, nose, lips. I couldn't tell you what every person I've walked past on the streets looks like, but anyone who stands out, or I can see is trying not to stand out, will stick. Like an imprint.'

She pictured Dmitri's face, and it made her shudder. To think that she had been just metres away from someone who'd not think twice to kill her. Who had tried to, and now still had Pavel. She started shivering.

The bleeding had stopped, that much she knew, but apart from that she didn't know. Didn't want to know. She closed her eyes. She'd forgotten how good it could feel to be taken care of. To feel safe. Warm. Dozy.

Simon's phone buzzed, and he put the bandage down to

answer it. Rory could only hear that it was a female voice at the other end of the line.

'Ma'am. You were right. The drawings? It's all the same guy. Nope, not two different guys. One guy. '

'Yeah, will do. She's even met him. Sorokin called him Dmitri. Turns out he came to the Casino that night. Our guy must have been too busy to notice.'

'Thank you, ma'am. It was a team effort, really. But thanks. I appreciate that. We're taking them both out. The boy is unharmed. I'll get as much out of her as I can before I get her out,' he said and hung up.

'Get what out of me?' Rory looked at Simon.

'I need that description of Dmitri, we'll need you to sit down with a sketch artist. A good one. In return I will get you to wherever you want to go.'

'That's it, a description of Dmitri? And you get me and the boy to London?'

'If that's where you want to go, then yes.'

'What about a photo?'

Simon stared at her, incredulous. 'You have a photo of him? The man who never appears in photos, never been identified on CCTV.'

'Yeah. A couple actually. I took them when he came to the hotel. They're not great, one is his reflection in a window, the other from afar. But there's no doubt it's him. And one more thing, his left ring finger is shorter than the others, just a stub.'

Simon looked at her. 'You're unbelievable. I could kiss you right now,' he said. And did.

Maybe it was the morphine, or the bourbon. But the one kiss became two, and then a third. The next kiss lasted long enough for him to have caressed every inch of her back. And undone her bra.

29

'WHY IS SHE STILL ASLEEP?'

The nurse looked at Dmitri. 'It's not unusual, in older patients. It takes a lot out of them, major surgery like this. You're the son?'

'Yes.'

Another nurse came into the room. 'Can I take these vases? The lady next door just had a room full of guests and there are flowers everywhere.'

Dmitri looked at his mother's bedside table. There was one bouquet there that Sorokin's secretary had sent. Dmitri hadn't had time to pick anything up on his way over. He'd spent far too long treating his own patient.

'Sure. Take them. All of them.'

Dmitri sat down and took his mother's limp hand in his. The skin was coarse, with lumps of hard skin from using the garden tools. The wrinkles read like a map of her life. A young pioneer born just after the Great War, his mother had received awards for her labour on the collective farm before she married Dmitri's father. Two sons later she was widowed when Dmitri's father was sent to a labour camp for possession of a Bible and only lasted one harsh Siberian winter. His mother had never spoken of him, the memory too painful. It was only after the breakup of the Soviet Union that his father's picture had reappeared on the wall, next to an icon of Archangel Saint Michael.

Dmitri stroked his mother's hand. The hand that he had reached out for as a child, whenever he was afraid or ill. Whenever his brother was playing too rough and had left him with bruises and grazes. If only he'd had a regular job, been a bus driver or something. It would have given them something to talk about. As it was, their limited conversations were always about her vegetable garden and her neighbour and the neighbour's son. Not much to bond over.

Andrei, Dmitri's older brother, had been the talker. He could go on for hours on end entertaining their mother with talk about music, literature, sports. It was Andrei's copy of *Master and Margarita* Dmitri had been lugging around as a teenager. He was the one who should have been at the Monsters of Rock concert in Moscow in 1991. Dmitri had been there, listening to Metallica and AC/DC. Bands he only had heard of because of his older brother. But his older brother had chosen a different path by then. A very different path. And it had broken their mother's heart.

Andrei had been sent to Afghanistan towards the end of the war, but he never came back. At first they thought he was dead. Killed in battle. But his body was never returned and there was no posthumous award for bravery.

A few months later, Dmitri had met one of Andrei's fellow soldiers on the street. Andrei had deserted. Left his squad behind and joined the mujahideen in their battle. Taken his machine gun and ammunition with him, only to use it to kill his countrymen. Dmitri hadn't believed them at first. He ended up fighting them, to protect his family's honour. But he could see it. Andrei was always looking for new things, new experiences. Seeking answers to the big questions in life. If he had been allowed to go to church, it might never have happened. But as it was, he converted to Islam and stayed. Maybe he was still there. Living in the mountains, fighting another war.

Dmitri had wanted to talk to her about it. About Andrei. But his mother had just shut the door on it. Like she had done when she lost her husband. She cut off any contact with relatives, the shame and embarrassment was too much to bear. So it was just the two of them. Mama and Dima. He'd been a troublemaker since before Andrei disappeared, and it didn't get any better after. It was Sorokin who'd got him back on track with his life. He'd seen the boy behind the eager fists and big mouth. And the man he could become.

'Visiting hours are coming to an end, Sir. You can come back tomorrow? I'm sure she'll be better then.' The nurse smiled at him, that gentle smile that people used to put others at ease, but it didn't seem genuine. More like she was trying to shoo him out of the way.

'Of course. I'll be back tomorrow morning, before I have to travel for work. Tell her I was here, will you? If she wakes up later?' Dmitri reached into his jacket pocket and took out the small laminated icon she had given him years ago. His own version of the Archangel Saint Michael. He kissed it, made the sign of the cross and left it on her bedside table, leaning on the solitary flower vase.

30

DMITRI REACHED for his phone as he walked into the car park. Sorokin had called him four times just in the last hour.

'Dima! Finally. Where have you been?'

'I'm at the hospital, went to see my mother, remember?'

'Of course, of course. Did she get the flowers I sent?'

'Yes, thank you. Not sure if she's seen them yet, she was asleep the whole time I was there.' Dmitri had reached his car and got into the driver's seat. 'What's up, anything new?'

'Yes, we've intercepted some communication. Great news. It wasn't Volkov who found Pavel. It was Masha's PI. She just set up a meeting with her in London tomorrow morning.' Sorokin said.

'She? So it is a woman?' Dmitri keyed in the code to reveal the hidden compartment behind the car sat nav. He flicked through his passports and chose one he hadn't used in a while. Mikhail Rubin. 'I'll go. I don't like loose ends.'

'You're not going anywhere, I'm afraid. You're on the list.'

'List? What list?' Dmitri sat there looking at his Rubin passport. He'd done some pretty high profile jobs with that one. A government minister in Moldova, a bank executive in Switzerland.

'The one list you don't want to be on. The red list. Interpol.'

Dmitri let the passport slip out of his hand. 'But how? Everything went fine in DC.'

'I don't think they got you in DC. I think they got you here. And it might have been my fault. The two Americans at the casino? One of them has been communicating with the embassy. Volkov told me. Thought he would try to add some pressure to get me to slip up. But I've got a freelance team in London, no questions asked kind of guys. They'll tie things up for us.'

Dmitri found himself staring at the BMW logo on the steering wheel. He imagined what it looked like upside down, if he had ever looked at it when he was in the middle of a sharp turn. He didn't think so.

Sorokin cleared his throat. 'You've had a good run, Dima. The best, even. We both knew it had to end one day.'

We both thought my career would end up with me dead.

'The good thing is,' Sorokin continued. 'With us finally having found the key, we're on the home straight to never having to work again. You can retire to Venezuela or something. They have beautiful women there. Stunning.'

Dmitri thought about it. There weren't many countries an unmasked Russian assassin could live out his retirement these days. Not with the Yankees on his tail. Venezuela. Iran, maybe. Syria. North Korea. Cuba was no longer an option, they were far too friendly with the Americans these days. Venezuela would do though. If he could only convince his mother that it was a lot more exciting and desirable than anywhere Darya had been to. He'd have to come back for her when she was out of hospital.

'So, what can I do?' The feeling of uselessness was new to Dmitri. He felt the life he had meticulously constructed collapse and crash into piles of rubble.

'There is one thing, actually. You have to take our guest

with you to the Caribbean. Keep him healthy, in case we need him.'

'What?' Dmitri left the question hanging. He'd been demoted to nurse and babysitter. All because Sorokin had to go to the casino that night.

'I know it's not what you normally do, but there's a chance we need him to sign over the company. I'll know more when I find the papers, but for now, we need him alive. And well enough to sign papers in a few days' time.'

'Shouldn't I come with you to Italy? I can change my appearance enough to fool passport control.'

'I don't think it's worth the risk. And anyway, the Italians are our friends. The mafia has been profiting from us for decades. I don't expect any problems retrieving the documents. It's not like I can't handle myself.'

Dmitri had to smile. He'd seen the surveillance video of the assassination attempt in the Casino, and it was only thanks to Elena and the other female guest that Sorokin had left the place with only a few scratches and bruises. He could no more handle himself than Dmitri's mother could resist the urge to make her son feel guilty for something or other. Then he thought back to the night at the casino, the Americans sat on the sofa. The female guest Elena had cleaned up, the pretty girl with legs of a runner. Masha's PI. Damn. She must have found him through Sorokin, possibly with help from the Americans. It still didn't add up though.

'Dima, are you there?'

'Yes. Fine. I'll get him to the Caribbean. The jet is at Vnukovo, right?'

'Yes. And I've prepared the yacht for the month. There's another job to be done in the Caribbean. The lawyer son of one of the men on the latest sanctions list. It's the best cover I could come up with at such short notice. That bastard Volkov keeps snooping around.'

Dmitri hung up and sat back in his seat. This was it. There

was no going back now. He thought about his mother lying in the hospital bed and looked up at the windows. Despite Sorokin putting in a word and a lot of cash to get the best surgeon on the job, she'd still suffered a minor stroke during the surgery. They didn't know if her brain had been affected yet, or at least they pretended not to know.

————

DMITRI HAD BUNDLED Pavel onto the jet in a semi-conscious state and sat trying to listen to music. He always knew what he was doing before getting on a flight, and would spend parts of the flight going through the plans in his head. But this time, nothing. No information. He didn't like surprises. Maybe Volkov was someone who might have access to means of surveillance, leaving even Sorokin's encrypted email vulnerable.

Dmitri flicked through the playlist on his old, sim card free, mp3 player. As the first few notes of the double bass flooded through his ear canal, the noise of the engines faded into the background. He'd discovered the band, Phronesis, by chance. He'd been in London to neutralise an exiled oligarch, and had done the deed at King's Cross station, after the oligarch had just had a meeting with a journalist for the *Guardian*. It was easy enough, with the throng of people in London at rush hour and a slight push off the platform. Dmitri liked the irony of the man having met his death at a meeting with that left wing, anti-Russian rag.

Afterwards he'd dropped in to check out the new bands playing at London Jazz festival. The Phronesis trio had hit him right in the guts. Nailed him to the floor. The way the three musicians seemed to become one, before they went on separate musical journeys, and then merged again. He was amazed at how someone could be so in sync with another being, let alone two.

Dmitri looked out the window. Moscow was disappearing underneath him. The grey apartment blocks. The shiny new skyscrapers. The golden cupolas of the churches. He should have been at his mother's side, in case she woke up. When she woke up. But he was doing this for her. For them both. There would be no more assignments after this. No more hardship. No more cold winters.

Pavel let out a groan on the stretcher behind him and Dmitri got up to adjust the morphine.

31

HEATHROW AIRPORT, LONDON

RORY LOOKED AT HER WATCH. It was nine already. The flight had been uneventful, but it took longer than expected to get through border control with their new CIA issued passports. They were supposed to meet Masha at ten at Larkhall Park, and it might take them an hour to get there. Rory had prepared Sasha, told him that if they didn't get to the park in time today, they would have to wait until the following day. Those were the rules. No last minute text messages saying they were late, no WhatsApps.

The boy squinted as they left the terminal building. He'd slept the whole flight, had been asleep most of the previous day even, apart from wolfing down a couple of burgers. Rory held his hand. At least the boy felt safe with her. And soon his part of this nightmare would be over.

Rory thought back to the previous night, and Simon. She'd never even kissed an American before. Then she spotted the black cab.

'Amir, over here,' she said and waved.

Amir was her regular post-assignment pick up driver, an army vet who'd lost a leg in Afghanistan and the one who'd got Tom on Richard's team for the Russia job.

The cab drove over to them and a man folded himself out of the driver's seat. It wasn't Amir. Rory forgot to close her mouth. She'd thought she might have some time to prepare before she met Tom again, but here he was. All six foot of him, looking as fit as ever, but with longer stubble than she was used to.

'Rory, so good to see you,' he said and smiled broadly. 'I hope you don't mind me taking Amir's place, I got back early and heard about your falling out with the big man. Everything okay?'

'Hi Tom.' Rory looked from Tom to Sasha. 'Let's talk about that later. Sasha and I have a meeting to get to.'

'Hello Sasha, a pleasure to meet you, young man,' Tom said and put his hand out.

Sasha's hand disappeared in Tom's. 'You're in the best care, you know. They don't come much better than Rory.' Tom winked at the boy.

Sasha looked from Rory to Tom. Her ex-boyfriend must have seemed like a giant to the eleven-year-old. Six foot and built like a rugby player, he dwarfed Rory and the boy.

'Tom is a friend, Sasha, and a former colleague. He's going to take us to your sister.'

Tom opened the passenger door to let them climb in, but the boy paused.

'Are you a soldier?' Sasha asked.

'Yes.' Tom said. 'Yes I am. How did you guess?'

'My father was in Afghanistan. His eyes are always a bit sad, just like yours.' Sasha let go of Rory's hand and climbed into the back seat.

Tom and Rory exchanged glances before she followed the boy into the backseat. There were too many questions on Tom's face, but he would have to wait. There was enough food and drink for a group of grown men in the back, and both Sasha and Rory tucked into the sandwiches and crisps.

Rory noticed that the red light in the door was on, the one

indicating the driver could hear the conversation going on in the back. She wasn't worried about Tom listening in, would have appreciated his advice even, but now was not the time to discuss tactics for getting Pavel out. Her first job was to return Sasha to his sister. Rory was elated, but had to keep her excitement under control. This was the favourite part of her job; when the child got to see his mother, father, or as in this case, his sister, again. But they might be too late to meet up today.

'What's your family like, Sasha? Could you tell me a bit more about them?' she asked.

Sasha talked most of the way to South London. About family holidays, fishing trips, foraging for mushrooms, New Year celebrations. It became apparent that Pavel had been the dream father after he stopped drinking and got his second chance at parenting. Masha hadn't seen much of that side of her father, she had left Russia to study in the UK shortly after Sasha was born. Rory felt a bit sorry for her; she could understand where Masha's anger came from.

When the cab crossed Vauxhall Bridge, Rory looked at the time. They might be just in time for the rendezvous. It was a firm rule, never to wait for longer than ten minutes, so she hoped they'd get there in time. The building works going on around the new US embassy were extensive, so there was lots of heavy traffic in the area. But it didn't get much better when they turned down Wandsworth Road. There were red brake lights visible as far as she could see down the road.

'Any idea what's going on, Tom? More building works?'

'Not here, I think. We've passed the brunt of it. Maybe some roadworks or something.'

Rory looked at the time again. They were five minutes late now. Masha might leave before they got there. If she'd known Rory was bringing her brother, she probably would have waited forever, but Rory hadn't taken the risk. Even if her devices were safe, Masha's weren't.

Her thoughts were interrupted by the *thakathakathaka* of a helicopter overhead. A wave of cars came in the opposite direction, and then their own lane started moving again. They stopped a few blocks north of Larkhall Park, where they were meeting Masha.

'Looks like an accident,' Tom said, but Rory could hear the slight hesitation in his voice and noticed him looking at the helicopter above them.

An ambulance raced past them, so did a couple of police cars. And as they got closer to the park, they could see a sea of flashing lights, some reflected in the nearby shop windows. A grey lorry stood abandoned by a zebra crossing and a police officer was directing the cars ahead of them around the lorry.

'... and then, we went to London to see Masha, and we went to see them play. At White Hart lane. It was before they started building the new stadium, and we even had a tour of the stadium as well. Masha took a picture of me in front of Kane's shirt in the dressing room.' Sasha had gone through the last years of holidays, and Rory had interjected a few times to keep him talking.

'He's your favourite player then?'

'No, not now. That was when I was younger. Now I like Eriksson the best. He's got such a good eye for the game,' Sasha said.

'Ah, ok.' Rory had her hand on the handle to get out and walk the last bit, but paused. She exchanged glances with Tom in the rearview mirror.

'Just a second, love.' She patted Sasha's hand before she leaned forwards and looked through the front. There was someone lying under the lorry. Another person on a stretcher being carried into an ambulance. And a bloody Burberry trench coat was crumpled up next to the body on the ground. The patterned lining was unmistakable. Rory tried to stop herself from gasping.

Coincidences didn't happen.

What have I done?

I got Masha killed. And I brought her little brother to see it.

Rory scanned the crowds that had gathered around the lorry. Some school kids, a few elderly shoppers with their trolleys, and a group of builders. She hadn't seen any building sites at this stretch of the road. And they seemed to be as interested in looking at the onlookers as the paramedics working on the injured person. One of them was exchanging glances with the lorry driver as he was interviewed by a police officer.

If they knew about Masha coming to the park, they also knew it was to meet Rory. And they might also know about Sasha being there. Pavel's warning rang through her ears.

They'll hunt you down.

Tom turned his head to look at her. She nodded. And just as the group of builders scattered and started walking in different directions, Tom pressed a button. All the windows apart from the windscreen and the front side windows went black.

'What's happening? Did we get here too late?' Sasha interrupted his own story.

Outside the cab, Rory could see the men dressed as builders getting on buses and walking in between the queue of cars, peering through the windows. Rory had to close her eyes to stop herself from panicking. Someone had killed Masha. Or tried to kill Masha. If she was dead, would they have bothered with the ambulances? Who were these people? How did they pull this one off, and why would they do so now?

'Just an accident, but yes, we were too late.' Rory said in Russian. 'I'm sorry. We'll have to wait till tomorrow. To stay safe.' The lie made her squirm, but there was nothing else she could say. Not now. Not before she knew for sure.

Sasha's lips started quivering. 'Can we not call her, or go to her flat? I know where it is?'

'Not now. It's not safe now. Oh, sweetheart,' Rory shifted across to sit next to him and he leaned into her. 'I know you really wanted to see her. But my main priority is to keep you safe, and that's exactly what I am going to do.' She wrapped her arms around him and felt his tears soaking through her top.

'Take us to the tunnel, please,' she said to Tom.

'Are you sure? I mean, what if?'

'I don't believe in coincidences. Nor do you.'

'I'll make some calls,' Tom said.

Sasha had gone silent, his head leaning against her shoulder. He might not have bought her lie, but he still trusted her. They crawled through the South London streets, and finally sped up again as they reached a major road heading south. Rory found herself biting her nails. She hadn't done that since she was a child. Rory's assignment wasn't close to the end. It had only just begun.

THE BOY WAS fast asleep when they drove onto the channel tunnel train. Rory got out and climbed into the seat next to Tom for the crossing. He'd been on the phone while they were waiting for the train, to a friend who worked at King's College Hospital.

'She's alive. Critical condition, they don't know if she'll make it. But she has a good chance. The other woman is dead. A Sarah Gower, do you know her?'

Rory shook her head. She'd never heard the name before. 'They must have thought it was me.' She leaned forward, elbows on her knees and her face in her hands. Pavel was probably being tortured this very moment. And his daughter was fighting for her life in hospital.

'Rory, don't even go there. You are not responsible for this. You haven't killed anyone. And you cannot let yourself think so.' Tom turned his head and looked back at the sleeping boy in the back seat. 'Now, more than ever, you need to be focused. Use your energy to make a change for the better. Do not let yourself dwell on maybes and what ifs.'

Rory looked up at him. 'That sounds terribly familiar.'

'It should. It's what you told me after Vaseem was killed in Syria.'

Rory sat up and exhaled. 'Okay. Fine. I just.' She closed her eyes again. 'I don't know what to do, Tom. I just don't know.'

'Then let's talk it through. Tell me what's been going on, what this is all about.'

And she did. In a whisper she told him about leaving her job (*I know, it's the best laugh I've had in ages when Amir told me about that,* Tom said. *If there was ever any doubt about your sound judgment, that's proof enough.*) About meeting Masha and taking the job without proper due diligence. And about all that had happened in Moscow. The banya, the morgue, the drunk friend. And finally about finding Pavel and having to leave him behind, and then rescuing the boy. And about the key. The key to a safety deposit box in Italy. It had come to her on the airplane, just as she was falling asleep. Masha had given her an old picture of Pavel and two other men, one probably his boss, in front of a building wrapped in bougainvillea and with the name Mascherano on a sign. It was also the name of a restaurant she'd found online, near Verona in northern Italy. A restaurant with a private dining room in an old bank vault. Tom showed no reaction to anything, only when she mentioned that the bullet had hit her before it got to Pavel did a flicker of worry show in his face.

'So, what do I do now?' she said at the end.

Tom looked out the front window.

'You're not going to tell me are you? You're right. I know what to do,' she added.

'I was worried you'd say that. I'm coming with you,' he said as he turned back towards her.

Rory looked into his brown eyes. 'There's no time, Tom. I can't take Sasha with me, and I need to know he's with someone I can rely on.' She could see that Tom was looking for an alternative, any alternative, that would mean he could go with her. But there was none.

'And Masha?' he asked.

'I'll call Glass, see what she can do to help. She's a DCI now. At least the police won't think a Russian assassination attempt in the UK is far-fetched any more. Maybe they can withhold the names as well. Hopefully for long enough to buy me some time.'

'What if they get there first?'

'Then I'll deal with that. But if they think I'm dead, they might take their time.'

'That's a very big if.'

'Yes, it is.'

A wail from the back seat got them both to turn around.

'Papa! No, no! Let him go! Papa!'

Rory jumped out the door and into the back seat where Sasha had sat up screaming. His eyes looked wild with fear.

'Shh, it's ok, Sasha. You're ok. You're safe, Sasha. You're safe.' She wrapped herself around him and held him tight, but he kept screaming.

'No, go away, I want papa! Papa!' Sasha started throwing his arms around, hitting Rory in the face and an elbow struck her right kidney.

'Sash, please, your papa sent me to find you, to take you somewhere safe. I promised your papa I would keep you safe.' Rory adjusted her arms to hold Sasha's arms down and away from her face, and started stroking the boy's hair.

'I'm here to help you. To help your father, to help Masha. Please, Sasha. I'm here to help. Your papa asked me to help you.' Rory noticed Tom looking at the car in front of them and behind them, to see if the crying and screaming was attracting unwanted attention.

'No!' the boy screamed. 'No, no, no! Let me go!' The screaming made Rory's ears ring, but the boy's arms had stopped fighting.

'Your papa sent me to find you, to take you somewhere safe.'

'I want papa,' the boy said, his whole body shaking with each sob.

'I know, I know. And I will find him for you. But I have to make sure you're safe first. I promised your father I would.' She kept stroking his hair and used her free hand to wipe away the tears from his chin.

They sat there for a while, Rory rocking him back and forth.

'I promised him I would keep you safe.'

The train had reached the end of the tunnel, and they could see daylight outside the windows of the carriage again.

'Sash, sashenka. I need to tell you something. Masha is in hospital. That's why we can't go to see her.'

'Did they do it?'

'Yes, I think so. But she's somewhere safe now, and I'm going to get a friend to help her, to keep her safe until she is better. Okay?'

'Okay.' Sasha sat up, pulling away from Rory's embrace. He used his sleeve to wipe away the snot and tears.

'Now. We don't have much time. My friend Tom here is going to look after you whilst I try to find your father. Or rather to find what it is they want, the men who have him. So we can get your father back. It means I have to leave you for a day, maybe two, but I promise I'll be back for you.'

The boy's lower lip started quivering again.

'It's okay to be afraid, Sasha. But Tom is the best in the world at what he does. He's British Spetsnaz. And he plays chess, just like you. Just don't ask him about football. He's one of those guys who don't know anything about football. Probably doesn't even know who Harry Kane is.'

The left corner of Sasha's mouth twitched upwards in a half smile.

'That's better. Tom will look after you and take you to

Priya's house. Priya and her brother are the closest to family I have, and I will come and find you there as soon as I can. Okay? Now come here,' she said and pulled him in for a hug.

————

RORY GOT out of the car at the Calais train station and hugged Sasha one more time before she got out. Tom rolled down the driver's side window and nodded to her.

'I'd ask how you're planning to get him to Priya's house, but I assume you've got a plan already?' she asked.

'Mhm.'

'I'll be off then.' She hesitated for a second. There hadn't been any time to talk about them. About their relationship, or rather lack of one. She bit her lips and looked down at her shoes. There was no telling that the brown stains on them were blood, and not mud. Her blood. Pavel's blood. She should pick up some new clothes though. Or rather some second hand ones. Nothing screamed disguise so loud as a completely new outfit.

'And there's no point in me asking you to wait until I've got Sasha to the house, so I can come with you?'

Rory shook her head, but didn't look up.

'Take care of yourself then.'

Rory turned and walked away, giving Sasha a little wave. She could feel Tom's gaze on her back as she walked, pulled the cap he'd lent her further down her head and turned the corner into the ticket office.

Just before the train left, Rory got a phone out and dialled Glass's number.

'Hi Glass, Rory here. I've got a favour to ask. And not much time.'

DCI Glass didn't interrupt her a single time, just listened until the end.

'No probs, Rory. I'm on it. Godspeed or whatever that saying is.'

———

IT WAS dark by the time she got to Marseille. Rory was exhausted after looking over her shoulder the whole day. There was no time to do proper counterintelligence, and every time she spotted someone who looked at her a nanosecond too long, or looked like someone she'd seen before, she changed her appearance. A Paris second-hand shop had provided her with a range of clothes, from vintage chic to mom jeans and trainers, and she had even dyed her dark blonde hair brown on the way.

Rory had only had a few minutes here and there to check the news on one of her burner phones. A South London newspaper said both women had been killed after being hit by the lorry, no names released yet as next of kin hadn't been informed. And a large casino in Moscow had been ravaged by fire, killing its owner and several staff and customers. Not just any casino. Her casino. Where she'd saved Sorokin's life and seen Dmitri the first time. Another fire had torn through a market near Kievsky station. There was no need to guess which one. They were tying up loose ends.

33

DMITRI LOOKED at the hands in front of him. The skin had healed well over the last day, and there was no sign of infection. He had pulled the broken fingers straight, and had taped them to the ones that were ok.

'Take your shirt off, please. I need to change the dressing,' he said.

Pavel did as told. As he had done every four hours or so in the last few days. 'Thank you,' he said. 'Thank you, for looking after me.'

Dmitri had ignored the words the first few times. Then they had started to sting. The man he had tortured, starved and mutilated was thanking him. He had dismissed it as Stockholm syndrome at first. That Pavel had been so broken by his ordeal that he had started to become grateful to his captor. But that was before Dmitri caught himself smiling at Pavel when he thanked him. This was not a man with Stockholm syndrome. This was a man who was trying to make him, the captor, the one who started to identify and sympathise with his victim. And the worst of it was that Dmitri didn't just see it happening. He didn't manage to stop it. Pavel was getting to him.

Did he do it on purpose? Was he really that good? Dmitri didn't know for sure, but he did his best to keep his guard up. He might have to kill Pavel in the next day or two, if all went to plan.

'Ouch,' Pavel pulled back as Dmitri took the dressing off. It had got stuck in the skin as it healed, and when Dmitri pulled it off it revealed the raw skin underneath. The rough stitches Dmitri had sewn had done the job, and the bullet hole was closing up well on the chest. The back was taking longer, as Pavel spent most of the day lying down. But there was no sign of infection.

'You should try to sit up more, give the wound time to heal. And oxygen.'

Dmitri went into the bathroom and washed his hands in the marble basin. He turned off the gold plated taps and went back to his patient. Pavel was lying down again, on his side this time, staring out at the sea. The sun was shining, but Pavel had been confined to the cabin to make sure he didn't try to escape. Not that he'd have the faintest idea where to go, or how to get away. They hadn't seen land in days.

The weather had been decent, and Dmitri wasn't sea sick any more. He hadn't quite regained his appetite, so Pavel got generous portions of the best food the chef could think of. The crew didn't know what the situation was with the involuntary guest, but they were well enough paid to look the other way. Sorokin had dismissed all but the essential crew. The captain and his deputy, an engineer, a chef and a maid.

'I'll be back with lunch a bit later,' Dmitri said as he left the room.

'Thank you,' Pavel said again.

Dmitri locked the door after him and walked out onto the deck. The yacht was the biggest he'd ever been on. Sorokin had bought it a few years ago via some tax haven company, but given the catalogues Dmitri had seen him with at the club he had no doubt that Sorokin wanted an even bigger one for himself when all this was over. Maybe Dmitri should get one himself, if he could get rid of the sea sickness. Sailing in international waters might be his best option after that Interpol listing.

They were close now, just half a day away from their destination. Road Town, capital of British Virgin Islands. Dmitri looked at his phone but there was nothing from Sorokin. Not yet.

'Some champagne, Sir?' the maid said.

'Sure, why not. And could you get the jacuzzi ready?' Dmitri tapped the glass on the big fish tank in the main living room, sending the tropical fish in all directions.

Yeah. A super yacht and a life on the seas might just be the way to spend retirement. He certainly didn't intend to spend much of it in Russia. The constant jostling for positions and connections, fighting to get a share of the next big scam.

Dmitri thought about Pavel. How he was the man Dmitri had aspired to be. A hero. A true patriot. A family man. Someone less interested in positions and wealth who managed with what he had. But it was too late to choose that path now.

'The jacuzzi is ready, Sir. And I've left the rest of the bottle on the table next to it.' The maid hesitated for a bit. 'Is there, anything else I can do?'

'You're getting bored, aren't you?'

'Not at all, Sir. Not at all,' she said and retreated back below deck. She wasn't his type, too skinny, or Dmitri might have suggested that she joined him. He was pretty confident that she'd accept the invitation. He'd noticed her looking at him, at his well built frame. She must have been fed up with working for middle aged men with man boobs, he thought.

Dmitri went up to the jacuzzi at the back of the sun deck. The champagne was there, so was a stack of super soft towels and a silk dressing gown. He put his gun on the chair, unbuttoned his shirt, and took off his pants and trousers all in one.

Leaning back into the sea water, champagne flute in hand, he let himself relax for the first time in a decade. There was nothing he could do until Sorokin called. Nothing at all.

Not five minutes later, Dmitri was back out of the jacuzzi. Relaxing with not a care in the world wasn't his kind of thing. He had to do something. Anything. He put on his pants and went back inside. Thought about calling his mother, but he'd already rung the hospital twice today. And sent her flowers three times since getting up in the morning. She hadn't woken from her surgery yet. Not properly, at least. That was what the nurses told him.

He checked his phone again, to see if there were any emails or messages from Sorokin. Nothing. He got his shorts and went down to the gym. Metallica blasted through the speakers as he set the treadmill to a ten kilometre uphill climb.

He'd only made it halfway when his phone rang.

34

LAKE GARDA, ITALY

THE ROAD LEADING to the villa was lined with cypress trees, and there were vines covering the undulating hills around them. The sun had been up for a couple of hours already, but the place didn't open before lunch, so Rory had caught a few hours' sleep before she did the last leg of her journey. As she turned the corner and could see up the hill, the main house rose above the cypress, a cream coloured building with red tiled roof and a small tower on top, alongside a roof terrace.

A few days ago she hadn't even known that these kinds of private vaults even existed. And this one, Villa Mascherano, was a very peculiar one. Probably linked to the mafia in some way, or even owned by it. Whatever it was, it couldn't have been profitable as the building now housed a Michelin-starred restaurant and the main vault had been converted into the private dining room.

The photos she had seen online showed a large oak table set with silverware and crystal glasses, an art deco chandelier in the ceiling and the walls lined with deposit boxes.

There were some men unloading the contents of a van to the side of the villa, and above their shouting and swearing in Italian Rory could hear the faint humming of a propeller aeroplane. Maybe she had been wrong about there being no airport, maybe the Russians were here already?

She looked towards the sound. A sea plane. Of course. She could kick herself, but there was no time to dwell on errors of judgement.

As she got closer to the villa, one of the men paused and looked at her.

'Can I help you? The restaurant doesn't open till later.'

'I know, I was hoping you might be able to help me with something though.'

'We don't need any staff. Have all we need, thank you.'

'I'm not looking for a job,' Rory said. Then she did a double take. Those eyes, with the close set eyebrows. The jaw. She'd seen him before. Or someone very much like him. She did a mental scan of all the pictures of Pavel she'd got from the client. Tried to place the face. Of course. There had been three men in the photo. Pavel, his boss Lebedev and the man she assumed was Mr. Mascherano. This was a younger version of him.

The man went back to unloading the van, handing his colleague a parma ham.

'I'm looking for your father,' she said.

Both men froze. 'What did you say?' the man whose face she'd recognised said.

'I'm looking for your father. He was a friend of my father. A long time ago. He left me something, here, in the vault.'

Both men looked her up and down, frowning. Rory stood still, tried to keep herself from trembling. If this was a mafia family, she could be on thin ice. There was only one way to find out.

'Take her inside, Gio. To the bar.'

Rory wasn't sure if it was a request or an order, but followed the second man up the back staircase to the main restaurant. It was eerily quiet, not a sound and not much light either.

'Arms out, legs apart,' the man said.

His hands searched her thoroughly. Too thoroughly for her liking. But she didn't let on. Show no weakness, she kept repeating to herself.

The door to the kitchens opened behind her.

'She's clean,' the second man said before heavy footsteps walked away.

Rory turned around, taking her time, and saw the silhouette of a man. A bit shorter than the one she'd assumed was his son, but similar build and shape of the head. She walked towards him, right hand stretched out to shake his, but stopped when he lifted his right hand up.

'*Basta, signorina.* That's close enough.'

Rory moved to the side a little so the light from the kitchen wasn't in her eyes when she looked at him. He had a white apron on, a butcher's apron, with red and brown stains on it. A meat cleaver in the left hand. And it was most definitely him. The left side of his face, from the ear to the eyebrow and down to the chin, had a huge burn scar. But the proportions were the same.

'My father, Pavel Abramov, was here decades ago. With his compatriot, Lebedev, of the Soviet Communist Party. They left something behind, in your vault, that my father wanted me to have,' she said.

When she mentioned Lebedev, the man narrowed his eyes. He had a long scar running down his left underarm, and seemed to favour one leg over the other. She'd read something online about an Emilio Mascherano having survived an assassination attempt, but wife and daughter had been killed.

'Did they now. Lebedev is dead, isn't he?'

'Yes, he is.'

'And how do I know you're not an impostor?'

'If I was, I wouldn't have the key with me.' Rory reached

into her bra and pulled out the small, rusty key. She held it up in front of her.

The man smiled for a second, but it didn't reach his eyes. 'We don't operate the vault any more. Or engage in any of our previous activities.'

'But you didn't empty the boxes, did you?'

'No. Most were collected almost twenty years ago. The few that weren't. Well. They're still there.'

Rory waited. She didn't know how to ask, what to ask, so decided to let him do the talking.

'I'll show you. But I don't want anything to do with whatever it is, understand? I left that world behind. I have a family, grandchildren. I don't want any trouble.'

'Of course.'

He led her down a spiral staircase to a dimly lit basement. Empty wine barrels with unlit wax candles on top lined the hallway that ended in a thick timber door.

'You need to go through the wine cellar, there's a doorway on the left. Given you have the key, I assume you know which box you're looking for? The records perished in a fire, the one meant to end me and my family for good. '

It didn't come across as a question.

'Thank you.' Rory didn't want to admit that she had no idea which box it was. There hadn't been a number on the key.

The thick timber door to the wine cellars itself had a heavy brown key in it, and it felt like a vacuum releasing as she pulled the door open. The smell of old things; wood, wine, cloth, came rushing towards her. There were rows and rows of wine bottles, the newer, less dusty ones filled the first sections she got to, but the older and rarer vintage ones, covered in layers of dust and old cobwebs, were to the left, at the far end of the cellars.

Feeling a little claustrophobic, Rory jammed the door open with a corkscrew, and went inside. The light was dim, atmospheric for a romantic dinner or wine tasting, but not at all practical. But as her eyes got used to the darkness, she manoeuvred her way to the back. Some of the rows had a barrel standing upright, with a few glasses on it and a cork screw. All set for impromptu wine tastings.

She found the entrance to the vault and walked inside, switching on the art deco chandelier. Three of the walls were covered in safety deposit boxes. She counted twenty rows on each side, with at least fifteen columns. The far end had fewer rows, but just as many columns. This could take some time. Some of the boxes were empty, with the small doors taken off, and had been made into shelves for dried flowers and candles. She prioritised the rows that were preserved. Unlikely that they'd light a candle under box still in use. That ruled out half the rows. Rory started from the top left and began working her way down, trying each lock to see if her key would fit. She could hear noises from above, coming from a newly made ventilation shaft, of what sounded like shouting and swearing, and assumed the men were busy unloading the van again.

Her fingers trembled as she tried lock after lock. Some were unlocked and she could see that the key hole was in the open position. But it was still taking too long. Far too long.

More shouting from above, and the sound of a big engine. Muscle car, or a vintage one, perhaps. Rory kept looking at the locks but the sounds from above were too much of a distraction. Something wasn't right. And she realised she'd skipped a row.

Back again. There. Two boxes side by side, both locked, second row from the top. She stood on tiptoes and spotted dust on top of the doors. She tried the first lock. The key went in, but wouldn't turn. The second one didn't turn either. She wriggled the key a bit, back and forth, and suddenly the levers caught. There was a small velvet bag inside, and it felt like jewellery. She took it out of the bag and looked at it. A necklace with matching earrings, set with diamonds, lots of them, and that blue precious stone. Sapphire.

Rory held it up to the light, took her nail to one of the diamonds. It looked real and like it could be worth a small fortune. But not worth killing so many people for. There was more shouting from above. Rory tiptoed again, and reached into the back of the box with her hand. There was an envelope at the back.

Then she heard a noise she had heard only a few days earlier.

Pop, pop.

Not a lock being unlocked.

Not a champagne cork at a casino table.

A gun.

A gun with a suppressor.

They were here.

35

RORY COULD FEEL A COLD DRAUGHT, sending a shiver down her spine as she took out the envelope she'd found in the second box. Then the cellar door slammed shut.

'Fuck.'

Slow steps, heavy, a man's shoe, came in her direction. There was a pause, then a few more steps, then another pause. He was looking for something. Or someone. He clearly hadn't been told where the vault was. Rory went to the doorway and snuck around the corner. The man was somewhere between her and the door. She tiptoed down a row of wine racks, trying to see where he was. At least there was only one.

The steps came closer, and Rory could feel her heart beat so hard that she was worried it was audible. She took long, controlled breaths, to help her stay calm. Whoever it was wouldn't be able to see as well as her, as her eyes had got used to the dim light. But there was no way she could get to the cellar door without being noticed. She put the envelope between two barrels and left the bag of jewellery on top of the nearest wine rack. She caught a glimpse of a beige blazer just before he rounded the corner and stared straight at her.

Not Dmitri the assassin.

Sorokin.

He was taller than she remembered, maybe because he wasn't surrounded by Amazonian models with six inch heels.

'Having a little wine tasting, are we? Not quite the done thing to sample the wine alone, is it?' Sorokin said in heavily accented Italian.

For a split second Rory thought she might have a chance, that Sorokin hadn't recognised her.

'I'm sorry, I was just,' Rory said, and took out a bottle of '82, as if to hand it over.

Sorokin came closer, and took the bottle. He examined the label, before he continued in English.

'A very good year, this one. I should probably take a few bottles home to Moscow. But let's try this one first, to make sure it's worth this Michelin star this place has.'

Sorokin grabbed the corkscrew from the barrel next to them, and screwed it into the cork, not letting go of Rory's eyes in the process. He took his time, and then pulled out the cork in one swift movement. Holding the bottle in his right hand, he turned the glasses over with his left. His gold watch fell down onto his wrist as he lifted and filled each one of them. There was no way of getting past him, and he had all the sharp objects within his reach. The bottle, the glasses and the corkscrew. He put the bottle and corkscrew down, picked up both glasses and handed one to her.

'To all the beautiful women in this world,' he said and swilled the glass under his nose before he drank it in one. 'What, do you not approve of my toast?'

Rory put the glass against her lips, and sipped at it.

'No, no, not like that. You empty the glass on a good toast. You don't just take a sip.'

She put the glass to her lips again, and downed it in one go.

'That's more like it. Now. Where were we? Yes. I was just

about to ask you how your game is these days. Won any good hands lately? You know, I was surprised to see you here. Not completely taken aback, but quite,' he said, and filled the glasses up again.

Rory swallowed. He was a middle-aged man. Probably not very healthy, but as ex-KGB he wouldn't be an easy opponent. And he had the swagger of someone who knew they were in charge.

'Let us drink to this: that we may suffer as much sorrow as there will be drops of wine left in our glasses,' he said, and put it right in front of Rory's face.

He stared at her as she emptied her glass again, before he took a sip of his. His jaws tightened.

'I have two questions for you. How did you find me here, and who do you work for?'

Rory opened her mouth to talk, but he put his finger on her lips.

'No, take your time. Think this through. I would rather have the right answer, than you trying to fob me off with lies and fabrications,' he said, and moved his right hand to her neck.

Rory grabbed the wrist, but it was as if she'd forgotten all her training. He pushed her against the wine rack, and used his left hand to search her waist for any weapons. Her outfit didn't have many other possible hiding places. Rory regretted not having brought a knife, if nothing else.

'I work for Masha, Pavel's daughter,' Rory said, trying to drag out her answer enough for someone to come to her assistance. But there were no sounds from above.

'We both know that Masha is dead. So who do you really work for?'

Sorokin lifted her upwards by the neck, so only her toes were still reaching the ground, his jaws tightening and the veins on his neck expanding.

Rory tried to mobilise her neck muscles, to stop the

crushing pressure on her windpipe, and grabbed at his hand with her own. He was way stronger than her, there was no way she could fight him off, not in such a small space and with his experience.

She felt the panic rushing through her, felt the bottles poke into her back, and started seeing white flashing spots around her. Sorokin slowly set her back down on her feet again, the vein on his neck pounding after having held her up for so long. Rory coughed, wanted to massage her neck, but he still held tightly around it.

'There's this guy, who works at the US embassy in Moscow. I don't know his name, at least not his real name,' she said. 'He's an agent, CIA, financial crime, NSA. I don't know which one. But he offered me twenty grand for any information on your colleague. The man with a missing finger. He's the one I'm looking for, not you,' she said, drawing out the words.

'And why would the Americans want to find him? Surely, if they knew who he was, they would just kill him? I think you might be making things up, little one, and you know what I said about that.' He lifted her up again, all the way off the floor now.

Her toes were trying to find something to stand on, but there was nothing. Her left hand grabbed on to the rack behind her, but the weight of her hand broke the bottle she was resting on, cutting her wrist in the process.

'That's a waste of good wine, don't you think?'

The flashing lights were appearing before her eyes again, her neck muscles trying and failing to keep the pressure off her windpipe. It wouldn't take much longer before she passed out, and she pulled her injured left hand up higher to get some of the weight off, ignoring the shards of glass that were piercing her skin. Their eyes were level now, and she could see the blood pumping at his temple, and on his neck. He might not be able to hold her up like that for much longer, but then she wouldn't stay conscious for much longer either. She closed her eyes for a second, and when she opened them again, she caught a quick glimpse of his ferocious glare. There would be no rescue.

'Now, we can do this the easy way; you answer my questions and I won't have to torture your father and throw him into this Icelandic volcano he's so interested in.' He put her down again.

Rory couldn't stop coughing and tears were gathering in her eyes. A whole cascade of thoughts floated through her mind. She hadn't talked to her father in weeks. Her last contact with him had been her cancelling lunch. And they didn't even share a surname. Not any more. Not since her mother died, and Rory had taken her maiden name.

It was ironic, really. That she was the one to die a violent death at enemy hands. Tom would never have been defeated by a middle-aged man. Then again, nor should she be. She had dealt with Richard. She could deal with this.

Rory gave a cough that convulsed through her body, making Sorokin step sideways to adjust his stance and avoid the spray. Her eyes were fixed on his neck, the blood being pumped through to his head.

She could feel it now, with her fingertips.

Another cough, a slight move sideways, and she grabbed tight around the wooden handle.

36

Before Rory knew it, before she'd even had a chance to think it through, she pushed away from the wine rack and threw her weight to the left. Using all the energy she had remaining, she pummelled the corkscrew in her right hand straight into Sorokin's carotid artery.

Bullseye.

Blood began to trickle out along the spiral of the corkscrew.

Sorokin grabbed onto her hand to stop her from tearing the corkscrew back out again, and her feet hit the floor with a thump.

It was no use though. She knew it, and so did he. This wasn't about him bleeding to death, though that would surely also happen. What they both knew was this; Rory had hit the carotid artery right where signals were sent back to his heart telling it how much blood it should send to the brain. Or in this case, how little.

Sorokin's eyes opened wide, and Rory could see the white all the way around his iris. His right hand was still on her neck, but the grip loosened and she could no longer see any movement in the vein on his temple.

Still holding on to the corkscrew with her right hand, she forced his fingers off her neck and he slowly slumped onto the floor in front of her, a slow *shuck* as the corkscrew came out of his neck. Blood sprayed onto the floor, like the cough of a tap once the plumber's been, and on her legs, but not for long. His heart had stopped beating.

Her ears were ringing. Then an eerie silence followed. Her right hand was covered in his blood, her left had a mix of her own and red wine.

She'd killed him.

She'd killed another human being.

Rory went through Sorokin's pockets and found a handkerchief and his phone. She didn't have much time, someone could come looking for him soon. She took his handkerchief and wiped her hands clean, then Sorokin's hand.

The phone was locked. An odd model she'd never seen before, probably some Russian make that was encrypted. Rory put Sorokin's limp thumb on the button, and the screen came to life. She went straight to the settings, to disable the locked screen function, but it was no use. The phone had been set up for Sorokin only. Rory cursed through her teeth, but started looking for something to get a decent fingerprint with. A bottle would work, but she might not get it out of the building without smudging it. The half bottle of wine she'd just drunk muddled her thoughts.

Her muscles shivered from the adrenaline as she ran back to the vault. Rory listened out for sounds from above, but there was nothing. She picked up a steak knife and went back where she'd come from. Only a minute later she was out of the wine cellar carrying the envelope, the phone and the bundled up red handkerchief.

As she approached the spiral staircase she could hear a chair moving in the restaurant above.

'Sit down!' a voice said in English. The Russian accent was unmistakable.

'Please. My son. He's all I have. Please, let me help him.'

Rory recognised the voice of the old man, Emilio. There was a cough and a wheezing sound.

'Sit down, or I'll shoot him again.'

Rory took her shoes off and took two steps at a time, as quietly as she could.

'*Mi figlio*, please. My boy.'

Rory poked her head just above the floor and saw the small group of people between the staircase and the kitchen. The Russian with the gun sat next to a table, his back towards her, the older Italian man sat opposite him and the two younger men were on the floor. She could see the son trying to catch his breath, blood pooling around him. The other man was motionless. Dead, or passed out.

Rory gestured to the old man and caught his eye. He needed no encouragement.

'*Mi figlio, mi figlio*. Please, let me help him. I am no threat to you, I have no weapons. Let me help my son, please. Take whatever you want, but don't take him away from me, please. He is all I have left,' he said and folded his hands in prayer.

'Shut up,' the Russian said and shifted in his seat. Rory made the most of the noise and picked up a large brass candlestick. Only three more metres, and she'd be right behind the Russian.

The son started coughing again, and it sounded like he was drowning in his own blood. The old man couldn't help but let out a yelp.

'Hail Mary, full of grace. Hail Mary, full of grace.' He kept rocking back and forth in his chair.

'Enough!' The Russian got up and pushed his own chair backwards. Rory had to step sideways to avoid being hit by it, and bumped into another chair. The sound made the Russian turn his head, and Rory made the most of his own movement when she whacked him on the temple with the candlestick. He went down with a thud, and landed at the feet of the son who was bleeding on the floor.

Emilio leapt out of his seat and grabbed the gun, firing two quick shots into the Russian's head. Then he aimed the gun at Rory.

She pretended not to notice the muzzle pointing at her and knelt down next to his son.

'I'm going to turn you on your side, ok? So you don't choke. And try to breathe normally. If you panic you'll just inhale the blood.' She turned him over on the side, facing his father, one arm and a leg on each side of the body to keep him stable. Then she put her fingers in his mouth to check the airways were clear, pulling his tongue forward. 'Are you going to call an ambulance or shall I do it?'

The old man looked at her as if he was trying to decide what to do.

The gun was still aimed at her head.

Rory still pretended it wasn't there.

She went on to examine the man on the floor and found the bullet wound, near the right lung, and grabbed a napkin from the table to stop the bleeding. The man gasped as she put pressure on it.

'Can you hold here while I check on his friend? He'll go into shock if we don't stop the bleeding.'

Emilio fished a mobile phone out of his pocket and dialled a number. Then he put the gun down and walked over to his son, phone in one hand, knelt down and put the other hand on top of Rory's.

'I need an ambulance. Villa Mascherano. My son has been shot.'

The other man was passed out, not dead. He'd been hit in the leg and the bruising on the left side of his head indicated that he'd hit his head when he fell.

'He'll be fine. Make the ambulance crew take care of your son first.' She got up and looked at Emilio.

He'd sat down on the floor and pulled his son onto his lap with his free arm. One hand keeping the pressure on the wound, the other stroking his face.

'I'm sorry. I didn't know this would happen.' Rory swallowed.

'The other one. The boss. Is he dead?'

'Yes.'

'Good.' Emilio nodded at the Russian lying on the floor. 'Unless you want to get involved, you might want to make a run for it now. Before the police arrive. There should be car keys in this guy's pockets, he was the one driving.'

'Thank you. And I'm so, so sorry.' She stood for a second, not knowing what to do, then turned and searched through the pockets of the dead Russian. She found a set of old fashioned keys and went to pick up her envelope and the handkerchief. 'I'm sorry. I ...'

Emilio interrupted her.

'You're not the one who came here with a gun.'

———

RORY STARTED the engine of the red vintage Porsche Speedster and felt the roar of the engine through her bones. Her hands had stopped shaking, but that was a result of a swig of the bottle of scotch she had taken with her rather than getting her nerves under control. She had rinsed her hands in it as well, and the smell of peat mixed with the scent of the leather seats. On the seat next to her were the papers from the safety deposit box, Sorokin's phone and a plastic bag. The handkerchief had soaked through, and she'd emptied a bin bag to put it in. She'd left the diamond jewellery as a small compensation to Emilio, though it wouldn't matter much if his son died.

Rory stepped on the accelerator and the wheels sent gravel into the rows of vines. She wanted to get as far away as she could before she made contact, in case Dmitri was nearby.

After a couple of hours on the motorway heading west back towards France, she stopped at a petrol station. She parked at the back, to avoid getting too much attention for the car, and got one of her burner phones out. She only had two unused ones left now, and would have to be cautious about using them. She had looked briefly at the papers before she left the villa, but hadn't really understood what they were. This time she took her time, and read them thoroughly.

Red Haven Corporation. This is to certify that the bearer is the owner of ten shares in Red Haven Corporation.

Rory recognised Pavel's name at the bottom, as company director, and there was another name, Enrique Loyola, listed as company secretary. The document had been issued in the British Virgin Islands, and each of the three shares were for a third of the company.

Bearer shares. Rory hadn't heard about the term before, but assumed it was something similar to bearer bonds. A way of hiding who owned a certain company, but also a high risk investment in the sense that whoever had the paper in his or her possession was also the owner. Easy to hide, but also easy to steal. It made sense that the Soviet Union had used it as a way of hiding their investments in the West in the 1980s. She googled the term to be sure.

A bearer share is an equity security wholly owned by whoever holds the physical stock certificate.

There was frequent mention of them in connection with the Panama Papers leak a few years earlier. But there was no mention of the Red Haven Corporation. Apart from a shop of some sort in India.

Rory put her burner phone away, put one of Sorokin's shirts over her clothes and drove west for another hour or so. Then she found a quiet spot not far from the motorway and got the other phone out. Sorokin's shirt. Sorokin's phone. And Sorokin's thumb.

She took the cut off thumb out of the plastic bag and used it to unlock the phone. It took a couple of attempts, the thumb was drying up already, but she managed in the end. There were a few new messages from different people. One was from a man named Volkov enquiring about the trip to Italy. Funny name. Mr Wolf. She wondered if it was a real name or a nickname.

Rory ignored the messages and went to recent phone calls. The missing calls were from hidden numbers, but she could see that Sorokin himself had called one number several times over the last few days. She looked at her fingers and tried to scrape away some blood from under the corner of a nail. Then she cleared her throat and pressed the button.

37

OFF THE COAST OF VENEZUELA

'Yes?' Dmitri was trying to slow his breathing, but couldn't hear what was said at the other end of the phone. 'Andrey Mikhailovich? I can't hear you, there must be a problem with the signal. Hang on a second.' Dmitri held the phone to his ear as he left the gym and walked out on the deck. 'Okay, this should be better. Are you still there?'

Then he heard a woman's voice.

'Who's this? Where's Sorokin?' he interrupted her.

'I'm afraid Sorokin is,' the voice paused. 'Gone.' The woman spoke decent Russian, but was no native speaker. Dmitri switched to English.

'Gone where? And who are you?'

'I am the one who's got the documents you want.'

Dmitri tried to place the voice. It didn't sound like one of Sorokin's girlfriends.

'I'd like to suggest a swap. You give me Pavel Abramov and I'll give you the documents.'

Dmitri tried to get his head around it.

'Where is Sorokin?'

'He's incapacitated.'

'What do you mean, incapacitated. Is he drunk?' He paced

around on the deck and picked up the half full champagne glass.

'He's dead. Got himself into a situation he couldn't handle, I'm afraid.'

Dmitri flung the glass into the doors to the living room. It shattered in a thousand pieces. He wanted to scream but had to stop himself from throwing the phone into the sea.

'Dead. At whose hands? Yours?' The sweat was running cold down his back despite the sun.

'Yes.'

'And now you want to talk? It's a bit late for talking, don't you think?'

'Too late for Sorokin, but not for us. Your friend left me no choice.'

Friend. Was that Sorokin had been to him? A friend? He'd started out as his boss and a father figure. And officially that was still the case. But they had become more like colleagues over the last decade. But friends? No. He would never have called Sorokin his friend.

'I appreciate that this might be a shock. Maybe I should call again a bit later?' The voice at the end of the line was cold. Detached. So matter of fact that Dmitri couldn't quite believe that she was telling the truth. Maybe it was one of Volkov's tricks? But Sorokin wouldn't have let anyone use his phone.

Dmitri went upstairs and sat down on the white leather sofa in the main living room. In front of him there was endless sea. To the left he could make out the outline of an island.

The island.

He picked at a patch of stubble he had missed when he shaved earlier that morning. There were only a couple of hairs poking out, but they made a slight sound as he scraped his thumb over them. 'Abramov for the documents. How do I know you have them?'

'I can send you a picture. They were in the safety deposit box you got the key for in Abramov's garage.'

Her. It was her. The woman Masha had hired. She was the one who'd tried and failed to break Pavel out. And she must have got to the garage, and perhaps the boy just before him. How, he didn't know. Maybe she had someone working for her. With her. She should have been dead by now. They should all be dead. Mitrofan, that stupid drunk, Masha, her PI.

'And who are you?'

'That doesn't matter.'

'It does to me. I like to know who I'm doing business with. If there is to be any business.'

'Masha Abramova hired me to find her brother and father. I'm just doing my job.'

Dmitri hung up. His head started spinning. Sorokin was gone. Dead. He didn't know why he was surprised, Sorokin had dodged a lot of bullets. But Dmitri was the one who should have gone first. The one who worked in the firing line.

He closed his eyes. What was the point?

His mother was in hospital, and she still hadn't woken up after her surgery.

His only colleague, or friend, as he had just been called, was dead. He had to get his head sorted. If Sorokin was dead, he would have to do the rest himself. Get the documents, take over the company and enjoy whatever money could buy.

A message came through, with a picture of three identical pieces of paper. It was only the top bit, but that was all he needed to see. Red Haven Corporation. Sorokin had got so close, after decades of searching for these three pieces of paper. And now he was dead.

Dmitri filled the other champagne glass and downed it in one go.

In a way it was easier this way. They had never talked about how to split the money. Dmitri had expected half, but thought Sorokin might have wanted a bigger share. If for no other reason than to reaffirm his seniority.

Dmitri got up. It was time to change the dressings again. Then he would sit down and figure out how it all would work.

Richest man in the world. Dmitri smiled to himself. He could get used to that. It was his turn, after all. He deserved this.

38

OUTSIDE MENTON, FRANCE

RORY DROVE up to the house, and parked in the shade of a plane tree. She sat for a while, couldn't get her hands to let go of the wheel. She had to pull herself together, at least when Sasha saw her.

She looked at herself in the rear view mirror. Bloodshot eyes, a bruise on one cheek. Dark red and purple finger marks on her neck. She'd bought new clothes on the way. Typical tourist stuff. A football shirt, a cheap Chinese copy of the blue Italian national team shirt, over denim shorts.

Priya came around the corner with secateurs in her hands, her curly hair tied up revealing sunburnt shoulders over a strapless dress.

'She's here!' Priya shouted to someone around the corner.

Rory grabbed Sorokin's phone and the plastic bag and got out of the car.

'Someone's travelling in style?' Priya said, but when she got close enough to see the state of her friend she stopped and put a hand in front of her mouth.

'Yeah. It's a long story.' Rory looked towards the house. 'Where is Sasha?'

'He's inside, playing chess.'

'So, who were you talking to just now?'

'My brother, of course. You could have told me who your client was, Rory. I remember meeting Sasha when he came to see her when we were at school. Are you sure it wouldn't be better to get the police involved in this one?'

'Sorry.' Rory said and went over to hug her friend. The familiar smell of her friend's hair brought tears to her eyes, but she blinked them away before Priya could see them.

'Tom's inside, playing chess with Sasha.'

'Ah. That makes sense.' The relief flooded through her. Tom and the boy were fine. One thing less to worry about.

Rory realised she kept touching her own neck, as if she had to make sure it was still there, still intact.

'Rory!' A familiar voice stopped her.

'Hi Shawn,' Rory said to the man who had just come around the corner.

He was barefoot, with a bright yellow shirt above his khaki shorts. As Rory leaned in for a hug, Shawn picked her up off the ground, and swirled her around. Like he had done every time they had met since she first became friends with his little sister. Rory winced as he put her down again.

'What's happened to you? Who did this?' Shawn's thumb touched her neck as he gently put her hair to the side.

Rory turned towards the door. 'Not now, Shawn. I need to talk to Sasha. And Tom.'

Rory left brother and sister standing there. They were the closest she had to family, apart from her dad. And they'd embraced Tom when she'd first introduced him to them. So much so that Shawn and Tom had become best friends and sailing buddies.

Rory looked at herself in the hallway mirror. She could make out every finger of Sorokin's hand. And she could still feel them. She found a silk scarf on the coat rack and tied it around her neck. It looked odd on top of the football shirt, but she didn't want to frighten the boy. Then she opened the door to the living room.

Music, their music, was playing on the stereo. It was a Kairos 4tet concert they had gone to on their first real date at the Soho Pizza Express jazz club. The simple, elegant piano intro of *Ell's Bells* followed by the male vocals brought back memories of lazy Sunday mornings in bed, together. Talking, making love, just being. But all she could feel was Sorokin's hand on her neck, and for a second she struggled to breathe.

Sasha and Tom were both immersed in their game, but Tom looked up when he heard the door shut behind her. Rory nodded to him, and gave a faint smile, but didn't make eye contact. She wasn't ready to deal with seeing him yet.

'Hi Sasha, who's winning?' she asked in Russian.

The boy turned to her with a smile. 'I am. For the first time!' he replied. The boy got up and ran over to Rory, who met him with open arms.

'It's good to see you so happy,' she said and gave him a good hug, even though the pain shot through her neck and into her back. 'And there is another reason to be happy today. Your sister got out of hospital, and my police friend tells me they have found a nice, safe house where you and she can stay,' Rory said as they both sat down on the sofa.

'Does she know I'm safe? Can I talk to her?'

'Soon, Sasha. And yes, she knows you're safe. Do you want to see how she's doing?'

Rory showed him the Instagram account with all the cats, and pointed out which one was illustrating Masha's situation. It was Glass's own cat, a big fat ginger tomcat, in different poses. First it was flat on the ground, eyes closed. Then it was on its side, one eye open. The next picture had the cat sprawled on the sofa, with a finger scratching it under the chin. The last picture showed the cat awake, alert, with a hand lying across it's back.

'There's a new picture that was just posted. Here.'

The cat was outside now, sitting in the sun.

'Classy,' Sasha said.

'Who's having dinner?' Priya shouted from the kitchen.

Sasha got up and disappeared towards the smell of food, leaving Tom and Rory alone in the room.

'How are you, Rory?' Tom came over, and lifted an arm, as if wanting to hug her.

Rory looked at the floor, at a small ant which had made his way inside. 'I'm fine,' she started. Then she exhaled. 'Who am I kidding. I'm not fine. I'm in way over my head. I've made a complete mess of things and people are dying because of it.'

'It sounds more like people are alive, because of what you've done.'

The voice from the kitchen rose again. 'Food is getting cold, guys!' Priya was serious about her cooking.

Rory and Tom joined the others at the big kitchen table. They kept the conversation going talking about the things Sasha had been up to. Tom and Shawn had taken him sailing, in a small dinghy, and they'd capsized twice. Sasha's English wasn't great, but good enough to follow the conversation. Rory knew the others were dying to quiz her about what had happened, and what would have to happen next. Tom kept looking at her neck. And at her hands. Rory was doing her best not to think about how close she had got to never seeing her friends again.

————

AFTER THE MEAL Priya took the boy to bed. He was a bit old for bedtime stories, but seemed to love the extra attention. And Priya's posh accent was just right for reading Harry Potter. Shawn cleaned up after dinner, leaving Rory and Tom at the kitchen table.

'Did you get it?'

'Yes. I got it.'

'What happened?'

Rory looked at her fingers. It seemed like Sorokin's blood was still stuck under her cuticles. She picked at a nail, trying to scratch it out.

Tom reached out for her and held her hand in his. 'Want to start from the beginning or the end?'

'I killed him, Tom. I killed a man.'

'Not before he tried to kill you, by the look of it.'

'True. But. I'm still responsible for his death.' Rory looked at her fingers again, and told the whole story of what had happened in the wine cellar. Tom just listened, not betraying any reaction he might have to what she was saying. Her cheeks were wet with tears at the end of it.

'Does his death make it more or less likely that Sasha's dad will be okay?'

'More, I think. Yes. A lot more likely.'

'Then you should put those other thoughts aside and focus on what you need to do to find Pavel again.'

'I know where he is. The other guy, Dmitri, has him. On a yacht somewhere in the Caribbean.'

'Did Sorokin tell you this before he died?'

'No. But I took his phone. And his thumb, so I will be able to unlock it.'

Tom looked at her, aghast. 'You've got his thumb with you?'

A glass crashed onto the worktop behind them and she jumped a mile. Shawn mumbled a 'Sorry, damn slippery those glasses.'

Rory frowned. 'Yes. I didn't want to risk getting a smudged print, so I cut it off with a steak knife. And then I called Dmitri.'

Tom looked at her, waiting.

'He said I've got 48 hours to bring him the documents,

and he will let Pavel go. If I don't, he'll kill Pavel and hunt me down and get the documents anyway.'

She paused. 'There's a flight this evening, from Nice. '

Priya had come back into the kitchen and had heard the last bit of conversation. Rory knew what they both would say. Call the police, leave it up to the professionals. But she knew that if she did, Pavel would die. She looked at Tom, hoping for some advice, and for him to tell her that she was doing the right thing.

'You can't let her go through with this, Tom. You've got to stop this, now, ' Priya said.

But Tom looked at Rory. 'You're the only one who can help Pavel right now. But I won't let you do it alone. I'm going with you.'

Rory looked at him. 'I can't let you do that, this isn't your …' she started, but stopped as Tom had already got up.

'Let's go. I'll just grab a few things, and we can buy tickets on the way to the airport. Shawn, don't drown the kid, will you?' Tom disappeared out of the room.

Priya looked both disappointed and relieved. 'You're both mad,' she said as she hugged Rory, not wanting to let her go. 'Completely bonkers. Promise me you'll come back.'

Rory loosened her friend's arms. 'If you don't hear from us within the next couple of days, call Glass. She's working at Islington Police station now. I don't know what sort of protection Masha has, but Glass will be able to put Sasha in touch with her. But only if you don't hear from me, okay? For now, he's safer here.'

THERE WAS BLOOD EVERYWHERE. Her hair and face was covered in it. Blood, or wine. She licked her lips, and wasn't sure what the taste was. Her white shirt had turned crimson, and the dark puddle on the floor was growing. She tried to wipe her hands on her skirt, or was she trying to steady her hands, to stop them from shaking? The smell of damp, and fermenting wine was tickling her nose. She wanted to run away, but was stuck. Couldn't move. What was holding her back? Who? She felt a warm hand close over hers, gripping hers. A big hand, giant, even. Was it leading her away?

'Rory, Rory,' the voice said.

She wanted to turn around, so see who it was, but it was all dark behind her.

'Rory. You need to raise your seat back. We're landing,' said the voice again.

Tom. It was Tom. The feeling of panic disappeared, like when on an early spring day the warm sun reappears after having been obscured by a cloud. She tried to open her eyes, they seemed glued together, and when she finally did manage to open them, it felt like her eyeballs had been rubbed with sandpaper.

'Here, have some water,' Tom said again. 'How are you feeling?'

Rory took a sip of the bottle he'd offered her, and looked at him.

'Tom.' Rory looked at him; it was a long time since they had been this close to one another.

'Yes. It's me. The same man who sat next to you when you fell asleep. You've been out the entire flight. Both flights.' Tom reached into the seat pocket in front of her and gave her a squishy roll wrapped in plastic. 'You missed breakfast.'

'Thanks?' She tore open the plastic and set her teeth into the spongy bread. She'd tasted far worse.

———

Rory didn't know what to expect when they landed. She had used the passport Simon, the CIA man, had given her in Moscow, and was sure he'd be alerted when they'd bought the tickets. Would Simon whisk her away off the plane before the other passengers? Would she be escorted by armed police, like a terrorist? Or maybe he hadn't been tracking the passport he gave her after all. Tom looked at her.

'You've got that look on your face. That 'I've been think-ing' look. The 'What if' look.' Tom paused, starting and stop-ping a few times, before he looked away from her. 'He'll be here, but you won't know it until he wants you to. Okay?'

'Yeah, you said. Just don't give me another of those 'he's not your friend' lectures, will you? I know that.' Rory bit the inside of her lips. She felt annoyed at herself for snapping at him like that. It wasn't like she and Tom were together any more. They hadn't been a couple, not really, since before his last tour of Syria. But she still felt a pang of guilt about what had happened with Simon. How she had felt. His hands on her skin. Then the plane hit the tarmac with a thump.

———

TOM DIDN'T EVEN LOOK at her when he put her bag on the seat he'd vacated. But he did let her get off the flight first. The heat embraced her as she walked down the stairs to the tarmac, and she was glad for the cap Tom had insisted on bringing for her. No police anywhere. No suspicious looking men in suits, with guns hidden under overcoats. But then it was the US Virgin islands, and summer. Tom walked next to her; she couldn't see if he was scanning the airfield and the terminal building or not, but was sure he was. They got to passport control, and the crowds from their plane seemed to be dwindling. Where she had expected long queues, they were met by a row of manned counters, with passport agents waiting. Her pulse jumped a little. She thought she'd had time to prepare, to go through her keep calm routine, before it was her turn to cross a border with a fake passport. Rory went to a male agent, and Tom followed her.

'One at a time, please. Stand behind the line, Sir.'

'We're travelling together,' Tom declared and put his own passport on the counter. The man scanned Rory's passport and his eyes were focused on the screen for a bit too long. He was reading something.

'Travelling together, you said?' the agent asked and looked at Tom's passport. He scanned both and typed something on the keyboard. 'Welcome to the Virgin Islands, Ma'am. And Sir.'

They walked through the baggage claim area, and through customs. Nothing. No one. Rory was about to turn to Tom and ask what they should do when she noticed a sign with her fake name on it. A guy in shorts and sunglasses stood there holding it, and gave her a little smile when he spotted her. Then his eyes fell on Tom next to her. The smile stiffened, but the man regained his composure and came towards them.

'Ms. Thompson. And Mr. Stanton? This way please.'

———

THE MAN LED them through the staff only doors and down-stairs to the basement. Rory got the chills; she was dressed for Caribbean summer, not this. Tom got a jacket out of his bag and put it over her shoulders.

She found it difficult to be around him now. Didn't know quite how to act, what Rory she should be. Rory the profes-sional was tough, blunt and to the point. She didn't waste time with pleasantries. But private Rory had softer edges. She quite enjoyed being looked after, being taken care of. It couldn't be any easier for him. They hadn't worked together since they hooked up in Russia, it wouldn't have been profes-sional. Or practical.

They walked through the dimly lit corridor and arrived at a hallway with several rooms going off it.

'Rory! So good to see you, I really appreciate you coming over here.' Simon stood at the door to one of the rooms. There wasn't much in it. Just a table, some chairs and a few elec-trical outlets.

'Hello, Simon.' She smiled, but tried to stay formal. 'This is Tom, my colleague.'

'Colleague? I thought you worked alone?' Simon did a quick assessment of his counterpart. 'Good to meet you, Tom. How was Syria?'

Tom took the hand and the two men gave each other a firm handshake. A very firm handshake. 'Good to meet you too, sir.'

Rory wasn't interested in wasting any time on a macho standoff. 'I don't know how well you are acquainted with the current scenario, Simon?'

'Not much. You're not the easiest person to track at the best of times. We lost you in Calais. I trust the boy is well?'

'Yes. He's fine.'

'And Sorokin is … gone?'

'Yes.'

Simon looked at her, waiting for more details, but when he got none he went to pick up a briefcase from the table in the corner.

'So, we've been trying to find Dmitri and think we got a sighting of him at a private airfield outside Caracas. There were a few private yachts moored up nearby, but we haven't been able to determine if he got on one of them or if he's still in mainland Venezuela.'

'I talked to him. Yesterday. He's at sea.' Rory was about to say more, but Tom's words kept spinning in her head. He is not your friend.

'You talked to him. To Dmitri?' Simon's mouth stayed open.

'Yes, I talked to him. He's got Pavel still. I'm here to trade the documents for him.'

'So you've got his phone number?'

'I have a means of contacting him.'

Rory could feel the contours of Sorokin's phone inside the belt on her trousers.

Simon looked like he was ready to pounce on her. 'What are you waiting for, we could track that right now. I can have a team take him out in the next hour, they're on standby already …'

'But how am I going to get Pavel out first?'

'Pavel? Out first? I'm not sure I follow you.'

'You can't send a team of commandos on board without having got Pavel away first. Dmitri will use him as a hostage.'

'I'm sure your friend here can explain to you how we sometimes need to make decisions like these. That by risking one man's life, we could save a lot of others. It's not a decision taken lightly, but there is no time to dwell on it. It is a responsibility that follows the kind of work that we do.

Dmitri is one of the most lethal assassins there are. And he has been for over two decades. It's time to stop him.'

Rory wasn't sure at what stage she had stopped listening. Or at least stopped paying attention. They had no intention of helping her rescue Pavel. They just wanted Dmitri. Dead or alive. Preferably alive, so they could interrogate the shit out of him. After what Dmitri had done to Pavel, it wasn't like he didn't deserve it. But she couldn't let them sacrifice Pavel to get Dmitri.

'I know this might be a very hard thing to do. I understand, believe you me.'

'What do you mean? Because I'm a woman? Women being predisposed to caring, not killing?

'I just meant that,' Simon paused, held his breath and then let it out again. 'It's just that you haven't exactly been in a position where you've had to make this kind of decision before. '

Rory cut him off. 'So you've done your little analysis of what kind of person I am? Well, who am I then? What pigeon hole have you stuffed me in?

Rory could see that Simon was trying to keep his cool, whilst she was clearly losing hers. Damn it. This guy was trying to get her to help with something that would get Pavel killed. And he was pinning her reluctance to do so on her being a woman?

Simon tried to say something, but she stopped him.

'The one for women you think can be convinced that it's all for the best, just leave it up to the professionals? The one for women who don't have jobs, they have 'hobbies'? You could at least show me the courtesy of acknowledging that you are asking me to deliberately fail my assignment, asking me to sign the death warrant of the man I am supposed to save. Save the misogyny and patronising …' Rory didn't get further. Tom had reached out to her, put a hand on her arm. She kept staring at Simon. He was clenching his jaws, but took the opportunity he had been offered.

'I'm sorry, I really am. I didn't mean for things to come across in that way. I have the utmost respect for you, and the work you do.' He paused, 'We never could have got this close without you. And if you want to know, we haven't stuffed you in any pigeon hole. We didn't have one that would fit your, uh, skillset. And I say that in a respectful way. Now. I will have to call my boss to explain the situation.' He left the room reaching out for the phone he'd left in the tray outside.

Tom and Rory looked at each other. She was about to open her mouth when he gestured to the light fitting.

'I know the room is under surveillance, Tom. I might've lost my temper, but I haven't lost my mind. I can't believe he'd try something like this.'

Coming back in, Simon looked like he might have had a scolding from his superiors for failing to get her onboard.

'Okay, we're going to let you run with this, for now. I assume you have a plan for how to do this swap?' Simon flared his nostrils as Rory nodded. 'We'll be on standby if you need any backup. But we're only holding back till tomorrow. That's all the time I could get you. Then we're going after him, wherever he might be, with or without your information. Can you live with that?'

Rory looked at Tom.

'It's your call,' Tom said. 'You're the one who knows how you want to play this.'

Tomorrow. Another deadline. It was the same deadline though, she only had twenty four hours left before Dmitri was going to kill Pavel anyway.

'Yes, I can live with that. And I can trust you to respect that, right?'

'Yes, of course,' Simon said. 'We're not the bad guys here. We want the same as you. If there is a chance of you getting Pavel out first, then go for it. But if we get any indication that you will fail, and Dmitri might get away, we're not holding back. And in twenty four hours, we take over.'

Rory stomped out of the room and Tom followed close behind.

'Oh, I almost forgot,' Simon said as Rory and Tom had reached the end of the corridor. 'There's a contract out for you, Rory. Some Russian put it out yesterday. One of Sorokin's friends, Volkov. Another one of the ex-KGB parliamentarians. Just thought you should know. Nothing you and your friend can't handle, I'm sure.'

Then the door closed between them.

Rory walked away as in a trance.

A contract. On her. Put out by Volkov. Mr Wolf.

40

OFF THE COAST OF ANGUILLA

DMITRI COULD HEAR the helicopter before he saw it. It came straight for the yacht and Dmitri went below deck to get his submachine gun. Then he ran up to the captain.

'What's going on? Who are they and why are you letting them land? Get them away.'

'Sir, I don't think that would be a good idea. You might want to talk to this man.' The captain looked from Dmitri to the gun in his hands and back again. 'Sir, I …'

Dmitri ignored him and went back outside and looked down at the helicopter deck. The man who climbed out of the helicopter was the same age as Sorokin. White hair and a very expensive suit. Volkov. The grey wolf. He walked with a confidence one would get from being used to having people obey him. He looked up towards Dmitri and pretended not to notice the submachine gun.

'Mr. Voznesensky. It's a pleasure to finally meet you,' he said as he took the steps two at a time and walked across the sun deck with his hand stretched out.

'That's close enough. Who are you?'

The man let his hand fall and looked around him. 'I think you know who I am. I'm your boss' closest associate. Or should I say your late boss'?' The man tilted his head. 'I am sorry for your loss. I understand you had known Andrei Mikhailovich for a very long time.'

Dmitri backed up against the glass doors as Volkov sat down in one of the reclining chairs. He reached for the champagne bottle and looked at the label. 'Not bad, this one. Though I dare say it's getting a little too warm in the sun. You should ask the maid to get you another one.'

'You're Volkov.' Dmitri spat the words out.

'Yes. The very one. Mikhail Volkov is my name. I am sorry not to have made your acquaintance before, but Sorokin kept you as his personal secret. Where are the others?'

'What others?'

'I was led to believe that Sorokin's whole team would be here. To reap the rewards of a particular scheme?'

'There's no team.'

'Really? Well I never. Sorokin had me fooled all these years then. Pretended he had a whole team of specially trained assassins ready to take out anyone at any time. But there was only you? You must have kept busy.'

'Why are you here?' Dmitri adjusted the strap on his machine gun so the muzzle pointed straight at his guest. He glanced back at the helicopter; there was only one other person there.

'He's just a pilot. No need to worry about him.' Volkov shuffled in his seat. 'Sorokin seemed to have found some important papers lately. Or at least discovered where these could be found. Papers of national security. You wouldn't happen to know where these are?'

Dmitri pursed his lips. 'National security, you say? No. I wouldn't know anything about that.'

'They're financial papers. And the Kremlin would like to have them. I am sure you wouldn't stand in the way of their recovery?'

'Of course not. You have a presidential order in place, I assume.'

Volkov squirmed in his seat.

What a piece of shit liar.

'Oh, it's not quite as official yet.'

Dmitri couldn't believe the man's nerve. To come to his yacht and make demands. He was minded to put the whole clip through that big mouth of his.

Volkov shifted in his chair again. 'How is your mother doing, by the way? She must have appreciated all the flowers you sent her. I gather her hip operation went well?'

Dmitri felt like he'd been punched in the stomach. His throat was tightening.

Volkov kept talking. 'Sorokin's secretary has been most helpful. She is distraught, poor thing. But she knew all his passwords. Can you imagine? Sorokin really did know how to surround himself with loyal staff.'

Dmitri just stood there. Taking it all in. Volkov had access to Sorokin's computers. His safe. But not his phone. The encrypted phone was in the hands of an unknown female operative. The same woman who had the documents. And Sorokin being who he was, he would never have put all the information on one device. Without the phone Volkov was half blind.

'My mother is as well as can be expected. Under the circumstances. I don't know if she's going to recover though. Surgery was tough for her. As I understand it, she might never wake up again.'

Dmitri hadn't wanted to admit it before. There was a reason he hadn't been able to talk to her when he'd phoned. The woman whose hand he'd held only a few days ago was all but gone. The nurses had tried telling him, but hadn't dared to force the subject.

'Oh, I am sorry.' Volkov looked bewildered. 'I'm sure something can be done for her.'

Dmitri put his hand on the pistol grip. 'You should probably go look for your important papers.'

'Oh, I will. I have lots of people looking for them, actually. But I thought it best to offer you the chance to help find them first.'

'Thank you for the opportunity. Now, I think it's time you leave.'

Volkov walked backwards down the stairs, watching the gun all the way.

'You might regret this. I have contacts to the very top, chief of staff, means at my disposal ...' Volkov tried to look threatening, but Dmitri was the one with forty dum-dum bullets ready to be fired.

'Enjoy your trip.'

41

'WHAT DOES THAT EVEN MEAN? A contract on me alive?' Rory was whispering, or more like hissing, to Tom as they walked through the terminal building. They were walking shoulder to shoulder, winding their way through the groups of bare-legged tourists.

'Let's just try to stay calm. We have some time before anyone but the CIA knows you're here,' Tom said. 'Let's use it, and get the hell out of this place at least. You've got twenty-four hours, and, assuming you haven't acquired a whole bunch of Russian enemies for life, it will all be over by tomorrow evening, when they've got Dmitri.'

'You think I should have let them take Dmitri straight away, don't you? Leave Pavel's life in their hands. Forget about it all, and go home?' Rory burst through the doors, leaving Tom to play catch up.

'No, I didn't say that,' he said, running a few steps to make up the distance.

'But you think so?'

'No, I don't think so either. I agree with Simon that some-times it is right to make that sort of decision. But not before you've tried to get Pavel out alive.'

They were headed towards the taxi rank, but stopped to remain out of earshot of the other travellers. A single palm tree stood near the kerb, its fronds swaying in the gentle breeze. St. Thomas and its airport had taken a beating in the hurricanes that had ravaged the Caribbean the previous year. The buildings had been rebuilt, but the surrounding nature would take much longer to recover. The turquoise waters of Lindbergh Bay stretched out to their right, a few bathers having a morning swim.

Tom looked at her, but she was looking at the sea. 'You and Pavel are the reason why they even know who Dmitri is.'

Rory squinted towards the sun. 'Thanks,' she said, and looked up at him. 'Any ideas how I can do both then, stay alive and get Pavel out? It's not like I can disappear, they will probably know where I'm heading pretty soon.'

'I have some ideas, yes.'

Rory had to smile. Need to know only. And she didn't need to know. Not yet.

———

AT SUNSET RORY and Tom walked down towards the white, sandy beach of Morningstar Bay. Tourists staying at the hotel on Frenchman's Reef above had left the beach for the day, the sun loungers were empty and stacked up, and people had started to reappear in their evening wear.

'Good to go?' Tom looked at her with an encouraging smile.

'Yeah. Good to go,' Rory replied. Then she reassembled the phone she'd taken from Sorokin and got out the tape with his fingerprint on it to unlock it. Tom had made it at Priya's house, and it worked on the first attempt. Easier than carrying the thumb around.

One new message.

Tom looked at her, with what she interpreted as a mix of

concern and admiration. He'd told her, as they walked to the bay, how he always knew she could do most anything. But that she'd still blown him away this time.

Rory opened the message and found a picture of Pavel and a newspaper, with today's date. He looked well. A lot better than he had been just days ago. Rory took the phone apart again and put it in the small waterproof bag with the documents. Then they both stripped down to their newly acquired swimwear.

As the tourists admired the setting sun, with their frozen cocktails and glasses of white wine, the silhouettes of Rory and Tom disappeared into the crystal clear water. There were several yachts tied up just off the shore, bobbing on the waves, and as the darkness of night embraced them, they swam out to a wooden sailboat, no bigger than a dinghy. It felt a bit like the Wayfarer Rory's grandfather had had, though she could barely see anything in the dark.

'Is this safe? To sail in this over open ocean at night?' Rory asked.

'It's better than safe,' Tom said. 'It's untraceable. Even the CIA will have trouble following us in the dark. And we've got the stars to help us.'

Tom managed to climb over the gunwale, and pulled Rory into the boat. Then they rigged the sails.

'There are hardly any navigational lights around in these waters, and people don't usually sail at night around here, so we should be pretty safe as long as we can navigate around the coast. And if we have anyone following us, we'll hear them easily.'

Under other circumstances, Rory would have loved this. Leaving the music and voices from the beach bar behind. The smell of the sea, the waves lapping up the sides of the boat, and only the sound of the wind in the sails and shrouds. But now, all she could do was think about Pavel, and Sasha and Masha who were waiting for news about him. It seemed from the photo that he'd had some medical treatment: he'd held the paper with both hands. She let herself drift off for a while, as Tom took the helm.

———

A BIG CRUISE SHIP, with rows and rows of lights, showed the way into Road Town. The streetlights lit the way up the winding roads of the hillside above the town itself. Light was beginning to appear over the horizon when they moored up near the yacht harbour on the outskirts of the town. They drove past brightly coloured shacks, some with the shop signs still on the street, advertising beach wear, clothes, sunglasses. A retired friend of Tom's had picked them up and brought them clothes, and they arrived in the centre dressed and ready for the day.

They found the office straight away, and ambled past, Tom's arm around her shoulders and hers around his waist. Rory didn't feel like a honeymoon couple, but there was no reason not to pretend and play it safe. If she could delay any positive sighting of her for as long as possible, it would give would-be kidnappers less time to prepare an attack. The Russians, whoever they were, Dmitri or Sorokin's partners, didn't know she was working with someone. She hadn't even known, just twenty-four hours earlier.

The building had a blue facade, and was two stories high. Or was there a third floor, set back from the top? Some green foliage indicated there was. All the windows were tinted, and the entrance door was blacked out as well. Loyola Associates Limited, it said on the door. There were CCTV cameras covering the door from both sides. A wine merchant across the road. The entrance was on the south side, facing other buildings, but it would be visible from the south east. Both from the water and the hillside above. From the west there were buildings in the way. No obvious sniper positions.

Anything you can see, can see you. Tom's mantra was in her head.

They both looked at the tall, office-like building towards the southern tip of the peninsula. It would be the most obvious point for a sniper. The top half of it was visible from the entrance, leaving a lot of possible windows to shoot from.

They finished their recce before daylight, and went to a nearby hotel and blended in with the tourists just waking up for breakfast. On the way, they both made some phone calls.

'Anything?' Rory asked as she sipped at a glass of fresh orange juice.

'Good news or bad news first?' Tom replied.

'Bad first, please.' Rory was trying to stop her knee from trembling.

'There is indeed a contract out. And it's big. Ten million dollars.'

Rory swallowed.

'Okay. And the good news?'

'They want you alive. It is very specific about that.' Tom looked towards the sea. 'This place will be swamped with hitmen as soon as they know you're here.' Tom furrowed his brows as he looked at Rory. 'Sorry. I didn't mean it like that.' He reached for her hand, but she pulled it away.

For a while it felt like it was just the two of them in the busy restaurant. Rory and Tom. And a long silence.

'I think you should leave,' Rory said.

'What do you mean?'

'This isn't what you signed up for. I asked you to help me with a hostage situation. This is different. I can't let you take this risk because of a job I took on. This is my doing, and if it is my undoing, then that's on me. You should go home.'

'You know I'd never do that, right? Leave you here, alone?'

'I know you wouldn't want to. But I also know that you're sensible enough to see that this isn't your battle.'

'Come on, Rory. You're wasting our time. I'm staying. End of.'

This time he didn't let her move her hands away, and held them in both of his as he looked into her eyes. His hands were warm, comforting, and there was a lump in her throat as she muttered a 'Thanks.'

'How did it go at your end?' Tom asked.

'You mean Sam? She's going to talk to the Eastern Europe Editor. They worked together in Moscow, so I'm pretty sure they'll let her look into it. They haven't been the lead on the big tax havens stories because of that *New York Times/Guardian* cooperation, so they're keen to get the scoop, if there is one.'

'So that's your insurance in place then. Good. Let's just hope you won't have to use it.'

42

ROAD TOWN, BRITISH VIRGIN ISLANDS

RORY GOT to the door at five minutes past nine. With the tinted windows it was hard to see if there was anyone in there or not, but she thought she could see some movement.

She pulled the door to her and went in. The reception was on the right. A lavish bouquet of fresh lilies stood on the otherwise empty desk, and the only decoration on the back wall was a black and white sailing calendar.

'Good morning, how may I help you?' the smiling face behind the counter said to her. A young man, with expensive tastes, judging by the Fendi leather briefcase next to his chair.

'Good morning, I was hoping to have a meeting with Mr. Loyola?'

'Have you got an appointment?' the man asked, narrowing his eyes.

He couldn't see her Loboutins from where he was sitting, which might explain the less than welcoming attitude.

'No, I'm afraid not. But he's been managing a company for me for a while, there's just a few little things I would like to talk to him about. And I'd rather not discuss these on the phone or by email, if you know what I mean.'

The receptionist was still looking at her, as if expecting more.

'Perhaps you would like to have the company name?' Rory continued. 'I assume this is a safe area? Or is that a mobile phone I see on your desk? You've taken the batteries out, right?'

The questions put the receptionist off balance. He quickly put the phone in a metal drawer. 'I do apologise. We had a few journalists snooping around after the Panama Papers a few years back, so we're still cautious as I'm sure you can understand. I'm afraid this isn't a safe to talk room, madam. If you would like to go into the waiting room, just a second, I'll buzz you in, and someone will come to talk to you there. It's the room on the left,' he said as the buzzer sounded and the door clicked open.

Rory walked into the waiting room, and the door closed behind her. It wasn't what she had expected from a firm that managed companies for the super rich. There was a water cooler and some glasses, but a few of them seemed to have been used already. The bottle was empty, and a stack of new ones were on a rack in the corner.

Rory had to resist her urge to replace the empty bottle with a new one. There was a small camera in the corner opposite the door, and she had no need to make herself stand out any more than necessary. Whoever sat on the other side would now be able to tell anyone where she was. If they knew who she was. And who to tell. The clock was ticking.

A young woman, probably early twenties, maybe even younger, appeared. She wore a black pencil skirt and a not so modest blouse.

'Madam, how can we help you today?'

'As I mentioned to your receptionist, I would like to see Mr Loyola? Regarding a company he's been managing for a while?'

'Yes, unfortunately he is busy all day with meetings. He

doesn't really deal with regular clients any more. Perhaps you could see one of our junior associates, I'm sure they can arrange whatever you need doing.'

'No, I'd rather talk to Mr Loyola himself. He set up the company, so I think it's best I talk to him.'

'Can I ask what the name of the company is?'

'Red Haven.'

The woman opposite her froze, and her eyes dilated. 'Oh.- Won't be a moment.' The woman turned on her heels and left the room.

Rory didn't know what to make of that.

————

'THIS WAY PLEASE,' The woman said as she opened the door to a room much more like what Rory had expected, Loyola's penthouse office. There was indeed a third floor to the building, with a large roof terrace in front. To the right of the door a bottle of champagne was perspiring in a bucket of ice. A large vase was filled with fresh lilies.

'Welcome,' the man in the pinstripe suit said, his arm outstretched and ready to shake her hand. 'Champagne? Or is it too early? We've got some excellent Ceylon tea,' he continued.

'Thank you, Mr. Loyola. Tea would be lovely,' Rory replied. The woman left the room and came back with two cups. Rory let her eyes linger on the younger woman as she left the room again, and made a point of not hiding it.

'Your daughter?'

Loyola twisted in his chair. 'Yes. She's learning the ropes before she goes off to law school in the US.'

'You must be very proud of her, Mr. Loyola.'

'Ricky, call me Ricky, please. Now, how can I help you today, Madam?'

Rory took out the bearer shares. 'I'd like to see how my company is doing, please.'

'Of course. let's just see,' the lawyer said and pulled the papers towards him. He got out a magnifying glass and looked at the different stamps and seals. 'Apologies, need to be on the safe side these days.' Then he typed something on his keyboard, and turned the screen towards her. It was a list of investments, the original ones above the line, and more recent ones below.

'I'm sure you know this, but it was set up to use any dividends to make new investments, in any company over a certain value on the NASDAQ stock exchange. So the list is quite long,' he said and scrolled down, reading out company names, some of which Rory recognised. Others she'd never heard of. But the ones she did recognise were all big technology firms. Intel. Microsoft. Apple. Cisco. Even Facebook was on there. And Alphabet, the new Google company.

Rory was getting fidgety, this was taking too long. But Tom had agreed. She had to know more about the company the bearer shares made her the temporary owner of before she met Dmitri. It was a bizarre situation. She hadn't even heard about bearer shares a week ago. Now she was in possession of the three pieces of paper that made her the owner of a company that had been established to hide Soviet investments in the West.

Loyola clicked on another page. Current market cap. She couldn't believe her eyes. Had to swallow hard, and took an extra breath. Then she counted the digits. Six, seven, eight, nine, ten. At least ten digits. Or were the last two numbers decimals? She looked again. Counted again. Nope. Ten digits. The lawyer was also clearly impressed.

'That's looking even better than I remembered it. I check in once a year, with these self driving investment vehicles. It runs itself, pretty much, but just to make sure.' The company was as old as her, and Loyola was probably racking his brain as to how she came to be in possession of the shares. And Rory, on the other hand, understood why he'd named his daughter after the company. Must have helped pay for his expensive tastes. And his daughter's upcoming law school.

'I would have kept you updated, of course, but we never had a name for this account?' Loyola looked at Rory, tilting his head and smiling, and left the question hanging in the air.

'No, that was the intention,' she replied with a smile.

His smile started to fade.

'However, I was wondering if you could do one more thing for me, before I leave.'

'Of course, madam.'

———

As Rory and Mr. Loyola walked towards the exit, she turned to say goodbye to the receptionist. But he looked away, pretending to look through some papers. His phone was back out of the drawer, and was vibrating on the desk.

'You not going to get that, Carlos? You're playing hard to get, eh?' Loyola winked at the receptionist. The receptionist's hands were trembling now, and he kept glancing at the door to the street. Rory paused for a second, giving the receptionist an opportunity to say something, but he just kept looking at his phone.

He'd sold her out. Or was she getting paranoid?

'Thanks again, Mr. Loyola. I really appreciate you being able to do all this straight away.'

'Not at all. Any time, my dear lady. I'm at your service any time.'

Rory had gone through this next bit time and time again with Tom. If she'd been spotted, if her location had been revealed by someone, the most vulnerable time would be as she left the building. She would have the sun in her eyes, and there might not be anyone or anything else around that she could hide behind. On the positive side, the bright sunshine would also be reflecting off the glass door, so any sniper would pause a fraction of a second before he or she looked at her through the scope. That was the fraction of a second she would have to make the most of.

43

RORY PUSHED the door open and leapt into the street, knowing that any cars around would be approaching the corner of the road slowly. A local cab driver still had to step on the brakes, and gesticulated at her. There were only a few other people in the street; a middle aged couple in matching breton shirts came from the marina, a woman was sweeping the pavement outside the wine shop opposite the lawyer's offices and a guy from the garage was having a smoke.

As Rory walked towards the marina, where the speedboat was waiting, she knew she was out of sight of the tall office building to her south. She'd be visible, and an easy shot, from the hillside both in front of her and behind her, but Tom had rejected those options as sniper terrain. There was no knowing she'd cross the road and be in sight from either side. The next time she'd be in view from the tower would be as she turned left on the next corner.

They'd hired a twin engine speed boat for the day. It had taken a large chunk out of Rory's dollar stack, but at least they knew there wouldn't be many faster boats on the island.

Rory had a quick look at her watch. It was 11am. They still had three hours to get Pavel out. All she had to do now was to get to the swap, trade the papers for Pavel. And stay alive for long enough for Sam to do her bit at the FT newsroom. Then this would all be over.

She could hear a car approaching from the back, it was slowing down next to her. She used the windows on the wine shop to check it out. A maroon sedan of some sort. Probably a rental. It had the steering wheel on the left, like in the UK, so it must be a British brand. Vauxhall maybe. There was nothing else obvious about it. The two men inside seemed to be heading for the garage. Which was a bit odd, if it was indeed a rental. The car pulled onto the pavement twenty metres ahead of her, as if driving onto the ramp, and the mechanic came out to talk to the driver. They all looked at her.

Rory wanted to walk away, to turn around and run, but maybe they were just staring because she was a lone female wearing a skirt. It wouldn't be the first time. She kept walking, aiming to look oblivious to the attention she was about to get. The car had its back wheels in the road, so she would have to walk on the inside of it. She considered taking her sunglasses off; it was dark inside the car shop. But before her left hand had reached her glasses, someone grabbed her arm and dragged her into the garage. She screamed, but the sound was muffled by revving of a muscle car that was on the rollers now above her. The man had pushed her front first against the side wall, and proceeded to put a cloth over her mouth. She instinctively inhaled, to fill her lungs with air, but stopped. Petrol. And chloroform.

She slowed her breath, knowing that it would take up to a minute for it to knock her out even if she was inhaling it, and tried to see if there was more than one attacker. There'd have to be, she had seen at least two in the car. But all she could see was darkness. She could feel the body of the man pressing her against the wall.

Probably six foot, maybe a bit less. Lots of bulk, but not

too much muscle. Professional at something, but not at kidnapping. She could feel his right leg between hers, and decided to go for it. She forced her right stiletto heel onto where his foot must be, and put all her weight on it. The man's scream mixed with the engine sound from above. The petrol stained cloth, and the pungent scent of the chloroform disappeared from her face and her hands were free. As she turned around, she used her stiletto for the second time, and whacked her heel on her attacker's head as he knelt behind her, clutching his foot.

She was right. He wasn't alone.

The two guys from the car were standing in between her and the street. They looked at the guy on the ground, but he wasn't moving. Then they looked back at her.

Rory had lost her right shoe when she knocked the first guy out, and kicked the left one away from her. The floor had puddles of engine oil, and it stuck to the soles of her bare feet. One down, two to go. Her gun was in the handbag lying just inside the frame of the metal shutters. She decided to ignore it. There was no chance she could get to it first, and she would prefer if they didn't have a closer look at the papers in there either.

The driver of the maroon car came towards her.

'We can do this the easy way, or the hard way.' He was fiddling with a spring-loaded knife in his left hand. 'You can either get in the car on your own, or...' He nodded to his knife. He sounded American, from a Southern state.

'You wouldn't kill me, you need me alive,' Rory replied.

'Alive, yeah. But no saying for how long you'd need to stay alive.'

'And why would I get into the car voluntarily if you're just going to kill me later anyway?' she said, hoping that Tom would come to her rescue.

'Pain, sweetheart. Pain. It comes in different levels. Right now our friend there ain't feeling it. But he will when he wakes up. And he's not going to be too friendly with you then, so maybe we should just go now, and you won't have to face that?'

Rory looked from the talking man to the other one. It was the passenger she was most worried about. The glint in his eyes made her think he'd enjoy whatever came next. He had that unhealthy look skinny people sometimes get. And was the bulk in his jacket a beer belly or was there a gun there?

Where was Tom? Rory had taken far too long to get to the corner, he must know that she was in trouble by now.

'Drop the shutters,' the driver said and took another step towards Rory. The clanging sound as the shutters rolled down reverberated through the space. She noticed a shade ducking under the shutters before they hit the tarmac, but it disappeared as the lights flickered on above them.

Both men moved towards her, and Rory noticed the gold teeth in the skinny guy's lower jaw. The tattoos winding their way up his neck, trying to escape from his grey t-shirt. He had a wheel wrench in his right hand, and slammed it into the car lift. The sound clanged around the shop, making Rory jump.

The two men smirked.

'Her beginner's luck has run out. Might as well let the boss know we've got her.' The driver gave a little chuckle. 'In case we need to get her to the drop before she bleeds out.'

The driver still had the knife in his hand, but Rory was focused on the passenger. He lunged towards her, making her jump back, knocking over the oil drip pan next to her. He smiled as she slipped and almost fell on the oily floor. She couldn't go backwards, the wall was just a metre away. The driver blocked any escape to the side.

The passenger threw a few punches in the air between them first. Playing with her. Then he threw a left jab that clipped her cheek, and followed it with a right hand punch headed straight for her nose.

All his force was in that one fist. The knockout punch.

Rory instinctively lifted her right elbow up to protect her face and put her hand on her neck. His fist only grazed her elbow, but hard enough to throw her off balance. She shot forward, closing the gap between them, putting her raised elbow between his head and his shoulder.

Before he could get his left arm around her, she'd given him two quick jabs in the kidney.

He let out a groan. That hurt. But not enough.

The driver was coming to his aid. The passenger grabbed hold of her with his right arm, and when his left arm followed to lock the grip, she bit his underarm as hard as she could. She could taste the metallic, warm liquid as she pierced the skin, and her assailant pushed her away.

'Fucking bitch, she's a bloody vampire that cunt. Give me the knife, Carter, give me the knife!' he yelled to the driver.

They were both coming for her now. Rory tried to dive in between them, but Carter, the driver, got hold of her, and before she'd had time to think he had her in a headlock. Her head was under his right arm, and his left hand held onto his right wrist. She could feel the pressure on her neck. They both wobbled a bit on the oily floor. If they both fell like this, she'd break her neck. No doubt about it.

Carter was laughing now. 'Look what I've got!'

The passenger was laughing too. Then he kicked her in the side. She had only had an instant to prepare, but had flexed her core muscles to avoid the worst of the effect. It still hurt like hell.

She was completely at their mercy like this.

They knew it.

She knew it.

But what they didn't know was that she had practiced this, and hundreds of other scenarios, so many times that her muscles were ready to act even before her brain had sent the signals. Rory twisted her head to the right, towards Carter's body, to relieve the pressure on her neck. Then she grabbed onto his left arm, took a step to the side, and got her right leg behind his left, and swung around. They both landed on the floor, Rory on top of Carter, who was still holding on to her neck with both arms.

She could feel the strain on her neck, the muscles working as hard as they could to stop anything tearing. She put her left arm on Carter's exposed neck and tried to shift her weight onto it, to get him to let go of her head. But he wouldn't.

She took another kick to the side. The passenger was grabbing her legs, then let go again.

Her feet slipped on the oil as she made another attempt, her forehead rubbing against the coarse floor as she tried to shift her weight. The man was too heavy, and she was too light.

And the other one will get me while I'm here on the floor, struggling.

There was a clanging sound behind her, metal hitting the legs of the car ramp, a gun going off.

'Hang in there, Rory!'

Tom's voice.

Then her feet found a patch of floor with no oil on it. Her toes were scraping against the ground as she forced her body forward, upwards, then sideways, towards Carter's neck. Her arm landed exactly where she wanted it to. Right on his windpipe, and with all her weight on it. His grip started to loosen, and she managed to twist her head enough to see Tom fighting it out with the passenger. The grip loosened even more, and she did a final push down with her right arm, hearing a crack as Carter let out a wheezing gasp for air. Kneeling on all four, above the limp body, her ears were ringing as she caught her breath.

'Rory, are you ok? Let me help you get up,' Tom said behind her.

'I'm ok. Just need to find my feet.' Rory sat back on her legs for a second, and took Tom's hand to steady her when she got up.

'The other two?' she asked, rubbing her sore neck and shoulders.

'Out. For now. The guy you got first had his phone out though.'

'They were going to call their boss.'

'Ah. Won't be long till he sends reinforcements then. Let's go. Can you walk?'

'Yeah, I think so.' Rory stepped over the men on the ground, and grabbed her bag. She had a pair of trainers in it, rubber soled and much better suited for being on a boat than her heels had been. A thin cardigan covered the marks on her arms and the black top.

Tom gave her a damp cloth. It reeked of oil. Rory frowned.

'Just to get the worst blood and dirt off your face,' he said and grabbed a jacket that was on a hook on the wall.

Then he stopped in front of her again. 'You missed a bit,' he said, and wiped the corner of her mouth with his thumb. It came off bright red. 'Took a good chunk out there, didn't you?'

Rory wanted to sit down, recover, and get her head around things, but there was no time.

Could she take any more of this?

44

BACK OUT IN the blazing sun, Tom led the way. She took a quick look in both directions, but didn't spot anything out of the ordinary. Then she caught up with Tom.

'Not too fast, there might be others around,' he said, and held an arm out to keep her behind him.

The road curved to the left, around a boat storage facility. Once they'd reached the corner, they would be back in the open, visible from the building they'd dubbed sniper tower. Rory's pulse was still racing, she tried to slow it down by regulating her breathing, but failed.

'I don't like this, this doesn't feel right, Rory. Let's go back to the car shop,' Tom said.

'Back and do what? We're 150 metres away from the boat. That's less than 30 seconds out in the open,' Rory replied.

'No, we're going back,' Tom said.

As they turned around, they got a stiff smile and a shake of the head as they almost bumped into the middle aged couple dressed in breton, now carrying what looked like a paper bag from a local bakery.

'Sorry,' Rory said as she walked around them.

'It's not that I don't trust your judgment, Tom. But I'm

running out of time. If there's a sniper, he or she is probably not working with the guys back there, so won't know when we're coming. I've got to get to Pavel in time, or this was all in vain,' she said.

Tom ran back to the garage and jumped into the driver's seat of the sedan. He wrung it around and stopped next to Rory, and she reached for the passenger side door.

'Get into the back, Rory. Flat on the floor.'

Tom drove the car around the corner, and a single bullet crashed through the driver side window, clipped Tom's neck and disappeared into the rear seat. Tom spun around and reversed towards the marina buildings and the big boat storage hangar.

Another bullet hit the car, shattering the rear window before it hit the back of the passenger seat.

Where Rory had intended to sit.

Tom reversed across some flowerbeds and found a narrow gap that led to the seaside, where they'd be out of sight from the tower.

Wide-eyed marina staff stared at them as Rory and Tom leapt from the car. They ran down the wooden ramp to the pontoon and Rory untied the speed boat from its moorings whilst Tom started up the engine. The twin engines roared, then Tom backed out and towards the sea. Rory sat on the floor at first, out of sight, but got up in time to see blue lights from a police car headed for the peninsula.

'That bullet was meant for me,' she said and touched Tom's neck. Her fingers were smeared with blood.

'Yes, but it wasn't you who fired it. It's just a graze, I've had worse.' Tom reached for her hand. 'Time to strap in,' he said.

The boat had special seats to protect them from the shock of hitting waves at high speed, and as soon as Rory had buckled up, Tom gave it full throttle. They raced out of the bay, past the cruise ships and a ferry that had just left the city.

They were headed straight for Peter Island, and it felt like the boat was flying, the engines' roars sending it into flight. As they crossed the waves from an earlier ferry, the boat really did fly: for what felt like several seconds it was suspended in the air, before it hit the water again. The seats absorbed some of the shock, but Rory grabbed onto the armrests.

'I'd like to get there in one piece, Tom.'

'Sorry. Just keen to get as much distance between us and the last known sighting.'

As they reached the far side of Peter Island, the southern-most tip, Rory looked around.

'He's not here. He said he would be here, with Pavel. There's less than an hour left.'

They went closer to the southern side of the private island, trying to see if the superyacht might be moored close to the shores. But there was no boat big enough to be the one Dmitri had mentioned.

'You can literally see over to US territory from here,' Tom said. 'I'm sure he just wanted a bit more distance between himself and your American friends.'

Rory reached for the phone again.

45

'THERE! That's it. Must be it,' Rory said.

The large, grey yacht cut through the waves, white foam in its wake.

'It looks smaller than I'd thought,' she said to Tom.

'That's because we're still far away. You see that boat on the lower deck? I bet that's as big as the one we're in. Which is good, because you don't want him seeing us yet.'

Rory got the wetsuit ready, and started pulling it up her legs. It was on the small side, the closest size she'd found, so she had to work hard to get it over her hips. It was a shorty suit, with elbow length arms and mid-thigh legs. She didn't want to make Dmitri worry about her being armed.

'Are you sure you want to do this?' Tom asked her.

Again.

She looked at him, eyebrows raised.

'It's just. You could reach out to the Americans, and they'll have a team of Navy SEALs here in less than half an hour. Or I could come with you.'

'You know as well as I do that escalating this situation is not in anyone's interest. Not mine, not Pavel's. Everything Dmitri has done so far has made sense. Common sense. I think there's a good chance that this trade will go just as we've agreed.'

'But,' Tom tried.

'But if it doesn't, then there's always plan B,' she said, grabbing the plastic folder from her bag. She put it in the sailing bag and sealed it up. Apart from the papers, she didn't bring anything. No gun, no knives. No exploding watch or pens with poison darts.

Rory wasn't sure what the common sense scenario was any more. But she did know that getting on a paddleboard with possibly the most valuable pieces of paper in the world in a bag, ready to trade them for a man she'd barely met, wasn't it. She paddled on along the shore for a bit, then out towards the massive yacht. As she got closer, she saw the silhouette of a man coming out from the top deck. He looked at her through binoculars at first. It must have looked odd from the shore, but Rory slowly turned around on the paddleboard, trying not to capsize. To demonstrate that she wasn't carrying. She got back up on the board and waited. The man disappeared from sight. Rory wanted to get closer, but Tom had convinced her that it was better if she kept her distance until she had seen Pavel alive. There was no point in risking her life for a man who was already dead. The silhouette reappeared, and pulled another one along with him. The second man was limping a little, but seemed otherwise fine. Rory paddled over the last stretch, her bad shoulder beginning to feel the strain, and grabbed onto the ladder at the back of the yacht. With the bag over her shoulder she climbed up to the gunwale and onto the lower deck.

There was not a soul in sight. A yacht this size would normally have a big crew, but it looked deserted. She climbed up the stairs to the middle deck, then onto the top one. As she got to the top deck, she could feel Tom watching her from far away. Rory stood there, next to a covered up jacuzzi, waiting for a minute, then there was movement from inside.

'Over here,' Dmitri said in Russian.

Rory walked into the opulent living room. The comforting feeling of knowing Tom could see her disappeared. A huge, white leather sofa half circled a glass table with flowers that could do with some fresh water. In front of the sofa there was floor to ceiling glass, giving the impression that she could step right into the endless sea at the other side of the glass. On the right was a pair of hand carved ivory tusks, with a buddha in various poses. To the left was Dmitri. And Pavel. They were both looking at her as she took in the surroundings. Pavel had his thumbs tied together with a cable tie, and was sitting down on a chair. He looked at her, as if searching for any sign that she had managed to get his children to safety. Rory gave a slight nod, that she hoped Dmitri would just see as a nervous tic. Dmitri stood behind Pavel, out of sight from the outside, a gun in his right hand and probably one on his left ankle, judging by the slight lump in his trousers, just above his shoe.

'Have you got the papers?' Dmitri demanded.

Rory took the waterproof bag off her shoulder, slowly, and unfolded the top. The folder was still dry. She took the documents out of the folder and held them out in front of her, worried that if she spoke, her voice would betray how scared she was. She walked towards Dmitri, but he pointed to the table with his gun.

'Over there. In front of him,' Dmitri said, nodding to Pavel.

Three sheets was all there was. Three pieces of paper with a decorative border around the edge, signatures in blue ink. Three sheets that gave the owner, or the bearer, the right to claim a fortune beyond belief, a fortune that had multiplied a hundredfold since the original investment in 1991. The investment that was meant to keep the Soviet economy growing with the value of American and other western technology companies. Enough money to put the holder high up on the Forbes billionaires of the world list.

'Read it out,' Dmitri said to Pavel, nudging him with the barrel of the gun. 'Skip the details, though.'

'Red Haven Corporation. This is to certify that the bearer is the owner of ten shares in Red Haven Corporation. It says there are thirty shares in total. It's signed by myself, as president, and the lawyer as the company secretary,' Pavel said with a frown.

'Signed by you?' Dmitri raised his voice a fraction.

'Yes.' Pavel's eyes looked over the bearer shares again, his pupils shifting back and forth. His surprise seemed genuine. 'I can't remember doing it, but Lebedev did get me to sign papers on lots of occasions, as a way of hiding the Soviet government involvement.' Pavel pushed the sheets to the back of the table, where Dmitri could see them.

Rory waited, trying to keep her breathing slow and relaxed.

'I've kept my part of the bargain. Now if you don't mind, I'll take what I came for,' she said and walked towards Pavel. Pavel leant forward, to try to get up, but the hand with the gun pushed him down again.

'Not so fast, little lady.'

46

DMITRI LOOKED at the papers again. He found it difficult to understand that this was all it took. Three pieces of paper. Three bearer shares. And he was now one of the richest men in the world, if Sorokin's estimates had been correct. But Sorokin would never get to experience what unlimited wealth could do. Dmitri looked back at the woman in front of him. Under other circumstances he'd have asked her out for a drink, hoping he'd get to take her home after. But as it was, all he wanted was to put a bullet in her head. She'd killed the only person he'd ever cared about, aside from his mother.

It hadn't occurred to him before that Sorokin had become so much more than a boss and business partner. He'd become his family. Dmitri found it difficult to contain his anger and frustration. He was stuck here, on the boat, with a prisoner who had slowly turned him and a woman who'd outmanoeuvred Sorokin. It was all unfamiliar territory.

'How do I know these aren't fake?'

'Why would I give you fake documents? Given the size of your yacht I can only assume that you have a whole team of lawyers waiting to analyse this before you release Pavel. It would be pretty stupid of me to show up unarmed and with fake papers in that scenario. So no. I can't prove that the papers aren't fake. But it won't take your lawyers long to figure out that they aren't.'

Lawyers. Sorokin would have had a team of them here, if he'd only been here. Dmitri didn't know any lawyers, but what the girl said made sense.

'Wait outside,' he said and got the girl to close the doors after her. Then he held the bearer shares up to the light, all three of them. He felt the paper, the slight indentations where each of them had been signed. They looked old enough, the fonts were different to modern fonts. The company name was correct. The name of the lawyer as well. Sorokin had sent the details over so Dmitri would have time to scout the offices before they went there to claim their reward. Then he nodded to the girl who came back in.

'Get up,' Dmitri said to Pavel, gesturing with the muzzle of his gun.

Pavel held onto the table as he got up. He'd got a lot stronger over the last few days, but suddenly seemed frail again. Dmitri reached out a hand to steady him, but pulled back when he saw the expression on the girl's face. She'd noticed. She'd seen what he himself would have seen if their roles were reversed. That he, Dmitri the professional assassin, was worried about his prisoner's wellbeing.

'Do you need help walking?' the girl asked Pavel.

'Keep away, please. He'll come to you. Outside.' Dmitri shrugged it off. He was a professional. Detachment was his thing. It was what would make him able to do what he was about to do. He just had to get both of them to the back of the boat first, he didn't want to have to spend hours washing the blood away. The remaining staff were loyal enough, but killing someone straight in front of them was too much. Dmitri put a paper weight on top of the documents and followed the two others outside.

The water glistened in the sunshine, and the paddle board

the girl had arrived on was wobbling on the waves two floors down. He could just let them go. That was the deal, after all. Maybe they would just disappear and let him enjoy his wealth. But would a man of Pavel's integrity let that happen? And would the girl, whatever her motivation was, just let it go? Dmitri didn't think so. The girl reached out a hand to help Pavel down the stairs.

'Move away, please. Now. He can walk.'

The girl paused and looked at Dmitri. 'How do I know you won't just shoot us in the back once we step off the boat?'

'You don't. You'll just have to trust me, won't you? If I wanted to kill you, I could have done so already.'

Dmitri was no poker player, and knew that the girl was trying to read him. His frustration grew, but they were on the last steps towards the lower deck now. Then Pavel slipped and fell down the steps.

Dmitri's instinct was to keep away, but he rushed down the steps to Pavel's side to help him get back up. That was when the girl pounced on him.

47

RORY LEAPT FORWARD as Dmitri knelt down to help Pavel. She kicked the gun out of Dmitri's hand and threw herself on the floor after it. Dmitri pushed Pavel aside and reached for his ankle before the other gun had even hit the deck.

The first bullet grazed Rory's hip before it went through the deck. She rolled sideways to avoid the next one and reached out for the other gun.

Pavel was back on his feet and came at Dmitri from behind, throwing a fist towards the back of Dmitri's head. But Dmitri ducked and used Pavel's momentum to throw him into the railing at the back of the boat. Pavel looked like he might fall overboard, but managed to steady himself.

Rory had the gun in her hand, aimed at Dmitri, and leapt back up on her feet. She stood there, staring at Dmitri, who was now aiming at her forehead. Rory stared right back and raised her arm up in front of her. She pointed the gun right between Dmitri's eyes, and stared at the same point, making it impossible for him to make eye contact. The yacht was tilting gently from side to side, the sun burning in the sky above them. Rory moved sideways, not letting Dmitri out of her sight, until she reached Pavel.

'Get on the paddle board and head for the shore. Now.'

'But what about you?' Pavel asked.

Dmitri changed his aim from Rory to Pavel. 'He's not going anywhere.'

'Yes he is. He's getting off the boat, either before or after we kill each other. And if it's all the same to you, I think he should get to go before.'

Dmitri moved his arm again and aimed back at Rory. She'd never stared down the barrel of a gun before. Never looked into the black hole, knowing there was a bullet in there, waiting for the striker to hit the primer. She wondered what it would feel like. Or if she'd even have time to feel anything. Her left shoulder began to ache, as if triggered by the memory of the bullet that grazed her in Moscow. This bullet would go straight through her head, there was no way Dmitri would miss by more than a centimetre at this range. Nor would she.

She swallowed. 'This can't be how you had intended your retirement to end. Richest man in the world, and you haven't even had a chance to open the champagne. Let us get off the boat, and you can drink as many bottles as you want. Every bottle ever made, if you should want to.'

Rory could see that he was thinking, assessing his options. He still had the upper hand, he could kill Pavel before she had time to fire her gun. She decided to level the playing field.

'If you don't let us get off the boat, you get nothing. Nothing, apart from a lot of people chasing you down looking for a fortune you don't have. It's not easy to hide without money.'

Dmitri stood motionless, and Rory had to adjust her stance to keep her arm straight.

'The documents are real, but they're worthless. I transferred all the holdings to a different company, in my name.

And you'll only get it if I sign off on the papers to transfer it back.'

'You stole my money.' Dmitri narrowed his eyes.

'I got myself insurance.'

48

DMITRI LOOKED AT THE GIRL. The gun, his gun, in her hand. Aiming at him. His thumb ached after her kick. He wasn't about to let on though. And the adrenalin flowing meant he'd only feel the real pain later. If there was to be a later. He could always kill Pavel, and hope she hesitated for long enough to miss if he ducked. But she must have made the same calculation. She had just lowered her gun and aimed straight at his heart.

'Come on,' the girl said. 'Neither of us planned to die today. Put the gun down, and we will leave your boat and you alone. The company holdings can be returned with a stroke of a pen, and we can all live happily ever after.'

Dmitri wondered if there could ever be a happily ever after for anyone at the top of the rich list. Maybe Pavel had got it right. Just enough money to look after his family, enough to enjoy life, but not enough for anyone to want to take it from you.

He realised he was tired. So tired. He hadn't slept properly in weeks.

'I want you to transfer the holdings now. By phone.'

'I'm sure that can be done. But let Pavel go first.'

'Not till I have my money.'

'You have me. Let him go back to his children.'

'Children? Masha is dead. You might have found Alexandr, but she is as dead as can be.'

Dmitri noticed Pavel standing up straight when he mentioned the names of the children. 'They're all dead,' Dmitri continued. 'Ivan. Mitrofan. The Chechens. And so will you be.'

Dmitri wasn't about to lose out to some wannabe GI Jane.

'Masha isn't dead. She's alive and well in a safe house. Far away from people like you.'

Dmitri looked at Pavel and back at the girl. Was she telling the truth? Maybe. But the look in Pavel's eyes had changed. There was no plea for pity any more. No sign of fragility. Just pure hatred. Rage. The girl had noticed it too. She held her left arm out, in front of Pavel, as if trying to hold him back.

'Pavel, don't. He's just playing with you. Your children are ok. They're safe.'

'You're nothing but scum,' Pavel said, spitting as he talked. 'Sewage. Filth. How do you live with it, plundering your country, your fellow Russians? Killing women and children, for what? So that you can get a slightly bigger yacht?'

Dmitri couldn't help it. Couldn't stop himself. 'I have given everything for my country. Sacrificed it all. Whilst you were drowning your sorrows in the gutters, I was defending our country from all the traitors and western enemies.' He looked at Pavel, then back at the girl. Losing his temper was not him. This, having a gun pointed at him, being called scum, was not him. He was a hero. How could Pavel not see? 'The cold war wasn't over in 1991. It just changed. The Russian people, our culture, our heritage, is as beleaguered and under threat as ever,' Dmitri said.

'Oh come on. There's no war against Russia. The only war there is, and there should be, is against tyranny and corruption. The war we should be fighting is against people like you, the corrupt elites. You're not fighting for the people. You're fighting for yourself and the select few at the top of the pyramid.' Pavel was shouting now. 'Vermin is what you are. Vermin!'

Dmitri felt his pulse racing, and a drop of sweat trickled down his forehead and into his left eye. He'd dropped his aim a few times already, and the girl had edged closer to him each time. Pavel knew him too well and kept shooting off arguments that hit where it hurt.

'My children were no threat to you. None whatsoever.' Pavel lowered his voice. 'He's eleven years old, my boy. Loves football. Ice hockey. Playing chess. Just a little boy.'

Dmitri straightened his arm again, aiming the gun first at Rory, then at Pavel. His hand was getting clammy and he could see her adjusting her grip on the gun as well. She kept looking at his hand, and as much as he wanted to hide it, his thumb kept twitching. That kick had done some damage.

'Let him go back to his children. And we can sort out the rest,' Rory tried again. 'We'll put down the guns and transfer the ownership. It'll all be done in a few minutes.'

Dmitri weighed up the options. Having Pavel around had exposed his weaknesses. But letting him go limited his options.

'Make the call now.' Dmitri put the gun in his left hand as he reached for the phone. 'You. Give it to her,' he said to Pavel.

Pavel walked over, no sign of previous ailments, and put himself on Dmitri's right, making him have to move his head to look from one to the other. A movement at the corner of his eyes made him turn back. Rory had adjusted her stance, moving just enough to make Dmitri look back at her, and that was when it happened.

Pavel grabbed Dmitri by the wrist and spun around, throwing him off balance. The phone fell on the deck.

Dmitri pulled the trigger, but Rory had shifted sideways when Pavel attacked. He wrestled with Pavel, trying to get a clean hit in that would send his patient back to la-la-land. The girl would never dare shoot at them, she'd be too afraid she might hit Pavel. Dmitri still had the gun in his hand, but Pavel had grabbed his left hand with both of his, and forced it into the air.

Then he heard the shot. A sound he had heard so many times before. Not from the gun in his hand, but his other gun, in Rory's hand. The pain shot up his leg from the knee and he lost his balance, slumping sideways towards the deck.

Pavel didn't hesitate. He forced the gun Dmitri was still holding onto towards his head. Then he squeezed the fingers together, forcing the trigger in.

Dmitri tried to stop him, tried to push the gun away.

He was stronger than this.

He should have been stronger than this.

The last thing he saw, or thought he saw, was his mother in the hospital bed. Frail and grey, cheeks sunken, a wrinkled old hand all alone.

49

RORY HADN'T KNOWN what to make of the verbal fight taking place in front of her. But whatever was going on, it worked. And when Pavel grabbed Dmitri's hand, she knew what she had to do. Level the playing field. She'd aimed and pulled the trigger. The bullet went straight through Dmitri's knee, and he slumped towards the floor.

It was the advantage Pavel needed.

The lower deck was no pretty sight. Brain matter was splattered all over the sides and the stairs. Pavel was covered in it, and on his knees, shaking. Crying. She knelt down next to him. Put her hand around his shoulder.

'It's over. It's over now.'

'Is it? For who?'

They left the body lying there. Rory took both guns and chambered a round in the smaller one, a Glock. It fit better in her hand. A couple of seagulls came floating by to check out the day's catch as they climbed the stairs, but Pavel went back down to chase them away and threw the jacuzzi cover on top of what remained of Dmitri.

They both climbed to the top and Rory handed Pavel the

larger gun, a Russian make she hadn't seen before. It was the one she'd used to shoot Dmitri's knee.

The captain and the other staff members had gathered in the wheelhouse and backed away, arms in the air, as Pavel moved towards them with the gun in front of him. The wheelhouse looked like it belonged on a spaceship. Integrated touch screens below the sleek, shiny surfaces. Two seats in the middle of the room, with a small console in between them.

A captain, his second in command, a cook and a maid or cleaner stood at the port side. Three men and one woman. The cook had a meat cleaver in his hand. Rory looked him in the eyes, then down at the knife and lifted her eyebrows. The cook knelt down, put it on the floor and pushed it gently towards her.

'Thank you.' She found some water in a small fridge and gave the bottle to Pavel.

'Where's the radio?' she asked the captain.

The man in the white shirt and hat pointed to the middle console. It was the only thing that didn't have a reflective surface. Rory picked up the speaker mic and checked that the radio was set to channel 16.

'Tom, are you there? It's over. He's dead. Dmitri is dead.'

She sent the message over the emergency channel, which she knew would be monitored by Simon and his colleagues too. Although they'd probably seen it all via satellite imaging, she wanted to make sure. Then she looked at the captain again.

'Set the course due west.'

'West? But that will take us to …'

'US territory. Yes it will. I'm sure they will treat you fairly if you cooperate. Or just send you back if you don't.'

The captain looked at Pavel.

'I've been kept on this yacht against my will, and you all knew about it. Don't look to me for sympathy,' he said.

Rory walked over to the windows and saw Tom and the speedboat approaching, leaving a trail of white froth behind it. 'Will you be ok?' she asked Pavel. 'I can stay if you want me to.'

'No, you should go. It's not over yet. Not for you, at least. And I can handle these guys. I dealt with a pack of mujahideen back in the day. This is nothing.'

Rory ran back down the steps to the lower deck and dived into the water. She let herself relax for a second, the cool water embracing her, before she swam back to the surface and over to Tom and the speedboat.

Tom grabbed Rory by the arms and lifted her into the speedboat. He pulled her close and held onto her, stroking her wet hair again and again. 'That was a stupid thing to do. I should never have let you do that. Never.'

Rory leaned back and looked him in the eyes. 'That wasn't your decision to make.'

'I know. But still. I should have tied you up and never let you leave my side. And jumping into shark-infested water like that, with open wounds? That was even more stupid.'

Rory laughed. 'Isn't that just a myth, that sharks are attracted to human blood? I thought they were only interested in fish blood?'

'Maybe,' Tom said and planted another kiss on her lips. 'I still want you out of that water.'

'It's not over, you know.'

'I know.' He pulled a towel out from a bag. 'But it's a lot closer to being over than it was just an hour ago.' Then he gave her a mobile phone and steered the boat back towards the islands they'd come from. Away from the yacht with Dmitri's dead body, away from Pavel.

A few minutes later Rory looked back towards the yacht. Two helicopters were circling above it. She grabbed the binoculars. Black clad commandos were rappelling down on the upper deck with automatic rifles in their arms. Pavel was there, the yacht crew walking out on the deck in front of him, their arms high up in the air. Pavel threw his gun over the side and lifted his arms up as well. One of the black clad men walked over to him, Simon perhaps, with an open hand as a greeting.

'Everything going okay back there?' Tom asked.

'Yeah. Looks like it.'

'You'd better make that call then. It's his personal number, got it through a friend in the foreign service.'

Rory looked at the phone. How do you even begin to bargain with the person who put a contract out on you?

'I need to send that email first, to Sam. I need to know her story is ready to print. I can't face this guy alone.'

50

OUTSIDE ROAD TOWN, BVI

Tom brushed her hair aside and pulled Rory towards him.

'Come back to me,' he said and planted a kiss on her forehead.

'I intend to.' Rory walked into the hotel lobby, picked up a copy of the day's *Financial Times* and headed towards the gardens. There was a flurry of paparazzi that waited by the swimming pool, and they paid no heed to the security guard who tried to make them disperse. Rory took off her sandals and dress and walked towards the deep end of the pool in a gold bikini, newspaper still in her hand. The bruises had healed over the last 48 hours, but the bullet-wound from Moscow was still bright read. A couple of the photographers snapped her as she walked, before they realised she wasn't one of the famous, or even infamous, wedding guests they were waiting for. She sat down on the edge of the pool and let her feet cool in the clear water. The six star hotel rose up in front of her, and she nodded to Tom, who sat on a fifth floor balcony with a rifle hidden under a towel. Then she unfolded the newspaper and found the page she needed. The picture showed a man in his late forties, maybe early fifties, attending a funeral in

Moscow. Sorokin's funeral. She left it open, on the edge of the pool.

Rory looked up to see the same grey-haired man walking towards her. Potbelly first, spindly white legs and arms after. The face was wrinkle free, but the tiny speedo he was wearing did him no favours. He awkwardly made his way through the throng of photographers, and a group of young women laughed as they took his picture on their phones.

'Miss Conroy, I presume?' he said in almost perfect English.

'A pleasure to meet you, Mr Volkov,' she replied in Russian.

He looked around and tried to frown but his forehead remained still. Then he sat down next to her.

'Looking for your colleagues?' Rory asked.

'No. I know where they are. I was looking for yours.' He leant his head back and filled his lungs. 'Beautiful place. Shame about the paparazzi though. But I guess that was the point of choosing this location to meet?'

'Certainly was.'

'Not a bad idea. Who's getting married?'

'Some Hollywood couple. Said to be the most photographed event this year.'

'I don't doubt it. I don't doubt it.' He shifted a bit and pulled in his waist a little. 'So, where do we go from here?'

'I would very much like it if you could stop the assassins you sent after me.'

'And what do I get?'

A group of young men came swimming towards them, throwing a ball. It landed at Rory's feet, splashing water on both her and Volkov. A tanned young man smiled at Rory as she threw it back.

'You get to be the one who returns the lost Soviet fortune to the Russian people. You get to be the hero.'

'I don't much care about being a hero.'

'I think you'd like it a lot better than being known as the crook who tried to steal it for yourself.'

Volkov pursed his lips. 'And how do you propose to return this wealth? If you're not passing it on to me, someone else will just take it instead. You know how Russia works. And the contract out on you still remains.'

'I've thought about that. And I have just the right person for the job. She's convalescing at the moment, but I'm sure she'll be eager to get on with it as soon as she's well enough.'

'Maria Pavlovich?' Volkov harrumphed and his jaw tensed up.

The two of them sat there for a while, and a waiter came over to ask if they wanted a drink. Rory shook her head and looked at Volkov.

'Really? You think I'd fall for that? What were you going to put in it? Sedatives?'

'Just a test, nothing personal. But I see that you might be more useful alive. At least for Russia, if not for myself.' He pushed himself forward and into the water. 'Give me a couple of minutes.'

He swam across the pool and over to a man in his late thirties in a beige linen shirt and Ray Bans. The two men talked for a while, both facing away from Rory so she wouldn't be able to lip read. The conversation ended with the shirt clad man picking up his phone and walking away talking to someone. He tried, but failed, to avoid being snapped by the paparazzi who didn't want to miss out on pictures of any of the many celebrity guests. Volkov came swimming back to Rory and put his arms on the edge of the pool.

'It is done. The contract is cancelled. And we're looking forward to working with Ms. Pavlovich. You might want to wait a few minutes before you get up, so the guys have time to get word out about you being off limits.'

Rory wasn't going to let Volkov get the pleasure of seeing

her afraid, so she just smiled curtly at him. 'Thanks for your cooperation. Much appreciated.'

'Can I just ask you one thing,' he said as he turned around. 'Why not take the money for yourself? With that kind of fortune you could buy any assassin off, or get good enough security to eliminate any threats to you or your loved ones.'

'It's not my money to take. Never was.'

Volkov turned and swam away. Rory made the 'all okay' sign to Tom on his balcony. She sat for a few more minutes to soak up the sun before she got up and walked back to her clothes. By the time she'd got dressed again Tom was waiting for her in the lobby, the yellow top of a Veuve Clicquot in the bag over his shoulder, two champagne flutes in his hand.

51

ONE WEEK LATER, LONDON

SASHA HELD TIGHTLY onto Rory's hand as they walked through Battersea Park with Tom. Past the running tracks and the cafe. There were children and dogs running around them, but Rory wasn't interested in dogs today. This was, as she would tell anyone who bothered to listen, the favourite part of her job.

She could see Pavel and his daughter Masha sat on a bench by the lake, a pair of crutches resting against the railing in front of them. Any disagreements between them; gone. Not forgotten, but forgiven. Rory paused and squeezed Sasha's hand. The boy let go of hers and walked towards the bench at first, then started to run. Pavel had barely got up before the boy threw himself around his neck, and Masha joined them soon after. They stood there for a while, huddled together. Crying, laughing. Tom pulled Rory in for a hug, and leaned down to kiss her. She looked into his eyes through her own tears.

'Let's go home,' she said and turned towards Tom's flat on the other side of the river.

When they started walking away, Masha turned around and started hobbling towards them on her crutches.

'I wanted to say thank you, again. And to apologise. I had no idea what I was getting you into. And I should have told you everything from the start.'

Rory gave her a hug. 'That doesn't matter now. The important thing is that you are all alive and well.'

'Thanks to you,' Sasha came over and hugged Rory so hard she had to ask him to go easy on her.

'You're getting stronger, young man. Take care of your father, now, will you?'

'Always,' Sasha said.

Pavel took Rory by the arm and led her away from the others. 'Miss Rory, I can never begin to thank you for your help. But I want you to have this. It's the key to a locker at Zurich Airport. If you ever need a little extra, there is something there waiting for you.'

Rory objected. 'Your daughter has already paid me in full, I couldn't possibly …'

'You don't even know what it is, so don't try to say no. I won't have it.' Then he walked back to his children and led them back to the lake. The ducks welcomed them with quacks and waddling, and Pavel gave Sasha a bag of breadcrumbs to feed them.

Tom reached out for Rory's hand and they started walking again.

'You might want to speed up a little, Roro. We're going to be late for Sunday lunch with your dad.'

AUTHOR'S NOTE

Covering Russia as a journalist, I would hear a lot of crazy stories. In the passenger seat on endless car journeys; in train compartments; in the banya; over a cup of tea or a succession of vodka toasts: people would tell me things. Stories I could never write about in the newspaper, because there were no documents or corroborating sources. This book is an attempt to capture some of it, and has a real life mystery as its starting point.

One of the stories I heard was about a Soviet Communist Party official who fell out of a window just after the coup in 1991. The dead man had been involved in managing the foreign wealth of the Communist Party, and although the money was said to have been recovered while Yeltsin was president, a lot of people aren't sure they found it all. My book imagines: "what if some of it's still out there... and what if someone knows where?"

The main characters are inspired by people I've met, worked with or interviewed. Rory is as brave as the journalists and human rights activists I have met working in conflict zones. Dmitri is as patriotic as the policemen I met in El Paso,

USA. And Sorokin is as corrupt as - well - a lot of the government officials I've met in the former Soviet Union, Central America, Asia and, frankly, all over the world.

AFTERWORD

Liked it?

Thank you for reading this far! I hope you enjoyed it, and if you liked what you read, please do leave me a review at Amazon or on goodreads. That will help motivate me to finish the next book about Rory. If you've spotted any errors, I would really appreciate it if you could let me know on **mettemcleod@gmail.com**.

Please Note

This book was written in British English. UK spellings and punctuation have been used throughout.

ACKNOWLEDGEMENTS

To Peter, my first and best reader. Thank you for helping me to write more good.

I began writing fiction while volunteering at San Francisco's Litquake festival, and would like to thank all the writers I met there, especially Meghan. I would not have dared to start writing fiction were it not for them and the Californian attitude they embodied. I was made to appreciate the saying: Failure is just one step closer to success.

Katy Darby, who did a beautiful job editing the book. Any remaining errors are all mine.

Zoë Sharp, my mentor, friend and fountain of knowledge. Not sure if I would have got this published without you.

Thanks to Matt @optimist.works for the beautiful cover.

My teachers at City University MA course: Claire McGowan, William Ryan, and Laura Wilson.

My writing group: Clara, Franziska, Clive, David, and Mike – thanks for the drinks, the drama and the writerly support. Thanks to the rest of the City Uni alumni, both published and yet to be published.

All the other people I've met in the crime writer community in the UK; from Crimefest, through Harrogate and

Capital Crime. Thanks to Caroline, for the delicious New Zealand white wine and equally good conversations. Thanks to Vicki, for Harrogate companionship. Thanks to Adam for writerly advice.

And thanks to Gina – for bubbles and unshakeable belief.

ABOUT THE AUTHOR

Mette McLeod grew up in Norway and trained at the Norwegian Defense Intelligence and Security School before being recruited to the Intelligence Service. She retrained and became a journalist reporting from all over the world, including two years as a correspondent in Moscow. Her writing is inspired by people she has met, real events and situations.

McLeod is an alumnus of the MA Creative Writing (Crime/Thriller) at City University London. She lives in Bergen, Norway, with her husband, two children and a Welsh lurcher. Visit her website **www.MetteMcLeod.com**

 twitter.com/mettemcleod

Printed in Great Britain
by Amazon